Death in Irish Accents

The Dublin Driver Mysteries by Catie Murphy

DEAD IN DUBLIN

DEATH ON THE GREEN

DEATH OF AN IRISH MUMMY

DEATH IN IRISH ACCENTS

Death in Irish Accents

CATIE MURPHY

www.kensingtonbooks.com

KENSINGTON BOOKS are published by

Kensington Publishing Corp.
119 West 40th Street
New York, NY 10018

All Kensington titles, imprints, and distributed lines are available at special quantity discounts for bulk purchases for sales promotion, premiums, fund-raising, educational, or institutional use.

Special book excerpts or customized printings can also be created to fit specific needs. For details, write or phone the office of the Kensington Sales Manager: Attn.: Sales Department. Kensington Publishing Corp., 119 West 40th Street, New York, NY 10018. Phone: 1-800-221-2647.

The K and Teapot logo is a trademark of Kensington Publishing Corp.

First Printing: March 2023
ISBN: 978-1-4967-4005-2

ISBN: 978-1-4967-4006-9 (ebook)

10 9 8 7 6 5 4 3 2 1

Printed in the United States of America

Pronunciation Guide

Irish names will often trip up English-speaking readers because we try to map English letter sounds and combinations onto a language never intended to use them. The trickier words in Death in Irish Accents are pronounced as follows:

Bláthnaid - Blawnid

Sadhbh - Sighv

Niamh = Neev

Aibhilín Ní Gallachóir = Evelyn Nee Gallaher

An Garda Síochána – ahn garda sheeowkana

(guardians of the peace/police)

Drogheda – draHEHda

Dún Laoighaire – dun leary

CHAPTER 1

A body fell out of the closet when the barista opened it.

The barista screamed, throwing herself backward, and landed in a sprawl across Megan Malone's lap. Coffee went everywhere. Megan, too startled to even yell, grabbed the barista to make sure she didn't bounce to the floor the way the—

The way the body had done. Megan said, "Oh god," under her breath. Immediately beside her, her girlfriend made a hideous, high-pitched squeak that was almost worse than the barista's screams. Like Megan, Jelena had grabbed the barista—Anie—but Megan had taken most of the girl's weight. Jelena scrambled backward, right over the arm of their couch, as the body dropped into the couch directly beneath the closet, then bounced off and hit the coffee table with a truly horrible crunch. Then it . . . slithered . . . to the floor, limbs

flopping around with a stomach-turning loose-
ness.

Either it was very fresh, Megan thought with a
sort of clinically investigative detachment, or it
was . . . not fresh at all.

Anie, the barista, was still shrieking. Jelena had
landed hard on the floor and crouched there, hands
clenched against her mouth to stop her own
screams. Everyone else in the café was coming to
see what had happened, people climbing on the
wide arms of the café's couches and pounding up
the stairs from the lower floor. Alarmed faces
started appearing at the top of the stairs, stacked
one above another like a comedy sketch as they
peered around at the nook-like space at the back
of the café where Megan, Jelena, Anie and the
dead girl were. The dead girl had fallen—well,
landed—between two of the deep couches and the
square coffee table at right angles to them.

Jelena, through the fists knotted at her mouth,
whispered, "This is not possible," and part of
Megan had to agree. This was her fourth body in
the past three years. That sort of thing had been
within the bounds of reason when she was in the
military, working as a combat medic and driving
ambulances, but it was not what anybody expected
as a limo driver in Dublin.

The other part of her thought they'd better
clear the room before anybody started taking pictures, although it was almost certainly too late for
that. She got Anie off her lap and stood, raising
her voice. "Max? Can you get everybody out of
here, please?" Her Texan accent sounded particularly noticeable to her right then, but it usually did

when she felt she had to be pushy about something. An American accent worked wonders for being pushy in Ireland.

Another of the baristas, a good-looking young white man, stuttered, "I—yes, okay, yes—" and began to herd patrons out of the café. A third barista went downstairs and Megan could hear him calling, "Sorry, lads, Accents has to close for a while. If you're waiting on your drinks, we'll refund your money at the till."

Somebody downstairs said, "What *happened*," and the barista, Liam, said, "There's been an accident," in a grim tone. After a few seconds, the lingering patrons from downstairs began to exit, craning their necks to see what was going on in the little alcove. One of them said, "Oh, *shit*," and scurried out with their phone already at their ear.

Jelena wrapped her hand around Megan's upper arm. "Megan, we have to *go*."

"I can't." Megan gave Jelena an apologetic glance, seeing the anger and worry in the other woman's brilliant blue eyes. "Honestly, I can't, Yella. Paul's going to have a fit over me even being here, but if I leave the scene before I call him . . ."

"Megan." Jelena's voice filled with strain, and Megan shrugged helplessly.

"I'm sorry. I really am. It's not like I mean for this to keep happening. Let me call Paul." She took her phone out, but Anie, whose crimson-dyed hair made her currently starkly-pale face look desperately unhealthy, clutched Megan's other arm.

"That's right, you've dealt with this kind of thing before. What do we do?" She got to her feet unsteadily, her gaze averted from the body at their feet. Most of the café had cleared out by then, with only the staff and a couple customers getting their money back remaining. "Is this going to ruin the business? Oh, God, I'd better call the owners. What am I going to say to them?"

"I don't know, Anie. I'm sorry." Megan glanced briefly at the body, which didn't seem to be leaking any blood, despite having hit the table hard on its way down. It—she—was young, with thickly curled, naturally red hair, and a host of freckles still visible after death. Megan didn't know if that was normal or not. She looked back across the café, where at least half the patrons were still gathered outside the plate glass front windows, and said, "Does anybody know who she is?" to the handful of people remaining in the café.

"She's a writer," Anie whispered. "Part of a group that's in here all the time. Bláthnaid. She liked a flat white and the peanut butter cake."

"Bláthnaid." Megan mentally spelled the name in her head, because it was one of those that didn't look anything like it sounded, at least to American ears. She heard *Blaw-nid*, but the spelling had a T-H where the W sound was, for heaven's sake. Then, idiotically, she added, "The peanut butter cake is amazing," as if she couldn't quite get her mind to work clearly beyond asinine agreements. "When was—"

"Megan." Jelena's voice sharpened. "Megan, just call Detective Bourke so we can go. You shouldn't get mixed up in this. Not again."

"Right. Yeah, okay, sorry." Megan actually dialed the detective this time, grimacing in anticipation of him picking up. He had once, lightheartedly, said that Megan only rang when she'd discovered a body. The rest of the time, she texted. He was unfortunately pretty much right about that, so she wasn't looking forward to him answering this call.

He did so on the third ring, with a wary, "Megan . . . ?"

"I'm at Accents Café on Stephen Street Lower and a dead body just fell in my lap."

The silence went on so long she checked to see if her phone had disconnected. Then, obviously through his teeth, Paul Bourke said, "Do not *touch* anything and do not *speak* to anyone until I get there," and hung up.

Megan put her phone in her pocket again and said, "He's mad at me," to the remaining people in the café, as a general statement. Then she looked at the set of Jelena's jaw, and thought it wasn't Detective Garda Paul Bourke who was *mad* at her. Although neither of them were exactly mad at her, probably. It wasn't like she planned this. But she did say, "I'm sorry," to Jelena, very softly.

Color rose in the pretty Polish woman's heart-shaped face, staining it pink. "When he comes here, Megan, we have to leave. When he's done talking to you. You can't . . ."

"Solve another mystery?" Megan supplied with a weak smile. "I don't know, my track record is pretty good so far."

Jelena's skin flushed to red. "This isn't your job. It's not the kind of thing you should be getting involved in. It makes me worry for you."

"I know. I know." Megan offered Jelena her hand, and pulled her into a hug when Jelena reluctantly accepted it. "I don't see how this could possibly have anything to do with me, though. It'll be fine, babe. I promise."

"Okay." The word, muffled against Megan's shoulder, sounded resigned. "Next time we're going to a different café after the gym, though."

Megan grinned. "Oh, come on, what are the odds that somebody else is going to get killed here? We're probably safer staying—"

"Killed here?" Anie had come back from calling the owners and stopped, frozen, just before the step leading up to the section Megan and Jelena stood on. "You think she was *killed*? Like, murdered?"

Megan, somewhat insensitively, said, "Well, she didn't put herself into that closet, Anie," and the young woman paled so sharply she had to sit down. A stab of guilt shot through Megan. She generally forgot that she was technically old enough to be most of the staff's mother. Being fortysomething was supposed to feel grown-up, but Megan had come to the reluctant conclusion that most people never actually felt grown-up. They just got older, and spent a lot of their time being vaguely surprised that they no longer shared the same life experiences as a twenty-five-year-old.

And honestly, her own life's experience up to the ages that the staff were was probably significantly different from theirs too, which made unthinkingly callous or cynical statements come a little easier, maybe. She, after all, had been in the Army for five years when she was Anie's age. Megan mumbled, "Sorry," and Anie nodded, although Jelena gave her a somewhat appalled look.

Megan said, "Sorry" again, and meant it.

Anie whispered, "It's okay. Of course you're right, I just didn't think—who would kill Bláthnaid? She was nice."

"I don't know. The guards will be here soon. Detective Bourke is only fifteen minutes away, even on foot." Just as she said that, a tallish, slender man in a camel-colored trench coat strode up to the door, flashing a badge and scattering at least half of the remaining crowd outside. He entered, brushing dampness from sandy red hair with one hand, and glancing around the café in a quick, professional assessment before his gaze landed on Megan and went flat.

Megan's shoulders slumped and she shot Jelena another apologetic look before taking a few steps toward the plainclothes detective. "Paul. Sorry, I mean, Detective Bourke. I'm, uh . . . really sorry."

Bourke shook his head in weary acceptance. "I feel like I should just be grateful it's been over a year since I found you neck-deep in a crime scene. What happened?"

Megan gestured toward Anie. "She asked if we could scoot over so she could get some supplies out of the closet—"

Bourke's gaze went to the closet, which still hung open. Normally hidden behind eight-inch-deep bookshelves, it filled the upper half of the wall above the couches, and was probably a couple feet deep and a good six feet high. Megan said, "I usually sit downstairs. I didn't even know there was a closet there. I thought it was just bookshelves. So we scooted over and she opened it and . . . Bláthnaid fell out."

"Bláthnaid? You know her?" Bourke's notepad was out now, its orange cover flashing as he flipped it open to start writing. He'd had a different-colored pad for every case Megan had ever seen him work on, and she assumed there was some kind of organizational or file-keeping method to the color schemes.

"No, no, Anie told me her name." Megan gestured toward the barista again. "And then I called you. Honestly, I did," she added defensively, at Bourke's skeptical glance. "You got here fast." It couldn't have been more than four or five minutes since the body had fallen out of the closet.

"I was at the top of Grafton Street," Bourke replied shortly. Megan had a momentary impulse to discuss which end was really the "top" of the street, but given that Bourke had arrived so quickly, he clearly meant he'd been closer to St. Stephen's Green. "What are *you* doing here?"

"Accents is my favorite café. They make better mochas than anywhere else I've ever been. Jelena and I came here after working out this morning."

"And you just happened to be here for the discovery of a body." Bourke sighed and gave Jelena a brief nod of greeting, which she returned before casting an unhappy but accepting glance at Megan.

"I'll be outside."

"Jelena, I'm sorry, I—"

Jelena lifted a hand, cutting off the apology, and went outside. Bourke followed her with his gaze, then raised his eyebrows at Megan. "Trouble in paradise?"

"There wasn't until five minutes ago! She wasn't

happy the last couple times this happened, but we hadn't been seeing each other very long then, and nothing like this has happened in over a year now—"

"Exactly fourteen months," Bourke said. "To the day. Cherise Williams's funeral was fourteen months ago today."

Megan looked askance at him. "You just know that off the top of your head?"

"I counted it out on my way over here." He pointed toward Jelena with his chin. "I'm actually going to need to talk to her, you know."

"I don't think that's occurred to her, but I don't think she's planning to leave without me unless I'm here a long time, so . . ."

"You have no reason to be here a long time," Bourke said. "You're not an investigating officer. You're a witness, at most. So tell me what you know and then, for God's sake, go away and don't get involved in this, okay, Megan?"

"This time I don't see how I possibly could. And I've told you what I know," Megan added with a sigh. "Anie opened the cupboard and the body fell out. Everybody screamed—"

"You didn't," Anie put in, and Megan blinked at her, then smiled ruefully.

"Maybe not on the outside. I was trying to keep you from hitting the floor. Anyway," she said to Bourke, "then I called you. That was pretty much it."

Bourke looked down at her for a long moment, nearly-blond eyebrows drawn down over pale blue eyes as he waited for the other shoe to drop.

For once, though, Megan didn't have another shoe. The dead girl wasn't her client, or a friend of her client's, or connected to her in any way. She couldn't blame him for expecting a link, though. He'd been the investigating officer on her first murder—that sounded all wrong—and they'd gotten to be friends, so she'd called him when she'd found herself neck-deep in a second, and then a third, murder mess.

But she wasn't involved in this one, so she spread her hands in as good an approximation of innocence as she could manage. "Honestly, that's all I know."

"And you're just going to leave instead of hanging around on the edges of my investigation, trying to overhear something and look into it yourself?"

Megan's face heated, although her brief smile was full of admission. "Obviously, I'm not gonna lie and say I'd never do such a thing. I totally would. But Jelena would kill me, and I'd rather have a girlfriend who still speaks to me than another notch on my murder belt." She winced as Paul's eyes popped. "That came out wrong."

"You think? All right." The detective exhaled. "Send Jelena in for a minute to talk to me, but I don't think there's much more she's going to be able to tell me. I'll interview the staff and learn more ab . . ." He trailed off, frowning. "I don't have to tell you what I'm doing for my job."

Megan produced a wide, cheesy grin. "No. But if you wanted to keep me up to date on the details . . ."

"My boss would demote me." Bourke turned away, and Megan, actually feeling a little guilty, scurried out of the café. An Garda Síochána—the

Irish police force—was not, as an institution, fond of her, and Paul's boss specifically would be happier if Megan returned to the States and never complicated another Irish murder investigation in her life. Megan thought the ins and outs of the messes she kept getting into were fascinating, but she genuinely didn't want to cause Paul any trouble, and Jelena . . .

Jelena was leaning in the alleyway just beside the café, her arms folded and a worried scowl settling on her delicate features. Megan murmured, "Sorry," again as she found her. "Paul wants to talk to you real quick."

"We go on double *dates* with him and Niamh, Megan, we don't—" Jelena's protest ended in a splutter and a waving of her hands, but she went inside, leaving Megan to cringe guiltily again. Even she had to admit it was kind of weird to be interviewed about suspicious deaths by somebody she hung out with for Friday night pizza, but at least she'd gone through it before. Jelena hadn't.

Of course, if it was weird for them, it had to be a lot harder for Paul, who also probably had to justify to his boss why he spent his spare time hanging out with somebody who kept being connected to murders. Megan said "Ugh," out loud, and thumped her head against the alley wall. Then, also aloud, she said, "But you're *not* connected to this one," and nodded firmly, like all she needed was a good talking-to.

Her phone rang, startling her, and she took it out to see her boss's name coming up with the Leprechaun Limos emblem as the image. Megan answered with as wary an "Orla?" as Paul's "Megan?"

had been earlier, and was broadsided by Orla's most an-American-is-listening-to-me Irish accent.

"Megan? Have you plans for the afternoon? I've a new client who's asking for you specifically."

"A *new* client?" Megan echoed, surprised. "Usually only Carmen asks for me by name."

"Oh," Orla said, her voice dropping to a grim mutter, "she's not asking by name, no. She's asking for 'the murder driver.' "

CHAPTER 2

"Oh my god," Megan said faintly. "Tell her I don't exist? You've never heard of a murder driver?"

"I knew you'd cause me no end of trouble," Orla hissed.

Megan, contrary to the last, said, "Now that's not fair. You're getting clients because of me!" and rather thought she deserved Orla's outraged sound of dismissal. "Why does she want the murder driver? I mean, me?"

"I don't know," Orla said, her inner-city Dublin accent growing stronger. "Says she's a writer, and a famous one at that. She's got fierce notions, if you ask me."

Megan said, "I take it she's left the office," and Orla snorted.

"She only rang. It was other clients who were in. Will yis take the job or not?"

"Is it only for today? I have St. Patrick's Day plans."

"Sure and it's only Tuesday," Orla said. "Maybe a bit tomorrow. Nothing on the Thursday."

"Okay, because there can't be. Jelena's in the parade and she'll kill me if I can't come help. I've had this weekend scheduled off since last August."

"I know," Orla said irritably. "All prepared, that's you. Cillian was devastated he couldn't bring his niece to the parade due to work, and that's on you."

"Heh. First, you could close business for the weekend, so, no, it's not on me."

Orla squawked with outrage. "D'yis know how much money's to be made on the holida—"

Megan, who did know, spoke over her. "Second, Cillian's niece is not yet two years of age. She won't remember anyway. What time today?"

"He had grandstand seats!" Orla protested, as if she cared a whit about Cillian's holiday plans. Having gotten her way, she went on briskly. "Half eleven, if you can make it, at the Avoca House in Drumcondra. I've told her there's a premium on hiring you, so be on time."

"Orla, half the reason you hired me is I'm an annoyingly punctual American." She glanced at the time, which was just past ten. "I know where that B and B is. I should be able to make that, yeah." She hung up, shaking her head in disbelief. Her boss was as mean as a rattlesnake and had never met an opportunity that she couldn't squeeze an extra bit of cash from, but putting a premium on "the murder driver" seemed rich.

Then again, maybe a so-called famous writer also seemed rich. Heavens knew Orla had a real knack for recognizing which clients she could bilk while simultaneously convincing them that they were getting value for their money. As far as Megan could tell, sometimes that value was just in knowing they were paying outrageous rates and were therefore obviously getting preferential treatment. Orla seemed to work on the assumption that they didn't have to be informed there was no real level of service change between what they got and what less wealthy clients got.

"Em, you all right there?" One of the café patrons who hadn't scattered peered around the alley corner at her, and Megan gave the guy a weak smile.

"Yeah, fine, sorry."

"Did you know her, then?" He tipped his head back toward the café, and Megan shook her head.

"No. Did you?" As soon as she spoke, she figured she shouldn't have, but fortunately, the young man shook his head no.

"Nah, I wouldn't be a regular like."

"Yeah, me either, or not enough of one to recognize her." Megan had been in Ireland for years now, and still sometimes had to bite back the impulse to ask "like what?" or "so what?" when a native-born Irish person ended a sentence with "like" or "so" in that way. She figured the hanging word was some vestigial aspect of the Irish language making itself known in Hibernian English, but none of her Irish-speaking friends had ever been able to pinpoint its origin.

That hadn't stopped her from picking it up, particularly if she was trying to sound a bit more Irish herself, but she still noticed it on occasion.

"Poor girl," the young man was saying. "D'ye think she's been dead long?"

Megan nearly answered "not long enough to start smelling," then decided this was exactly the kind of thing Detective Bourke didn't want her talking to random strangers about. "No idea. Hey, I'm Megan Malone." She offered a hand, and the kid, who was probably in his early twenties, shook it.

"Sean Murphy. That's a very Irish name for an accent like that."

Megan grinned. "Yeah, I get that a lot."

"Are ye long here, Megan Malone?"

"Almost five years."

Sean clicked his tongue. "You don't talk to enough Irish people, if your accent is still hanging on so strongly."

"You're probably right." Megan pushed away from the alley wall as Jelena came back out of the café. "Nice to meet you, Sean. Take care."

"Investigating?" Jelena murmured as they walked away.

Megan glanced back over her shoulder. The young man was heading the other direction, up toward St. Stephen's Green. "No. Or I don't think so, anyway. He wanted to know what I thought about the dead girl, so I got his name in case it's important later."

Jelena frowned. "That's investigating."

"Well, I'll tell Paul and that'll be it, okay? Orla called and has a job for me this afternoon."

"*Just* this afternoon, right? We have plans this week."

Megan smiled up at her. "I reminded her, and reminded her that I took this weekend off eight months ago." They reached the corner and she glanced both ways: Aungier Street to the left, George's Street to the right, the name changing at the intersection where they stood.

That was standard for Dublin, as if they had too many notable people and not enough streets to name them after. An Irish cousin of Megan's, visiting America, had exclaimed gleefully at how easy the street signs were to read and follow, which hadn't made any sense to her until she'd been in Dublin for a while. Just north of where they stood, one of the city's main arteries changed names five times in as many blocks, but the only street signs were bolted to the sides of buildings and covered in grime. Megan had learned the hard way that in Ireland, if you didn't already know where you were going, you might never get there. Especially in a relatively fast-moving vehicle. "Which way are you going? Back to Rathmines with me?"

"No, I'm going over to Chapters Books. They've got something in for me. You'd better take the bus home. The dogs will want a walk before you go to work."

"You are as wise as you are beautiful." Megan stole a kiss.

Jelena laughed. "It's true, I am."

"Okay. I'll see you later. And I promise I won't get any more involved in that murder. I mean, that suspicious death."

"You'd better not." Jelena returned the stolen

kiss, then cut across the street to head north across Temple Bar. Megan walked up to the next bus stop heading south, and watched the familiar street slip away under the bus's wheels as it brought her home. She still thought of the little house she shared with Jelena as "the new house with the garden," although they'd been there over a year now. Her puppies, Dip and Thong, were properly dogs now, and long-since accustomed to the ritual of being fed and left in their comfortable little house in the garden when Megan had to work. Megan herself had finally learned to put them out *before* she showered and got ready for work, so she didn't show up at the Leprechaun Limos garage with fine white dog hairs all over her black uniform.

The Lincoln Continental she liked best was waiting for her, and she cut through early afternoon traffic toward Drumcondra in the north city, taking the fastest route but slowing as she drove through the B and B's neighborhood so she could admire the expensive houses with their promise of large back gardens. She wouldn't half mind living in that area herself, although she'd never be able to afford it. She pulled up to the Avoca House, a handsome building with a two-tone exterior, red brick on the lower floor and gray stony spackle on the upper. A middle-aged white lady huddled just inside the entryway, avoiding the increasingly bad weather. She was broadly built, in a way that Megan thought would have been described as "a battleship" in the days of corsets, and wore an unbuckled raincoat against the misty day. As soon as Megan pulled up, she rushed to the car, yanked open the back door, and jumped in before Megan could even kill the engine, much less get out and hold the door like the limo service offered. "Megan Malone? The murder driver?"

The woman had a distinct Midwest accent and an air of excited expectation that Megan suddenly didn't want to meet. For the space of a heartbeat, she considered just becoming an actual murder driver and killing the woman instead of answering her questions. Explaining that to Jelena or Paul seemed like more effort that it was worth, though, so she sighed, smiled, and said, "I'm Megan Malone with Leprechaun Limos, yes."

"Oh, terrific. I'm Claire. Gosh, I'm so excited to meet you! I got to Ireland last week, you know, I wanted to come in for the St. Patrick's Day parade, everybody wants to be in Dublin for that, and someone in the writing group I'm in here mentioned you and I just had to meet you! Tell me, how do you keep getting mixed up in all these murders? Are you scared to take a new job, these days? Has anyone close to you died? Do you think the spate of deaths is over?"

"Ma'am," Megan said when Claire paused for breath, "did you want me to drive you somewhere?"

"Oh! Yes, out to Trim Castle, please. I'm writing a historical romance set there. How *did* you get tangled up in so many murders?"

"A series of unfortunate coincidences, that's all. I'm sure you understand I can't discuss things due to client confidentiality." Given that one of the incidents she'd investigated had ended up on international news, Megan was stretching the idea of client confidentiality beyond credibility, but it was worth a shot.

Claire laughed merrily. "Well, maybe I'll get lucky and you'll get involved with one while I'm here!"

Since two of the murders she'd been mixed up in had been her clients, Megan thought that perhaps this one should *not* hope for that, but kept her tongue behind her teeth. Instead she said, "So you're here for research?" as she pulled out of the parking lot and turned north toward Trim.

"Just a little thing I'm working on, before I go on book tour." Claire waved a hand, dismissing the research's importance. "I usually write historical romance—that's why I'm going to Trim—but I want to do something modern, something exciting. I'm sure you can understand that you seem like a wonderful inspiration. Tell me, do you work with the local police? What are they called? An Garda . . . something? See-oh-can-uh?"

"Ahn," Megan replied, almost against her will. "'A-N' in Irish means *the* and it's pronounced *ahn*, with a short A. And it's shee-oh-kah-nuh, sheokanuh. An Garda Síochána. It means the peace guards, or guardians of the peace."

Claire had a surprisingly girlish laugh for someone who reminded Megan of a battleship. She clapped her hands, obviously delighted, and repeated the phrase a couple of times before asking, "So you speak Gaelic?"

Megan had to give her credit for trying, at least. The last American she'd driven—well, not the last one, but the last notable one, even if she'd been notable partially for ending up dead—had been either unwilling or unable to even hear the difference in how she said things, and how the Irish said them, much less try to correct herself. "It's Irish. The English word for the Irish language is Irish. The Irish word for the Irish language is Gaelic, which looks pretty much like *Gaelic* to non-Irish speakers and is pronounced that way in some of the dialects. I learned it as *gwaylgah.* All that said . . . no, I don't speak Irish."

The last confession got a bit of a laugh, but Megan caught a glimpse in the rearview mirror of her client's eyelashes fluttering rapidly. Then she took out her phone and made notes, murmuring, "Gaelic, gwaylgah, sheeohkanuh," as she did so. "This is great, thank you. So what's it like working with An Garda Síochána?"

Megan chuckled as she took them out of the neighborhood and up Drumcondra Road toward the M50, which was the fastest, if not the prettiest, way to get to Trim. "Good try, but I never said I did. Have you been to Ireland before?"

"Nope. I have some friends here, or at least, an old acquaintance," and she sang, "be forgot, and never brought to mind," in a passable alto before continuing: "And I hadn't really brought her to mind for years, except she contacted me last year about mentoring a young woman, which was a big ask, honestly, from somebody I barely remembered, but I'm glad she reached out, because Bláthnaid is really talented and—"

Megan's hands went icy on the steering wheel,

and blood rushed through her ears, drowning out Claire's cheerful conversation. Even her vision narrowed, dark and dangerous enough that she moved into the slower lane of traffic and dropped to the lowest speed she dared without actually pulling over. She'd driven at least a kilometer, maybe two, before the pounding of blood through her body lessened enough for her to manage, "I'm sorry, did you say Bláthnaid?" somewhere in the middle of Claire's monologue.

"Oh!" Claire's expression, visible in the mirror, went concerned. "Did I mess it up again? I chatted with her in text forever before we ever actually spoke, and I've been saying her name all wrong every time it comes out. *Blawnid*," she said carefully. "Did I say *Blath-nayd* again? It must drive her nuts, having people get it wrong all the time. She said it was unusual even here, and it would obviously be a train wreck at home. I'd probably change my name. Nobody can mess up Claire, you know?"

"Megan's hard to mess up, too," Megan agreed hoarsely. "No, it's fine, I was just, um, surprised. Because, uh. Because it's an unusual name."

Claire appeared to accept the weak excuse and went back to chattering happily as the rush of blood filled Megan's ears again.

Bláthnaid *wasn't* a common name, even in Ireland. The odds of Bláthnaid the dead writer at Accents Café being unrelated to Claire's mentee Bláthnaid were slim, at best.

Megan pulled back into the faster lane of traffic, suddenly intent on getting to Trim. The sooner there, the sooner back again, and the sooner she could hand Claire off to some other driver. Because if Claire somehow dragged Megan more deeply into Bláthnaid's death, Detective Bourke and Jelena were going to draw straws on which one of them got to kill her.

CHAPTER 3

"Bláthnaid's a darling," Claire went on. "Very young, you know, but I'm getting to that age when everyone seems young, even old people, in that 'suddenly seventy doesn't seem so old anymore' way, right? She's taken my advice very seriously. It's flattering, of course, but then I worry that I might be steering her in the wrong direction."

"Why's that?" Megan asked hoarsely. She might as well get what she could out of Claire while the woman was prepared to speak freely to her. She could report back to Paul, after all, which would be *helpful*. Not investigative or busybodying or whatever. Just *helpful*.

Maybe if she told herself that enough times, she'd start to believe it.

Claire waved a hand expansively, a couple of rings catching the light in the rearview mirror. "Partly it's that I want people to write what speaks to them, you understand? The book of their heart, and all of that. But I also want people who are serious about writing to understand how incredibly hard it is to make a living as a writer."

"Really?" Megan glanced at her in the mirror. "I thought writing was profitable."

"Do you really want to know the truth about that?"

"Well, now I do!"

Claire grinned. "Okay, then. It's only profitable for a very small number of very lucky people. Most writers make less than ten grand a book, and that's usually paid out over twelve to eighteen months. Sometimes longer. You might get more money later, if you 'earn out,' which means your book sells enough for the publisher to recoup the advance they paid you up front. But that can take years."

Megan's eyebrows popped upward. "Holy cow. How does anybody make a living as a writer?"

"Mostly they don't," Claire admitted. "There's a reason writers keep their day jobs. So any time I give anyone advice I worry that it's wrong. I want Bláthnaid to write what she's passionate about, but I don't want her to think doing that means she'll automatically be successful. And that's hard for anybody to hear, whether they're just starting out or have been in the game a long time."

"Do you think she's got what it takes?" Megan's stomach twisted guiltily at even asking, given that Bláthnaid would never have a chance to try.

Claire shrugged expressively. "She's a good writer, which helps. But whether you make a sale depends on so many things that have nothing to do with being good or not. I hope she'll succeed, though. I like seeing my name in the acknowledgments. Makes me feel like I did a little good in this world."

"You must see your name somewhere else, though," Megan said, almost absently. "If you're going on book tour?"

An explosive sigh sounded from the back seat. "Well, there's the irony. I'm one of the lucky ones who makes more than ten grand a book. But I can't tell you how to follow in my footsteps even if I wanted to, because there really is so much luck involved. I was in the right place at the right time with a good enough book, and somebody needed what I was doing just then, and took a chance on me. It's a crapshoot."

"I had no idea. I thought it was more . . ." Megan frowned vaguely at the road in front of them as she took the exit toward the town of Trim. "I don't know what I thought. Writers in movies and TV shows are—"

"Fictional?" Claire said, and Megan laughed. A little while later, as they pulled into a street-side parking spot below Trim Castle, Claire breathed, "Oh, *my*. Oh, you have to come check it out with me. It's more fun with someone. Unless you've seen it a hundred times. But you haven't, have you?" She made hopeful eyes from the back seat, and despite the fact that she was clearly going to cause Megan trouble, Megan couldn't help laughing.

"I've only been once, actually, and it was before I moved here. I'd love to come along." Only, she told herself again, because if she could get anything more useful out of Claire regarding her rela-

tionship with Bláthnaid, it would be good information to pass along to Detective Bourke.

"Yay!" Claire clapped her hands and climbed out
of the car before Megan could get the door. "Now—
oh, wait—does it cost more to have my driver
come along on my excursions with me? I'll pay for
your entry ticket, of course, but if it's more to have
you walking around with me instead of sitting in
the car then I'll call Mrs. Keegan and let her know
I'm happy to pay the increased charge."

"Ms. Keegan," Megan said absently. She couldn't
imagine anyone prepared to put up with Orla long
enough to marry her. Or Orla putting up with anyone long enough to marry them, either, to be fair.
"And no, it's fine, I enjoy exploring with clients.
I'm sure Orla would be happy to charge you more,
but it can be our little secret."

Claire dimpled in delight and clapped her
hands together again. "Hooray! And oh, this really
is fantastic, isn't it?" She took out her phone for
some pictures and Megan, gazing up toward the
castle, had to agree it was, in fact, fantastic.

The castle grounds were fronted by stone walls
that stood twice Megan's height, punctuated by
towers that ranged from modest to massive. The
largest was the Dublin Gate, which faced south
and had a gorgeous arched entry about five feet
off the ground, suggesting that once upon a time
there had been a moat and a bridge crossing into
the grounds there. That tower had to be at least
forty feet high, but the central castle loomed over
it, more than eighty feet tall of stonework walls
shaped in an intricate, twenty-sided cruciform. "The
walls are eleven feet thick, I think," Megan said,

trying to remember what she'd learned on the tour she'd done years earlier.

"These ones?" Claire goggled at the outer walls, but Megan shook her head.

"No, the actual castle walls. I don't know how thick these ones are. It's all greenery and lawn inside, too, which isn't how it would have been. I can't remember if there are any artist's renditions of how it might have looked when it was built."

"Let's go find out!" Claire marched ahead, leaving Megan to pay for the on-street parking with the company credit card before hurrying after her. A moment later they were within the castle walls, and for the next two hours Megan followed her client around, climbing alarmingly narrow stairs, peering at the countryside through slim windows meant for loosing arrows through, and listening to a knowledgeable guide highlight the castle's history. Claire took notes and asked questions until Megan's eyes glazed, but the guide, either delighted to be quizzed or in awe of a writer interviewing him, answered everything she asked and added details that had her writing more notes. Finally, the guide apologetically said he had another tour group to lead, and left them to their own devices.

Megan, feeling a little faint from Claire's enthusiasm, said, "You're very thorough," and Claire made a face.

"Thanks. If I'm lucky about two percent of this will make it onto the page. Writers are forever spending hours going down research holes for one sentence."

"That doesn't sound like a very efficient use of time," Megan said cautiously.

Claire laughed. "No, but writers are also forever doing whatever it takes to avoid the actual writing part of their job. Sometimes, when you're in the groove, it's great, but a lot of the time it's staring at a screen and trying to figure out how to get yourself out of the plot hole you've written yourself into."

"Hence the research," Megan guessed, and Claire grinned again.

"And the gazing out the window, and the cleaning the kitchen or the kitty litter, or, if you're really desperate, a midday shower. The best ideas always come in the shower, for some reason. Or in the middle of the night." Her expression went stern, and she pointed a finger at Megan. "If you ever think, 'This is such a great idea that I'll definitely remember it in the morning,' don't believe yourself. You have to write it down."

"In the unlikely event that I start writing books, I'll remember that," Megan promised. Claire was growing on her, despite the whole asking-for-the-murder-driver thing.

"You should, though. All your murders would make a great story." They left the castle grounds, Claire still taking notes as they returned to the car. "Can you drive me into downtown Dublin? I'm supposed to meet some friends at a café."

A knot formed in Megan's stomach again. "Sure. Which café?"

"Accents. It's on—"

"Stephen Street Lower." Megan's stomach turned

over. "I know it." And that almost certainly answered the question of whether Claire's Bláthnaid and the dead girl were one and the same.

Part of her thought she should tell Claire the truth. The rest of her thought she'd better text Paul as soon as she could, and, at a stoplight, she did. **Funny story, but my new client is a writer who was mentoring a young woman named Bláthnaid, and she just now asked if I'd take her to Accents.**

The phone rang about three seconds later, and Megan hit the *I can't answer your call right now* button, then sent a text that said **driving.**

Bourke texted back with a series of increasingly exploding head emojis followed by **Accents is closed for the day but I'll meet you outside of it. JAY-SUS, Megan!**

At the next stoplight, she texted **I know, I'm sorry** and drove back to Dublin feeling guilty over events she couldn't control.

There were far more people outside Accents than Megan expected, given that the body had been discovered a good six hours earlier. It slowed traffic, which was never fast on the narrow street, even farther, giving Megan plenty of time to glance around as they crept forward. The glass-fronted café itself was cordoned off, but people were gathered at the Chinese place across the street, spilling into the street itself, and in the alley to the café's side. Megan vaguely recognized a number of the gawkers as regulars, familiar strangers whose faces she knew in context of the café but might not be able to place away from it.

The group huddled in the alley were mostly women who spent so much time working in the front downstairs corner of the café that Megan had heard them call it their office. She knew they showed up with laptops, ordered coffees, and holed up for hours, and that one of them was American. The rest sounded Irish-born. They were clearly in distress, casting furtive looks into the street as Megan drove by in the Continental.

"Oh!" Claire leaned against her window, face almost smashed against it. "It's closed! What's going on?"

"I'm not sure." Megan was amazed that Claire couldn't hear the artificial, robotic stiffness in her voice. "Should I park in the garage around the corner, and we'll go see?" Bourke was going to kill her for inviting herself into whatever conversation he was about to have with Claire. Orla was going to kill her for getting involved with another client on the periphery of a murd—*a suspicious death*, Megan corrected herself firmly.

And Jelena was going to kill her for not walking away from the whole thing immediately. Megan bit back a sigh as Claire said, "Oh, yes, please! I know you're on the clock but I can't see how it matters if you're with me or sitting in the car; so yes, please come with me."

Possibly Claire was going to kill her, too, for not mentioning everything she knew about the mess at Accents. Then again, of all of them, Claire had the least reason to be concerned with Megan's involvement in yet another suspicious death. In fact, given that Claire had specifically asked for "the murder driver," she might well be delighted at the whole unfolding disaster.

Although presumably she would be less delighted that the young woman she was mentoring had turned up dead. Megan bit the inside of her cheek to keep herself from saying or doing anything besides pulling into the Park Rite on Drury Street. Claire was out of the car again before Megan could hold the door for her—Americans often were—and put her arm through Megan's to make sure they traveled at her desired pace down the stairs and around the corner toward the café. Together, they barged past the group gathered at the Chinese place, and Claire rushed across the street into the gathering in the alley. "Stephanie! What's going on?"

The American woman from the group turned the long way around to face Claire, giving her a moment to grimace visibly at the rest of her little crowd. Megan only caught a glimpse of the expression, and before she had time to process it, Stephanie was hugging Claire unhappily. "Claire, there's been an awful—something terrible has happened."

"What?" Claire returned the embrace, then shot a confused glance at the rest of the group. "What happened? Where's Bláthnaid? I know I'm late, but you're always here early in the day . . ."

"Bláthnaid is dead." The solitary man in the group spoke, his voice shaking. Megan had only seen him a few times, and thought he was possibly a new-ish addition to the group. He was younger than most of the women, tall, bearded, and had evil mastermind eyebrows that Megan rather envied.

Claire's jaw fell open. "Wh—at?"

"We don't know what happened," another woman said, her voice tight with suppressed emotion. "Apparently she was found in the café when they opened this morning."

Megan cast a glance upward, trying not to comment. "Found in the café when it opened" wasn't *exactly* wrong, after all.

Claire whispered, "Oh my God," and for some reason, her hand found Megan's, clutching it. Her fingers were icy and her palm sweaty. Megan resisted the urge to withdraw her hand and wipe it against her work trousers. "Oh my God, what happened? No, you said—you said you don't know." She put her other hand over her mouth, visibly trembling. "Oh my God." Then she released Megan's hand and ran for the street, where she vomited noisily. The crowd at the restaurant across the street made a united sound of disgust and suddenly dissipated.

Paul Bourke strode up as Claire went through another round of puking. He eyed her, then joined Megan in the alley, his pale eyebrows drawn down low as he indicated Claire. "That her?"

Megan nodded apologetically, and the American woman, Stephanie, said, "That's Claire Woodward. I knew her from a critique group back home before I moved over here, and we kept in casual contact. She emailed when she was coming over to do research, so she's been joining our writing club since she got here."

"Claire *Woodward?*" Megan echoed, looking in surprise at her vomiting client. "Wait, I know her. I mean, I know her stuff. She's kind of a big name, isn't she? They do movies based on her books. She wrote *Last Dance at Sunset*," she said to the detective. "The one Niamh was up for the lead in."

"Oh. *Oh.*" Bourke looked after Claire with a faint scowl. "She didn't like Niamh for it."

"Obviously, she's a heinous bitch," Megan said, inspired to defend her actress friend, even though Claire actually seemed like a perfectly nice person. Color flushed Bourke's golden-toned face and he choked on a laugh. Stephanie didn't even choke. She just laughed sharply, then covered her mouth and looked guilty.

"She *is* a heinous bitch," one of the other women said, if shakily. "She's been coming in with us for about a week now and she's awful."

"I swear she wasn't that bad, back before . . ." Stephanie trailed off apologetically.

"Before she got famous," the Irish woman supplied. "She's one of those that there's only one right way to write a book, and it's her way. Do you know how damaging that is for new writers to internalize?" She looked unhappily toward the café, as if she could see inside it. "Bláthnaid was new. She just started writing with us a little while ago."

"Well," Adrian said. "Two years ago."

"Thanks for reminding me I'm aged, Adrian."

"And you are?" Paul asked.

"Juliet McKenna. This is Adrian Tchaikovsky," she said, indicating the tall young man. "Stephanie Burgis is our resident American, and this is Sadhbh Flannagan."

Megan bit down on blurting, "Oh!" as she heard Stephanie's full name. Jelena had a stack of well-loved novels by Stephanie Burgis, and an ongoing hope that the last book in the series would be out soon. And Claire had said Stephanie was late in turning in the final book. The little bits of information clicked together with a ridiculous amount of satisfaction in completing a puzzle she hadn't even known she was trying to solve.

Bourke, thankfully not aware of Megan's thought process, noted the names down, saying, "Irish or English spelling for Sadhbh?"

"Irish." Which meant, Megan knew, that her name looked like a holy terror to English-reading eyes, although it was pronounced like *sigh* with a V on the end. Sadhbh was dark-haired, in her mid-twenties as Bláthnaid had been, and red-faced from weeping. Her voice was thick from tears, too, as she said, "Bláthnaid and me were college mates. We bonded over having impossible Irish names."

Bourke nodded, then gestured everyone a few steps farther down the alley. Claire hadn't rejoined them, but was still sitting numbly on the curb like she might throw up again. In her heart of hearts, Megan knew she should go help her client, even if it meant she might miss something.

She stayed put, saw Bourke noticing she stayed put, and decided to ignore that. Paul, in turn, clearly decided to ignore her, and directed his next question at Sadhbh, but was clearly prepared for any of the others to answer. "Tell me about the last time you saw her." Megan wasn't surprised when Juliet, who—from what Megan had seen of the group working together—seemed firmly grounded and business-oriented, spoke up.

"It would have been . . ." Juliet drew a deep breath, trying to settle herself. She was about Megan's height and had a round, kind face that offered a sad smile as Adrian put an arm around her shoulder. "It would have been Sunday evening, I'd say. She and Claire had a tiff, and Claire stormed off."

"What was the fight ab—" Megan snapped her mouth shut at Bourke's warning look.

"Claire's been mentoring Bláthnaid," Stephanie said. "Over the internet, but since she was coming here for research, and I was in this writing group with Bláthnaid, it all seemed like it was a nice tidy . . . whatever. I introduced them." She made a face that suggested she had regrets.

Bourke smiled briefly. "A nice tidy whatever? I thought writers were good with words."

"We are when we get to revise them before they go out to the public," Stephanie said with an equally brief smile. "The fight was my fault, I suppose. My editor was in Dublin a few weeks ago and I introduced Bláthnaid to her. They talked about her book, and my editor wanted to see the S and three—that's the synopsis and the first three chapters. Bláthnaid submitted them and was asked for the full manuscript last Friday, so she came in to our writing date pretty excited. It's a big moment, to have the full manuscript requested."

"So what went wrong?" Bourke's note-taking hesitated as Stephanie paused. The writers exchanged glances, obviously willing one another to be the one who broke whatever their bad news was.

"Claire brought in an ARC—that's an advance reader copy—of her newest book to the writing session Sunday night. It's what gets sent to reviewers and, in cases like hers, maybe to television and film producers, ahead of its publication," Adrian said as the silence drew on. "And Bláthnaid brought her manuscript in. None of us had read it."

"I'd read the first few chapters," Stephanie said. Adrian shrugged agreeably as Megan bit her tongue on curiosity and let Bourke ask the obvious question.

"And?"

"They were the same story," Stephanie said unhappily. "Almost word-for-word. It looks like Bláthnaid plagiarized Claire's work."

CHAPTER 4

Megan turned to look across the street at Claire Woodward, who was still pale and sweaty on the sidewalk's edge. "So that kind of makes her the primary suspect, doesn't it."

Paul hissed, "Megan!" and she winced apologetically as he gestured at her. "Go home, Megan!"

"I can't! She's my client!"

"Well, you can go—" He gestured again, obviously not intending anywhere in particular with the motion. "Over there! Go—be with your client!"

Megan reminded herself that she was a fully grown adult with a job that did not involve solving murders, and managed *not* to say "but all the interesting stuff is happening over here!"

Not out loud, at least. She slunk toward Claire, but halfway across the street, couldn't quite stop herself from stomping her feet with aggravation in the middle of the road before she crossed the rest of the way and sat down on the sidewalk beside her client.

Claire fixed her with an unhappy smile. "Sent away from your murder driver investigation, huh? I didn't do it, Megan."

"Nope." Megan held her hands up, palms out. "I'm definitely not getting involved. Paul will kill me. My girlfriend will kill me."

"And if you remind yourself of that enough times, maybe you'll believe it?"

Megan made a face. "Something like that, I guess. What, do writers have great insight into the hearts and minds of the people around them?"

"Not really, but doing a little dance of frustration in the middle of a street is kind of a dead giveaway."

Megan, trying to draw dignity around herself, said, "I was hoping nobody saw that."

Claire gave a soft laugh. "I don't think your detective did, if that helps."

"He's not my detective, but that's something, yeah." Questions bubbled up and Megan pressed her lips together, trying to keep them in.

Claire, staring at the gaggle of writers across the street, answered them anyway. "I had no idea Bláthnaid was trying to pass my work off as her own. I don't know how she could have imagined it would succeed. The book was already sold, after all. It's about to be published."

Voices rose in the group Paul was interviewing, with Bláthnaid's college friend Sadhbh pointing violently at Claire, who sighed. "She's telling him I stole Bláthnaid's work, not the other way around."

"Did you?" Megan grimaced as soon as she asked, but Claire only exhaled sadly.

"No, of course not. I don't blame you for asking, though. I assume the detective will, too."

"Probably. It's kind of the first thing that leaps to mind."

Claire nodded. "Maybe you should go ahead and leave me. I'm sure I can get back to the B and B on my own, and this could take all day, couldn't it?"

"Yeah . . ." Megan's shoulders dropped gloomily as she watched Paul take Sadhbh to the side for further interviewing. The other writers huddled closer, casting worried glances toward Claire without anyone visibly wanting to come talk to her. "I should probably call my boss, at least."

"And your girlfriend," Claire suggested.

Megan smiled crookedly. "I haven't figured out how to break this one to her yet. She doesn't like the whole 'Megan gets involved in murder cases' thing."

"Can you blame her?"

"Not at all. I'm not too crazy about it either." Megan glanced at Paul and Sadhbh in the covered alley and sighed. "Of course, it also turns out I kind of hate not being right in the middle of it, if I'm . . . well, you know. Right in the middle of it."

"Well, that's my fault," Claire said in an attempt at a brisk tone. "If I hadn't asked for the murder driver, you wouldn't be in this mess."

Megan dropped her head and said "Mmm," to

the ground. It wouldn't make Detective Bourke's job any easier if she let Claire know she'd already been neck- or, at least, lap-deep in the situation before Claire had asked for her. "I don't even see how you could have plagiarized Bláthnaid's work, if your book is going to be published soon and hers is only just now being considered."

"I write fast," Claire replied with a dramatic sigh. "I suppose it's possible I could have seen her premise and opening chapters, revised them to my own liking, and submitted them as a proposal to my editor. In that scenario, I could have made the sale and written the book, either using the material she sent me for workshopping and review or just on my own, and delivered it. Next thing you know, it's about to come out, and she's only just finished her own manuscript. I suppose I would have needed to write my own ending, if I'd done all this, so the books would diverge more at the end, I guess. But honestly, ideas are cheap, Megan. Even if I'd stolen Bláthnaid's exact premise, I would have written a completely different book anyway. Why would I take her actual story?"

Megan wrinkled her nose. "I don't know. Are ideas cheap? I thought coming up with an idea was the hard part of writing."

"I invite you to tell a writer you've got a great idea, so if they want to do the easy part and write the book you can split the profits," Claire said drolly. "No, making an idea work can be hard, but that's why writing is the hard part of writing. People kind of don't believe that. Almost everybody can put words down on a page with a pencil or a keyboard, so I think sometimes the physical act of being able to write gets mixed up with the idea of being able to write a book. And don't get me wrong, it's not like digging ditches, but telling a story that works is harder than just being able to form a sentence and put it down on a page. She really thinks I stole Bláthnaid's book," Claire ended sadly, nodding at Sadhbh, who had left Paul and returned to the group.

He beckoned Stephanie over and the American woman left the other writers with a brief, uncomfortable smile. Claire watched her a moment, then said, "She probably thinks I did it, too. She doesn't like me very much."

"I thought you were friends from way back."

"Well." Claire wobbled a hand back and forth. "Acquaintances. We were part of the same writing group back in Sacramento a million years ago. But it's mostly professional envy. My career took off and hers . . . well, it didn't stall. I just hit all the lists and some big money, and she didn't. It's not fair. She's at least as good a writer as I am, maybe better, but it happens. And I know she's way late on the last book in her series, so she probably gets some satisfaction out of seeing me in a bind."

"What about the rest of them?" Megan bit the inside of her cheek again. Maybe she could convince Paul she'd just been having a conversation, not investigating.

Claire shook her head. "I don't know them at all well. Juliet seems pretty cool. Serious about her work. She whips the rest of them into shape when they get together at the café to write. Adrian's a

nice kid. Not a great people person. He likes to repeat things to make sure he's got it right. That's
about all I know about either of them. I don't
think they have any particular reason to dislike
me, but I guess they'd rather think I was the bad
guy than their friend."

"Baddie," Megan said softly. "The Irish usually
say 'baddie' instead of 'bad guy.' " Mentioning that
helped her keep quiet on the fact that Juliet had
agreed with Megan's spurious comment about
Claire being a heinous bitch.

Just as well she wasn't investigating, Megan
thought. Her impulse toward discretion had apparently disappeared entirely since the last time
she'd been involved in a murder case. Probably Jelena's good influence. She smiled at the thought,
then took her phone out, but realized she had no
idea what to say to her girlfriend. Or her boss, for
that matter. After a minute she got up and moved
down the street to call Orla anyway, hoping inspiration would strike when she answered the phone.

"I know it's you, Megan, so what's the story?"
Orla said when she picked up.

"Funny thing about that murder driver re-
quest . . ."

"Oh," Orla said, sounding a lot like Jelena for a
moment. "Oh no."

"The client's alive," Megan said hastily. "But I
had a . . . ah." A momentary silence drew out while
she looked for a delicate way to phrase the news,
then broke as she decided she just couldn't. "I had
a dead girl fall in my lap this morning, and it turns
out the woman I'm driving this afternoon knew

her. So I guess I'm calling to see if I should . . . I don't know."

"Quit?" Orla demanded. "Move to a desert island so you don't drag anyone else to hell with you? Call a priest to have the devil stricken from your bones? Cast yourself—"

"All *right*, Orla, I get the idea. Do you want me to quit the job or not? She says she can get back to her B and B on her own, if it comes to it."

"Are you still with her?" Orla's voice turned canny. "If I can still charge her for the time spent, I don't see why you should rush back to the garage."

Megan thinned her lips and stared down the road toward the line of moving traffic on the larger street. "You're a terrible woman, Orla."

"But a rich one," Orla said, and hung up.

Megan stayed where she was a minute, still watching the traffic, then inhaled deeply and called Jelena, who answered with a worried, "Megan?"

"I'm fine. I just wanted to keep you in the loop." Megan made an actual clawing motion with her free hand, like she could pull the words back.

Jelena's silence held for a few long seconds before she said, "In the loop about what?" in a dangerously calm tone.

"The job I picked up this afternoon has a connection to the dead girl."

"*Megan!*"

"I know! I'm sorry!"

"You have to quit! Give the job to Cillian!"

"I talked to Orla," Megan said helplessly. "She said to stay on the job."

"You talked to *Orla* before me?"

"I can see now that that was a mistake."

"Megan, I swear to God." Jelena's silence felt daggered. "If this affects our plans this week . . ."

"It won't! It won't, Yella, I promise."

"You don't know that! You can't promise it!"

Megan sagged and sat on the sidewalk down the street from Claire, pushing her driver's hat back on her head to prod at her hairline. "You're right," she said more quietly. "I'm sorry. I'll call Orla and tell her she needs to give the job to somebody else."

"She'll say no," Jelena snapped. "She can charge extra for you."

"That's more or less what she said," Megan agreed, but shook her head. "No, you're right, though. I need to not do this. I'm sorry. I should have called you first, and I should have—"

A sigh came down the line. "Not been dying to know the whole story?"

Megan ducked her head guiltily. "Yeah, I guess so."

"Megan . . ." Jelena sighed again. "You might as well finish out today."

"No, it's fine, Claire said she could get home on her own. She's Claire Woodward," Megan added. "The writer?"

"The one who didn't want Niamh to be in her movie?" Jelena's voice turned tart. "Never mind, stay with her. Maybe you'll get her killed, too."

"Jelena!" Megan laughed. "That's awful!"

"I don't mean it." Jelena paused. "Mostly. Niamh really wanted that part."

"Yeah, but Claire can't really have blackballed her, can she? Writers don't have that kind of power in casting movies from their books, I don't think. Like, Anne Rice didn't want Tom Cruise to play Lestat, and look how that worked out for her."

"Niamh isn't as successful as Tom Cruise."

"Even Tom Cruise isn't as successful as Tom Cruise. But I don't know, maybe she's got her own production company. Do writers have production companies?"

"I work at a chocolate café, Megan," Jelena said ruefully. "I don't know what writers do and don't have."

"Me either." Megan looked back toward Claire, whose unhappy gaze was fixed on the other writers across the street. "Now I kind of want to ask, though."

Jelena made an explosive sound. "Well, go ask, then. Maybe it will cure your 'satiable curiosity.' "

"See, how did I ever get lucky enough to deserve a woman who quotes Kipling?"

"You're very cute and very lucky," Jelena said. "We'll talk tonight."

"Lucky, especially," Megan agreed. "Okay. Jelena?"

"Yeah?"

"Thank you."

Another sigh softened Jelena's voice. "Yeah. You're welcome. I'll see you later, skarbie." She hung up, leaving Megan to hope that, if she was still willing to use the Polish endearment that meant *babe*, maybe she wasn't *too* angry.

Claire said, "Everything okay?" as Megan came back to sit beside her again.

"More or less. Can I ask you something?" At Claire's open, inviting gesture, Megan said, "What's it like having movies made of your books?"

Claire gave a quick, surprised laugh. "It's amazing and super-annoying."

Megan's eyebrows rose. "Annoying?"

"People get mad at me if they don't like the casting, or if the movie changes the book's story at all, or . . . anything. They think writers have a lot of control over that, when really, unless you're also a producer, you don't have any at all, and hardly any novelists end up with production companies."

A little wave of relief swept through Megan as she thought of Niamh's disappointment over the role she hadn't gotten. "Right, yeah, I thought writers couldn't have anything to say about casting, not really."

"Right. Although after the first couple movies and one very bad television show, I talked to my agent and a lot of lawyers and started a production company." Claire smiled briefly. "Now I still have almost no control, but I get paid a lot more."

Megan's stomach dropped. "Oh. Almost no control means . . . ?"

"Well, like, there was an Irish woman up for the lead on my next movie, Niamh O'Sullivan? I just really thought they should cast an actual American. I get so tired of British actors taking iconically American roles, you know? All those American superhero characters who are played by Brits."

Megan had a momentary sensation of being surrounded by options for "which hill to die on." The one she chose, with effort, was, "Irish actors aren't synonymous with British actors. Different countries, you know. They fought a war about it and everything." And eight hundred years of resistance, but an all-out argument/lecture on Anglo-Irish relations was not what she wanted here.

"Oh, you know what I mean, though," Claire said with a wave of her hand. "I just wanted an American for the part, and the woman who got it is wonderful."

Megan folded her knuckles over her mouth and said, "Mm," through them. This was her own fault. She'd brought it up. Yelling a defense of Niamh wouldn't help either the case, the situation, or Niamh's career. Heaven forbid Niamh should get labeled "difficult" because her friends couldn't keep their mouths shut. Hollywood was hard enough for women of color.

Claire gave her a sideways smile, though. "You're Irish enough now to want the local girl to do well, huh? I don't mean anything against Ms. O'Sullivan. I can't even be sure the casting directors listened to me. I just had an opinion, that's all."

"Well, we all have those," Megan conceded, although it took an absurd amount of effort to sound pleasant. Orla would be rightfully furious if she got the company bad reviews by being a cow to a client. Across the street, Paul had finished talking to Adrian, and turned toward Megan and Claire where they sat. "Looks like you're up next."

Claire's clammy hand went to Megan's wrist. "Come with me?"

A brief war of desires took place in Megan's chest, almost making her laugh. "I'm not sure I should."

"He can send you away if he wants," Claire said with determination. "Come on." She got up, pulling Megan with her, and crossed the street.

Paul, who was in Claire's line of sight, gave Megan the most subtle of warning glares. She widened her eyes with an admittedly not-very-sincere innocence and shrugged. Paul said, "You're excused, Ms. Malone," and Claire, still clutching Megan's wrist, said, "I'd like her to stay. I've never been questioned by the police before. This is all awful."

"It's considerably worse for Bláthnaid O'Leary." Detective Bourke sighed. "All right. Keep your mouth shut, Megan."

Megan barely refrained from miming zipping her lips, and from the short, sharp look Bourke gave her before turning his full attention to Claire, thought he knew it. "Ms. Woodward, can you describe to me the exact nature of your relationship with the deceased?"

"I was her writing mentor," Claire said shakily. "Stephanie introduced us online about a year and a half ago because Bláthnaid"—and Megan could hear how carefully she said the name, trying to get it right—"was writing historical romance, like I do, and she thought I could give her some guidance."

"How closely did you work together?"

Claire shook her head. "Quite a bit in the first few weeks, as we—I, really—decided whether it would even work. I'm a terrible mentor, it turns out. I have the necessary skill set, but I put it off and feel guilty instead of actually doing the work. After the first blush wore off, we'd probably talk once a month or so. Bláthnaid would send me new material she was working on, and we'd discuss it or workshop it. We had some brainstorming sessions. It was all through email or online chat. I like brainstorming in chat rooms, where everything you say is all written down so you just have to scroll through to remember what you talked about."

"What chat service did you use?"

"The one that comes with Gmail, mostly. Why?"

Bourke ignored the question while Megan ignored the impulse to take notes on how he interrogated Claire. He was considerably better at this than she was. As if he'd been trained for it, and Megan was just some random person off the street who kept getting herself in over her head, or something. She sucked in her cheeks and looked down to keep from laughing. Paul ignored that, too. "When did you see Ms. O'Leary last?"

Claire took a shaky breath. "Sunday night. Well, evening, I guess. Eight or nine PM, a while before the café closed. They probably told you," she said with a nod toward the other writers, who had gathered to scowl suspiciously at Claire as she was interviewed. "I brought an early copy of my newest book in, and Bláthnaid brought in her book proposal that Stephanie's editor had just requested. And they were the same book." Her voice rose a lit-

tle with confusion, then broke. "I don't understand how she could have imagined that was going
to work."

"The obvious answer is that she didn't, and you
plagiarized her work, instead," Bourke replied
steadily.

Claire's shoulders slumped and she gestured
loosely at Megan. "I was telling her how that
could work, but honestly, Detective—is that the
right thing to call you?"

"It is."

"Honestly, Detective, if I'd gone to all the trouble of stealing her work and thought she was going
to expose me, wouldn't it have been smarter to kill
her before she showed anybody what she was working on? Then I could have deleted all her files, at
least the ones I'd seen, I guess, and pretended
total innocence."

The faintest hint of bemusement pulled at Paul's
mouth. "But you didn't."

"Because I didn't steal her book! Also, I wouldn't
kill anybody."

"But you did think through why one approach
for killing her would be smarter than another."

For a moment, Claire's nervousness turned to
exasperation. "I'm a novelist, Detective. We spend
a huge amount of time thinking through ap-
proaches for things we're never going to do. Honestly, you should see my search history."

"Thanks for the invitation. I'll take a look."

Claire's face fell comically as Paul went on,
"Where were you this morning between four and
eight AM, Ms. Woodward?"

"Sleeping at my B and B," she said unhappily. "By myself, so I guess that's not much of an alibi. Four hours is a long window for figuring out the time of death, isn't it?"

Megan, who had been wondering the same thing, dared a glance at Paul, who developed pained lines around his mouth. "Ms. Woodward, for the moment, you're free to go. You are not, however, free to leave the country. Megan, if I could have a moment?"

Megan, startled, said, "Sure," and Claire took an uncertain step or two toward the gathered writing group. A little to Megan's surprise, most of them indicated she should join them, and she hurried into the huddle, clearly in hopes of receiving, or offering, comfort.

"Did you talk to Ms. Keegan?"

"She swore at me and then told me I might as well stay on the job for the day, since she can over-charge Claire for this. Jelena's given me until the end of the day to satisfy my curiosity. I'm sorry, Paul. I'm really sorry."

He dismissed the apology. "How did what she said to me square up with what she'd told you?"

"Pretty well. She had some thoughts about the other writers in the group."

The pained tightness pinched his mouth again. "I'll want to hear about that later. Do you and Jelena have dinner plans?"

"I don't know. She said we'd talk tonight."

"Oh, you *are* in trouble. I'll text and ask her if I can drop in. In the meantime, Megan . . ."

She sighed. "Stay out of trouble?"

"That would be grand altogether, but clearly unrealistic. Just be prepared to tell me anything she says, whether it seems relevant or not."

Megan snapped a not-entirely-sarcastic salute. "Yes, sir."

"Ah, g'wan witcha." Paul, sounding very Irish indeed, waved her off, and Megan sheepishly went to collect her client.

CHAPTER 5

"Does he think I did it?" This time, a miserable Claire let Megan hold the car door for her. Closing the door and getting into the driver's seat gave Megan a moment to come up with the most politic answer as she met Claire's eyes in the rearview mirror.

"Even if he does, Detective Bourke wouldn't tell me, Claire. I'm not a police officer."

"But you're friends!"

"And as his friend, I wouldn't want him to tell me anything that would get him fired," Megan said firmly. "Claire, I'm sure it'll probably be fine. In the meantime, is there anywhere else I can bring you? Have you finished your research for the day?"

"You could show me the city walls," Claire said dismally. "I've got a dashing rescue scene in this book and it'd be helpful to get a sense of what they had to overcome to get into Dublin at the time."

"Walls like the ones at Trim," Megan said, but smiled at the other woman. "All right. I'll take you over to St. Audoen's in the Liberties. It's got the only remaining gate from the old walls, and there's a freestanding chunk of wall on Cornmarket that you can have a look at."

Claire, her voice small, as if she was reluctant and yet unable to be intrigued, said, "The Liberties?"

This, Megan thought, was most of the fun of chauffeuring tourists. She launched into a history lesson—the Liberties had been an abbey outside of the Dublin city walls, and granted the liberty to conduct trade there, hence the name—and had become the center for trades and craftsmen by the sixteenth century, with an international population that was reflected in street names even now. By the time they'd driven the ten minutes from the café to the Liberties, Claire had forgotten most of her worries and leaned forward, listening with delighted interest to Megan's lecture. "You could make a living doing this!"

"I do," Megan pointed out.

"I mean giving tours!"

Megan grinned as she found a parking spot. "I do."

A few minutes later, standing beneath the imposing square-framed arch of St. Audoen's Gate, Claire said, "Holy shit," with slow thoughtfulness. "You just don't really appreciate these things until you see them, do you? You read about the city walls in books, but it's hard to really imagine what having twenty-foot tall, six-foot wide walls surrounding a city must have been like. Even if the city is smaller than what we think of as a city. I mean, these are huge." She stepped inside the gate, spreading her arms and utterly failing to reach either side, from where she stood. "*Look on my works, ye mighty, and despair.*"

"Yeah, and just like Ozymandias, this is all that's left. You should go to Carcassonne in France sometime. The citadel there has been walled since about the same time Dublin's walls were built, but they're intact. Or at least, restored. I don't know how much of them is the actual original walls. It's pretty impressive, though."

Claire stepped out of the gate, her eyes sparkling. "Carcassonne, huh? I sense another historical romance coming up. So this is—what direction does this face?" She turned around, trying to get her bearings.

"North." Megan pointed toward the River Liffey, a couple of blocks away, and westward. "Trim is over there, northwest of here, if you're thinking about your dramatic rescue. I don't know what kinds of roads there were back in the day, though."

Claire waved a hand. "I'll figure it out, although it's farther than I thought. I was thinking ten miles or so. Thirty is a whole different thing, when you're traveling by horseback."

Megan cautiously said, "Is this—this isn't for the book that's coming out right now, right? The one . . . uhm."

"The one that's going to cause a lot of controversy?" Claire bared her teeth. "I hope that whole 'no such thing as bad publicity' thing is true. No, this is the next one." She fell silent a moment, then, much more quietly, said, "You'd better bring me back to my B and B, I think. I need to call my publicist and my editor and let them know what's going on. They're both supposed to be here this week, anyway. They're coming on tour with me, but they should probably know what they're walking into."

"When do they arrive?"

"Derek's coming in tonight and Kiki comes in tomorrow."

Megan drew a breath, realized she was about to volunteer to pick them up at the airport, and forced a cough to cover it. Claire's eyebrows drew down and Megan shook her head, wheezing, "Just need some water from the car. Sorry—I'm fine."

"Well, let's get you back to it, then." Claire gestured solicitously and Megan, eyes watering from the effort of not getting more involved, went where she was invited. Claire spent most of the drive back taking notes on her phone, leaving Megan to sift through everything she'd said and try to find useful tidbits to share with Paul.

Her phone buzzed just after she dropped Claire at the B and B with a text from Jelena saying **Paul and Niamh want to have dinner. Am I going to regret this?**

Megan made a face. **Hope not. I said I'd tell him anything Claire mentioned to me, in case it didn't match up to what she told him.**

Jelena sent back a resigned-looking emoticon, then a text saying **Takeaway, then? Since he probably doesn't want to be talking about an active murder case in the restaurant?**

I'm heading home, Megan wrote. **I could cook. Unless you think takeaway is safer.**

I think takeaway is faster, Jelena said. **You always want to make a slow-cooked American meal when you're feeding us Europeans. Stew. Chili. Barbecue ribs. You think we're missing out, otherwise.**

Megan laughed, said, "True dat," aloud, and texted **All of which sounds DELICIOUS, but I'll get Indian or something on the way home, then. You're a star, Yella.** Only after she'd put the phone down did she wonder why they'd had the entire conversation in text, since it would almost certainly have been faster to call. "Because phones are invasive," she informed herself as she pulled back into traffic.

The streets were filling up with tourists ahead of the holiday weekend, and driving back to Rathmines took most of an hour, more than half again as long as Megan had expected. Orla, scowling hugely, was at the reception desk when Megan brought the car in, and Megan paused on her way through. "What, didn't Claire's credit card clear, or something?"

"She's only after ringing asking for you for the whole of the holiday," Orla announced with a glare. "And you're going to give me some rubbish about having plans."

"Because I have plans! I've had plans for a year! I am not changing my plans so you can make a few hundred extra quid!"

Orla sniffed. "Selfish, if you ask me."

"I don't see how I can possibly be at fault here!" Megan left to the sound of Orla's grumbling and stopped for Asian fusion food on the way home. She put it on the kitchen table while she went to release the dogs from the back garden, and came back to Jelena, still in her coat and shoes, guiltily trying to hide the fact that she'd stolen a gyoza as soon as she got in the door.

Megan laughed. "Don't worry. I realized I was starving when I got to the restaurant and ordered enough for six teenagers."

"Mmm," Jelena said around the dumpling. "Never shop hungry."

"Or order food, apparently." Megan grinned, slipped Jelena's coat from her shoulders, and hung it up for her. "Any idea when Paul and Niamh will be here?"

"If it's not in the next couple minutes I'm going to eat all their food."

"If you can eat it all before they get here, I'll be very impressed." Megan put her hand out to Jelena to see if she was in trouble for the entire "involved in a murder again" thing, and to her relief, Jelena smiled ruefully and tugged her close for a kiss as the dogs bounded desperately around their knees, demanding acknowledgment.

"I know you don't mean to do this, Megan. I just wish it was easier for you to stay out of it when you find yourself involved."

"I don't know why it's not," Megan said in despair. "Somebody with any sense would run screaming in the other direction."

"Well," Jelena said affectionately, "you're American. Nobody expects you to have any sense."

"Hey!" Megan laughed out loud. Jelena grinned

and Megan sniffed. "I was *going* to tell you I'd met Stephanie Burgis, the woman who writes those big, fat fantasy novels you've got in the bedroom, but now I'm not going to."

Jelena's eyes brightened. "Really? Was she nice? Did you ask when her last book was going to be done?"

"Really, yes, and no, it didn't occur to me."

"Aw. Well, I'll just keep reading the fan fiction, then."

"There's fan fiction?"

"Oh, loads." Jelena finally bent to greet the dogs. "Yes, Dip. Yes, pup. I see you. Hello. Don't be rude. Hello, Thong. Yes, you're very cute. Now stop that," which was very close to the same conversation Megan had held with them in the back garden. Dip, who was the more dramatic of the two, fell over on his back and gave Jelena a mournful look, as if she had cast him away and in doing so, broken his heart. She giggled and he managed to assume an offended air as Thong, more politely, sat and wagged her tail so hard that everything from her shoulders down quivered. "That's a good girl." Jelena rubbed the dog's ears. Dip sat up to stare at both of them in deeply hurt disbelief as Jelena straightened. "Some of it's pretty good. The fic, I mean. The dogs, too, sometimes."

Megan laughed as a knock sounded on the door and Dip launched himself at it, not barking, but desperate to see who was there. Thong leaped after him, ran into Jelena's knees, corrected course, and crashed into her brother at the door. "Oh my God, dogs, it's just visitors!"

"Dip," Jelena said firmly. "Thong. Come here. You know you're not allowed to lick people to death at the door." Both dogs slunk back to her and sat at her feet, but all their attention was for the big revelation of the door opening. Megan, grinning, went to answer it, then laughed to see both Paul and Niamh with their gazes fixed warily downward, clearly in anticipation of being swarmed by Jack Russells.

"Jelena's finally taught them not to do that," Megan said by way of greeting. "Come on in." She smiled at Paul, and Niamh kissed her cheek as they came in.

"I hear you're up to all sorts of mischief again, young lady."

"It's not my fault! Events are conspiring against me!"

Niamh laughed as she shrugged her jacket off, a wonderful big, rich sound that made everybody around her smile, too. She had her hair up, curls dripping down in a style that reminded Megan of how Jelena often wore hers, and for a moment she had to look between the two other women. Jelena was several inches taller, but they both had the same delicate chins, high cheekbones, and large eyes. "I never realized you two look a lot alike," she said in surprise. "Different color palates, but other-wise . . ."

They regarded one another, Niamh saying, "You're not wrong," thoughtfully. "What I wouldn't give to be your height, though!"

Jelena laughed and gestured at Niamh's outfit.

"And what I wouldn't give to be able to borrow your wardrobe!"

Niamh did a little laughing spin, showing off a cropped blouse top and high-waisted trousers that fell long over what Megan guessed were tall heels. The short jacket she'd already abandoned was the same rich burgundy as the trousers, which, Megan thought, would look as good against Jelena's porcelain skin as it did against Niamh's tawny tones. "Oh, this old thing?"

"I've never seen you in 'that old thing' before," Megan said with confidence, and Paul grinned.

"No, you haven't. She got it last week. It's—who is it?"

"Prada."

"Oh, Prada," Jelena said with a roll of her eyes. "No big deal."

Paul shook his head. "After the internet declared she won—" and he put the word in air quotes— "the awards shows' red carpets last year, designers just started sending her things."

"It's very hard to be a movie star," Niamh said so solemnly that Megan giggled.

"She tries them all on and asks for my opinion," Paul went on with a momentarily glazed expression. "Some of them are desperately awful, but some are incredible."

Megan laughed. "Do you agree on which is which?"

"Not always. We agreed on that one, though. It's brilliant."

Niamh went to Jelena's side, trying to stand even taller in her heels so she'd match the Polish woman's height. "You could probably wear this. It'd just be shorter on you."

"The top is already cropped! I'd be indecent!"

"You'd only be gorgeous," Niamh assured her as Paul started poking in the takeaway bags.

"I don't know what's in all these, but it smells delicious."

"Ramen and teriyaki and . . . honestly, I think I ordered everything on the menu. I was starving. *Am* starving!" Megan started unloading the food while the dogs wound around Paul's shins, trying to see if he loved them. "Has your boss strung you up on the topic of me yet?"

Paul petted Thong and shooed the dogs away. "I've kept your name out of it so far. I didn't think it was necessary to say 'Megan Malone had a body fall on her at a café.' 'A café patron discovered the body' seemed sufficient."

"For both your own sake and mine."

"More mine," Paul admitted as he went to wash his hands. "Can I help?"

"Plates are in the cupboard to your left."

"Okay. Silverware?" He opened drawers until he found it, then stacked cutlery and tableware together to bring them to the table. A couple of minutes later they were all settled, with bits of conversation exchanged, and dogs laughed at, as they focused on dinner.

"All right," Paul eventually said, once dinner was finished and they'd resettled in the living room where the dogs kept creeping into their laps, like if they did it carefully enough they wouldn't be noticed. They were put back on the floor, but undeterred, tried again, until Paul gave up and kept Dip in his lap while Thong stared mournfully at Jelena. "What do you think, Megan?"

"I don't have an opinion." He eyed her and she sighed. "Okay, obviously I have an opinion, but I'm not supposed to, so I'm saying I don't."

"I wouldn't be able to sleep for wanting to hear it," Paul said dryly. "Do tell."

Megan shrugged. "I don't think she did it. For one thing, I've gone up stairs with her. She runs out of breath at half a flight. Wrestling a dead body into a closet above your head is harder than that. Or I assume it is," she added as Paul's eyebrows rose.

"Anything else?"

"I don't see what good it would do her. She's already Claire Woodward. Why would she steal somebody else's work? She says ideas are cheap, that if you gave her the exact same premise as Bláthnaid's book, she would write something totally different. What do *you* think?"

Paul grunted and bent his attention to scratching between Dip's ears. Thong, unable to take it anymore, crept into Megan's lap again with an apologetic gaze, and rolled over to expose her tummy. Megan mumbled, "Okay, fine, I'm not made of stone," and rubbed the little dog's belly fondly.

"It'd be easiest if it was her," Bourke said after a moment. "Motivation's there, opportunity's probably there—we're having the security cameras at her B and B checked to see if she really was there all night, which is not something I should be telling you—and I'd be lying if I said I didn't want it to be her because she stood in the way of Niamh's career."

Niamh's expression softened and she leaned over, touching her forehead to his briefly. "I told you not to worry your head about that. People get passed over for roles all the time. Even me," she said with a quick smile.

"Yeah, but they wouldn't all have the book's author on the morning talk shows saying it'd never be you if she had anything to say about it." Paul drew a deep breath and lifted one hand. "Now, see, now I'm doing the overprotective arsehole thing that I said I wouldn't do. I'm sorry. Anything else for my notes, Megan?"

"Um, yes." Megan snapped her fingers, trying to remember exactly what had been said. "She said to me earlier that she didn't want Bláthnaid to get stuck on the idea there's only one right way to write a book, but Ms. McKenna said that's how Claire is, that she thinks you have to do it her way. I have no idea if that's important. And her editor and publicist are coming in. Derek and Kiki. I don't know which is which. But she mentioned it and I did *not* volunteer to go pick them up—"

"Good!" Jelena and Paul spoke in unison, and Niamh laughed at the affronted expression Megan felt flicker across her own face.

"—but I thought you should know," she ended with as much dignity as she could. "Claire expects this to all turn into some kind of publicity for her new book. Can you keep her from talking about it all? Since it's an ongoing investigation?"

Paul muttered, "Jaysus. No, although I told her not to. It'll be all over the socials by now, though.

People will be asking her about it. It's always harder with high-profile suspects or victims. People want to be part of it, and that's the last thing I need."

"I could go skinny-dipping in Dalkey," Niamh volunteered. "Just strip off me kit and waltz right in. That'd distract everybody for a while."

"In *March*?" Paul turned to Niamh, whose laughter rolled across the room again.

"Now there's a man confident in his relationship," she said cheerfully. "Me naked in public, that's fine, it's just the weather he's concerned about." She leaned over to kiss him thoroughly enough that he cleared his throat and straightened his shirt unconsciously when it ended. "I've been working out for the next fil-um," she said, exaggerating the often-used Irish pronunciation of the word. "Probably no better time for candid nudes to escape onto the internet than now."

"Let's see if we can avoid that scenario," Paul said hoarsely. "Not that I'm unappreciative of the suggestion."

"Well, desperate times," Niamh said, still cheerfully. "No point in being a celebrity if you can't draw fire sometimes, right?"

"I wonder if other movie stars sit around having these discussions," Jelena said, amused. "'Hey lads, want me to jump naked into the sea so you can go about your business?'"

"I'll start asking," Niamh promised. "It'll be a good conversation starter with new coworkers."

"Okay, but you gotta tell me what Favorite Chris says," Megan said with a laugh.

"Oh, he's definitely a jump-naked-in-the-ocean type," Niamh said. "I don't even have to ask."

"Neither of us need to know this," Paul said to Jelena, who grinned.

"Probably not, and still somehow, this is the life we lead. All right, now, take your girlfriend home before she shares any more intimate industry secrets, and I, Detective Bourke, will do my best to keep *my* girlfriend from becoming any more involved with your murder mystery."

CHAPTER 6

Much, much too early the next morning, Jelena mumbled, "Megan, your phone is blowing up," and for a vague, dream-ridden moment, Megan envisioned it hissing and spitting sparks of smoke and fire. It took another several seconds to groggily realize the incessant buzzing wasn't her alarm, but a less-steady stream of incoming texts and missed call notifications.

Then her heart seized with panic, all the worst possible conclusions leaping to mind as she sat up and fumbled for the phone. None of the missed messages were from the States, though: nothing from her parents, or her friend Rafael in California. She collapsed back into bed, stomach swirling with sickness, and just lay there with the phone on her chest for a minute, waiting for her heart to slow down.

"Skarbie?" Jelena used a Polish word for *babe* as she lifted her head sleepily. "Everything okay?"

"Yeah. No. I dunno. No emergencies at home, though. In America, I mean."

"Okay." Jelena kissed her shoulder and flopped back down, clearly content to wait for whatever news was blowing Megan's phone up. It buzzed again and Megan made an effort to open the message this time.

This one was from Cillian, her coworker who doted on his niece, and said **Have you seen this?!** with a screenshot, and then a link, to one of the Irish tabloids.

The headline shrieked MURDER MYSTERY MAYHEM! with a slug of *Local "Murder Driver" Megan Malone at the scene of another crime!* beneath a photograph of Megan in her Leprechaun Limos uniform. The accompanying article had more to do with her murder driver history than Bláthnaid O'Leary's death, but Megan was fairly certain neither Detective Bourke nor An Garda Síochána in general would see it as her being uninvolved with the investigation. With a groan, she checked another message.

One was from her friend Fionnuala, whose restaurant had been where food critic Elizabeth Darr had died. It just said **Oh my god, Megan, are you okay?** but the next couple were from other people sending links and screenshots to different tabloid articles, and then, to Megan's total dismay, there was a link to a story on one of the respectable news sites. "It's only five-thirty," Megan said in disbelief. "They're Irish. What are they all even doing up at this hour?"

"Nothing that won't still be there in another hour." Jelena took the phone out of Megan's hands, set it on *silent*, and put it on her side of the bed. "Go back to sleep."

"It's all over the tabloids, Yella. More murder driver stuff."

Jelena pulled her down and tucked her back against herself. "Nothing you can do about it right now. Go back to sleep, Megan."

"I'm not sure I can," Megan said, and didn't wake up again until Jelena, damp and smelling of shampoo, kissed her forehead and murmured, "I have to go work on the float, bejb. Call if you need anything. Don't let Orla get to you. The dogs will want in, in a minute."

Megan put a hand out, catching her fingertips as she left, then curled up under the covers, pretending the phone didn't exist for another couple of minutes. Then, reluctantly, she rolled out of bed, went to get the dogs, showered, and finally picked up the phone, astonished to discover it was almost nine. She couldn't remember the last time she'd slept past seven.

"Of course, I don't remember the last time my alarm got turned off either," she said to the dogs. Thong leaned against her shins and Megan sat on the floor to go through her messages as both dogs tried to get in her lap. "Stop that, be careful. You'll both fit, if you're not pushy. There you go. See, that's better. Good pups." She tugged on Dip's ear and rubbed Thong's nose, then sighed and responded to the one message that said nothing more than a grim **call me.**

Paul Bourke picked up on the first ring. "Are you okay?"

"Are *you*? I've got about fifty texts from Orla saying I'm the devil herself and also that the company is booked out six months in advance now and can I pick up extra shifts because people want to be driven by the murder driver, but your captain must be spitting nails."

As if he couldn't quite stop himself, Bourke said, "She's not technically a captain," but for a woman who'd done a full twenty years in the military, Megan had proven hopeless on remembering the right terms for Irish police ranks, and Paul had more or less given up on trying to correct her. "She's furious, and I'm off the case."

Megan sat bolt upright, dislodging the dogs. "What? Because of me? What?! That's not fair, Paul, that's—"

"No, it's because of Niamh. I said I liked Woodward for it and that I'd get a mean satisfaction if it was herself indeed, and the chief wanted to know why that was, and I told her and she took me off the case."

Dip came nosing back toward Megan, tail down like he was afraid they'd done something wrong to get bumped off her lap. Megan put her hand out toward him and all was instantly forgiven, but she was less forgiving of Paul's boss. "She has to know you're not going to find Claire guilty if she's not, Paul."

"She wouldn't be wrong, though. I've a conflict of interest."

"You're not—you haven't been suspended or anything, have you?"

"No, just taken off the case. Young Dervla Reese is taking over. It's grand, Megan."

"Irish people use *grand* the same way Americans use *fine*, Paul. It can mean your leg is broken, your hair is on fire, and your dog died, but you wouldn't want to bother anybody about all of that."

He chuckled. "Ah, sure, you're not wrong, but there's not much to be done now, is there."

"Did you tell Niamh yet?"

"She's in London for the morning. Interviews."

"God, she must have gotten up before breakfast to make that. We shouldn't have kept you over so late last night."

"She gets by on four hours of sleep better than anybody I've ever met," Bourke admitted. "Then again, she's like a cat when she's not working. Sleeps twenty hours a day and lounges in the sunshine."

Megan said, "That must be very hard for you," and to her relief, he laughed.

"Occasionally it's like that bit in the movie, where Hugh Jackman's roommate comes in to see Julia Roberts in the tub, backs out, and comes back in again because he's just checking he wasn't seeing things."

Megan laughed. "Hugh Grant, not Jackman, but yeah."

"Jesus, they're not even the same nationality, are they. I've no business dating a movie star, Megan. I'm hopeless."

"I have to assume that's refreshing, Paul, or she wouldn't be dating you." Megan pulled her phone away from her ear as it buzzed with an incoming message. "Oh, God. Orla's after me. I don't want to be famous, Paul."

"Try being Niamh O'Sullivan's boyfriend," he said wryly. "Good luck with Orla."

"Mmph." Megan hung up, bent over the dogs for a minute to steel herself, then rang Orla. "I'm not picking up extra shifts."

"They're altogether desperate for you!"

"I don't care!"

"We'll talk about it," Orla said, as if she was making a great concession.

Despite herself, Megan laughed. "You don't let up, do you?"

"It's part of me charm." Orla put on an accent broad enough for an American cereal commercial, and Megan gave another snort of laughter before Orla, with a reluctant sigh, said, "Are ye all right, missus? I wouldn't like seeing my own face all over the tabloids so."

"It'll blow over in a couple of days," Megan said with more hope than certainty. "The parade's coming up. There'll be more interesting things than me. And the guards will get it solved and there'll be nothing to talk about."

"Until you get in another mess." Orla sounded satisfied at the prospect.

"Whose side are you on here?"

"My bank account's. Look, are you coming in to work or not? Yer wan's asked for you."

"My one? Claire Woodward?"

"That's the one," Orla agreed. "Out to Drogheda, she says, to look at the old fort and the St. Laurence Gate. Is she planning to invade?"

"I think she already has." Megan groaned and stood, dislodging the dogs. "All right. I can drive her today, but not tomorrow, Orla!"

"So you've said a hundred times. Grand so. You're expected at ten."

"That's barely an hour!"

"You should have called earlier." Orla hung up with a sniff and Megan, spluttering, went to shower.

Claire Woodward was much subdued when Megan arrived at her B and B a few minutes after ten that morning. "It's all over the papers," she said as she got in the car. "I knew there would be publicity, but I thought we could get out in front of it. Derek got in last night and has been on the phone nonstop ever since."

"Are you sure you want to go out to Drogheda?"

"The next book still needs to be written." Claire went quiet a moment, then said, "Could you repeat that, please? Drah-heh-dah?"

"Yeah." Megan gave her a brief smile in the rearview mirror. "Not Drog-head-uh. Just wait until you go to Dún 'La og hairy.' It's spelled L-A-O-G-H-A-I-R-E and pronounced *leary*. Dún Laoghaire."

Claire, a little desperately, said, "Why do the letters do such different things in Ireland?"

Megan breathed a laugh. "I get the impression that the short answer is that the old written Irish language smashed into old written Latin and left bits and pieces of both everywhere. There were a lot of sounds the Latin alphabet didn't have letters for, and a lot of letters the Irish language didn't have sounds for, so Irish, written in the standard modern English alphabet, looks like a hot mess to English-reading eyes. It's just a different language, that's all."

"Wow. What's the long answer?"

"It requires a dissertation." Megan glanced at Claire again. "Should we be picking your editor up, or anything?"

"Oh, no, he doesn't want to go stomping around forts doing research with me. Besides, he's . . ." Claire sighed. "Doing triage. Apparently there is such a thing as bad publicity."

"Oh. I'm sorry to hear that." Megan had no idea what to say beyond that.

"Yeah," Claire said. "Me, too. I understand why she'd copy me, I make a million dollars a book, bu—"

Megan, unable to help herself, said, "Oh my *God.* I thought you said most writers didn't even make ten thousand a book!"

"I also said I was one of the lucky ones."

"Yeah, but a million dollars? Really?"

"You'd think she would have murdered me, instead, right? Made all that money off my book after claiming I'd stolen it and was too dead to defend myself."

"That actually seems like a much better idea, yeah." Megan screwed her face up in a sort of revolted laugh. "Did you just come up with that? Are all writers so macabre? I thought you wrote historical romance!"

"I think most writers are at least somewhat macabre. It's like I told your detective. We're always plotting scenarios out. Most of them don't make it to the page, but with something like this, yeah, you kind of think 'Is this how I would do it?' And in this case, no, I wouldn't kill her, I'd have her kill me. Although I guess that would work out badly for me, so I should change the plot."

Megan grimaced. "Maybe it's good you're writing historical romance."

"Probably just as well." Claire was lower-key than usual as they visited the eight-hundred-year-old Millmount Fort overlooking Drogheda and the Boyne Valley, and as she stood inside the equally ancient towering St. Laurence Gate in the town itself. "There are hundreds of reasons I'd rather live today than back then, but it's still hard not to look at these old gates and walls and see the romance and strength in building fortifications like these. Protecting what was yours. Do you know where the abbey was?"

"No, but I have the power of the internet in my pocket." Megan took her phone out, then turned herself around to get pointed in the right direction. "What's left of it is a few blocks down to our left, or there's the bell tower of the old friary up there to the right." The tower was, it turned out, visible from where they stood. "Wiki says it's the highest point in Drogheda on this side of the River Boyne. The fort is higher."

"Well, let's go up and have a look." They walked up to find the belfry fenced off in a little park-like space between otherwise perfectly ordinary houses. A large ginger cat wound his way through the fence bars, gazing up at them with piteous orange eyes before sitting in front of Claire and meowing for attention. "Oh, you're friendly, aren't you, poor, hungry kitty?"

Megan, peering along the inside of the fence, grinned. "He's lying to you. There are at least four cans of food in there, and they're not all empty. I bet people feed him six times a day."

"Oh, how can you be so hard-hearted?"

"I have two dogs who try that on me every time I come home." Megan crouched to offer the cat her fingers, then rubbed between his ears when he deigned to visit her momentarily. "Not a bad life for you, huh, Jack? There's a good kitty." She rose again, squinting at darkening clouds above them. "I think we should go back to the car and drive around to the abbey. The weather's turning."

"Can we take the cat?" Claire petted him once more before they finished their explorations of the town's medieval sites. "I think I'd like to go back to Dublin. I'm usually good for a long day of researching, but nothing feels quite right, right now. Do you think the café is open again? Do you think the rest of them might be there?"

"We could drop by and see," Megan offered after a moment. Paul—or the guards in general— couldn't condemn her for just bringing her client where she wanted to go. "I mean, I could bring you there. But I'll ring to see if they're even open, first."

"Oh, that's a good idea. I always forget you can call and ask things, anymore. Even though I used to spend hours on the phone as a kid."

"Me, too." Megan smiled. "Big cultural shift since then." She called Accents as they walked back to the car and was told the café was open, although the barista sounded overwhelmed. "I think they're busy," Megan said when she hung up. "I guess having a body found on the premises is either really good or really bad for business."

"Maybe we shouldn't go by," Claire said quietly. "If they're that busy, the writing group probably isn't there anyway."

"You can decide on the way back to Dublin," Megan offered.

"Sure. I'd like to go. I just want to make sure everybody's okay." Claire's phone rang as they reached Dublin's outskirts and she answered briskly, but her shoulders slumped almost immediately as she listened to the person on the other end. "All right. I'll see you there in a little while." She hung up and met Megan's eyes in the mirror. "My publisher's lead public relations person just flew in to Dublin to talk about how we're going to deal with all of this, so if you can bring me back to the B and B after all . . . ?"

"Of course." Megan held the door for her when they got to the B and B. "Good luck with the PR guys. I hope you get some rest, Ms. Woodward."

The drive back through afternoon traffic went smoothly, but she didn't know she intended to stop by Accents on her own until she turned down Stephen Street Lower as if on autopilot. She went around the corner, idled the vehicle for a moment, and rang Orla. "I'm off the clock, but if you don't need the car back right away, I want to stay in town for a minute."

"I need it back by five," Orla said tartly. "Until

then, I suppose it's yours. As long as you pay for mileage."

"I'm not going off the normal drive back to the garage, just not heading straight back. But yes, if I go off the beaten path, I'll pay for mileage. I'd never dream of anything else." Megan pulled into the parking garage and went to find herself some gossip.

CHAPTER 7

She had to steel herself at the door, partly because of the number of people crowded into the little café, but more because of the astonishing noise they were making. Voices rose and fell over one another like they were climbing hills, laughter and expectation and curiosity driving it all. Even with the front door open, the atmosphere was muggy and slightly sour, too many bodies sweating in an enclosed space. People moved reluctantly as Megan shouldered her way in, and she found the end of the line, which went down the stairs, with some effort.

One of the baristas widened his eyes at her in recognition of both her familiar presence and the madhouse of the café as he came up the stairs with a tray of dirty cups and plates. A minute later the line shifted, and it occurred to Megan she should check to see if the writing group was even there before she committed to queuing for half an hour. She went farther downstairs, peering around the corner to search the lower room.

Adrian, the lone man in the writer's group, was alone in the front corner and surrounded by other peoples' belongings. There were several laptops besides his own, two different kinds of half-eaten cake, pots of tea, and newly filled coffee cups littered on the couch seats and table between them. Megan trotted the rest of the way downstairs and went over, not sure he'd remember her. "The rest of them abandoned you, huh?"

He looked up with a *these seats are taken* speech clearly prepared, then sagged and gestured toward a freestanding chair. "It's Megan, right? The murder driver."

Megan winced. "Yeah, I'm afraid so. Sorry, I just was—"

"Nosy?"

"I was trying to think of a more flattering way to say that, but yeah."

"Well, you might as well sit down. Juliet took Sadhbh out to have a breakdown and Stephanie's gone to the toilet. If you're here I don't look like I'm holding quite so many seats for myself, and . . ." He waved at the people sitting in, on, and by the couches and chairs in the downstairs. "It's busy."

"Thanks." Megan sat, then wished she'd ordered a coffee after all. "How are you all holding up?"

"Can't believe it, really. We're none of us getting any writing done. Even Juliet, and she's a proper taskmaster. Sadhbh keeps crying. She and Bláthnaid were tight."

"I got that impression." Megan sighed. "How are you doing?"

Adrian shrugged. "I wasn't that close with her, like. You'd think that would make it easier. I guess it does. I'm not in bits like Sadhbh. But we were friendly, and it sucks." He studied Megan for a minute, then half grinned. "Did that detective send you to talk to us?"

"Oh my God, no. We would both be in so much trouble if he had. No, I'm just . . ." Megan fell silent for a moment, then, not sure she was making a good decision, said, "I was there when they found her body, that's all. So I feel way more invested than I probably should."

"Oh, shit, no way." Adrian put his computer aside and leaned forward. "Were you really?"

"Yeah. And no, I'm not going to go into the details, but it was kind of awful. So, yeah, I guess I just want to know. And I'm definitely not supposed to be asking." She put on her best gimlet stare and said, in a fake deep voice, "And where were you between the hours of ten PM and six AM on Monday night, lad?"

A peculiar look of alarm swept Adrian's bearded face. "Ten? Sure and I was at the pub, wasn't I."

Megan was almost certain he hadn't looked nearly that worried when Bourke had talked to him. "Were you? With friends, maybe? What pub?"

"Sure, now, I don't know, I'd the drink taken, hadn't I?" Adrian shifted uncomfortably. "No, the Monday? I wouldn't have gone to the pub then. I'd have been at home, eating pizza."

Megan's eyebrows rose. "Takeaway or frozen?"

"Takeaway, the frozen stuff's shite."

"From where?"

The younger man's eyebrows rose uncertainly. "Domino's?"

Megan, gently, said, "You know the cops can check that, right?"

"A toastie," Adrian wailed. "I remember now, I was after eating a cheese toastie Monday night! By myself in my flat!"

"You can afford a flat of your own?" Megan asked, distracted.

Disbelief crossed Adrian's face, wiping away his consternation. "In this market? Of course not. I've two housemates. They were home," he said in a rush of obvious relief. "They *were* home."

"So you were at home Monday night. Watching television and eating a toastie. And they can verify that." Megan didn't really consider interrogation her strong suit, but Adrian was in a proper cold sweat, looking like he'd been caught red-handed at the murder scene. "Adrian, what kind of relationship *did* you have with Bláthnaid?"

"Nothing! I fancied her for a while, but she wasn't interested! Besides," he said viciously, "you ought to be asking Juliet, not me. Bláthnaid made a mess of her son's career."

Megan sat back, blinking. "Really? What happened?"

"He's an actor, right? Aaron. And they went out for a while, but she wouldn't accept it when they broke up. So Aaron was on set and Bláthnaid told them she was his girlfriend and they let her through, and she threw a wobbly over the breakup. Made a right fool of herself and him, too, and they threw them both off set and Aaron can't get work now.

Blacklisted, he is, because everyone's expecting that kind of behavior all the time, like. Jules was livid. Said she'd wring Bláthnaid's neck herself if she had the chance."

Megan gazed at him in astonishment. "Something tells me nobody mentioned that to Detective Bourke."

"Well, Jules wouldn't paint herself with that brush, would she? And we were none of us going to just say it where she could overhear. She's deadly," and for once Megan was fairly certain he meant it in terms of *dangerous*, not *cool*, which was how Dubs often used the word.

"How deadly?"

"Black belt in aikido deadly," Adrian said, then slumped in the couch as if he'd just realized how much he'd said.

"Thanks for telling me," Megan said. "I won't let on to the others."

He gave her a look crossed between grateful and furious, then picked up one of the half-eaten pieces of cake and turned his attention to eating it. The barista Megan had seen on the stairs came down and brought her a mocha she hadn't ordered, then winked. "You're good for it, and I know your order. Just pay up on your way out."

"You're a star, Liam!" She glanced at Adrian as she accepted the cup. "Is it all right if I stay a little while?"

He shrugged with resigned invitation. "If you're here to watch the things, I might go up to the toilet."

"Go on, I can keep an eye on it."

"Thanks." He got up and left, although she

heard his deep voice on the stairs and a few seconds later, the American in the group, Stephanie, came back to the couches.

"It's a madhouse up there. I'm surprised you got a coffee."

Megan lifted the little cup of chocolate chips that came with the mochas at Accents, then dumped them in and stirred. "The barista knows me well enough to bring me a mocha without me asking. I'll owe them my body weight in tips, later."

"Yeah, you will." Stephanie sat down, smiling. "Checking up on us for the guards?"

"No!" Megan thought she protested too much and couldn't help the embarrassed grin that followed. "No, this is a hundred percent for me. I'm beginning to accept that I'm hopelessly nosy."

Stephanie's eyebrows rose, although her smile didn't fade. "Not for Claire either?"

"Oh. Huh. No, although that seems more likely from a 'I don't want the guards to be any angrier at me than they are' perspective."

"I saw you on the news a couple of years ago when that golfer died," Stephanie said with a nod. "So this is like, what, your fourth murder?"

"Technically I think it's about the sixth, because more than one person keeps ending up dead, but . . . yeah." Megan sighed. "And for some reason the guards really hate that."

"Oh, I can't imagine why," Stephanie said in such an American tone that Megan laughed.

"I know, right? How long have you been here?"

"Here-here at Accents today or—yeah, I didn't think that's what you meant. Almost twenty years. You?"

"Oh, wow. You still sound pretty much as American as I do. Almost five, now."

"Yeah, I can't get rid of the accent. I can sound Irish," Stephanie said, effortlessly slipping into the accent and staying there for a few more words, "but I'm only ever after talking to people who live in my own head, and not enough of the Irish themselves. At least, that's what I say is the reason for still sounding American," she said, going back to her regular accent. "What's your excuse?"

"I drive a lot of Americans," Megan said. "I think I'd have to stop, to complete any kind of accent-based assimilation."

"Ever think about going back?"

Megan shook her head, and so did Stephanie. "Me either. It's like visiting a foreign country now. A very familiar foreign country, one where I know how everything works, but it's still foreign. I really miss Cheetos, though. The crunchy ones, not the fluffy ones."

"Oh my God. And root beer. You know you can get it over at the Candy Lab in Temple Bar, right?"

"Ugh, last time I was in they only had sugar-free stuff, which is disgusting. And they're really hit-and-miss for crunchy Cheetos," Stephanie said despondently. "They have weird flavored ones. I just want plain ol' Cheetos. And shredded coconut! You cannot get shredded coconut in this country!"

Megan laughed. "No? I don't ever use it, so I didn't know that."

"No, it's all, like, pulverized here. Desiccated, they call it. Little . . ." She held up her fingertips, pressed together so there was a tiny space between her nails. "Little flecks. Or you can get fingernail-sized flakes, and neither is right. I can't make my Christmas candies with it. And I never think about it while I'm home, so I never remember to bring any back with me. Just buckets of ibuprofen."

"Oh my God, right?" Megan laughed again, then tested her mocha with a careful sip that turned into a happy sigh. "They make such good mochas here."

"I'll take your word for it. I like my coffee dark and bitter, like my soul." Stephanie gestured at what was evidently her own coffee cup, then folded her arms around herself and leaned forward. "So what do the guards think?"

"I honestly don't know. I don't work with them. I just get tangled up in parallel." Megan watched the other woman's tight body language for a moment, then asked, "What do *you* think?"

"God, I wish I knew." Stephanie relaxed with a sigh. "I think it's awful. She was just a kid and it's making me suspicious of everybody. Even . . ." She whirled her hand at the empty seats and laptops around her. "Like, does it mean anything that Adrian asked her out a couple times and she said no? I didn't think it did. I thought he'd taken the hint. But now there's a whole, you know, rejected stalker boyfriend thing running through my head. Did she and Sadhbh have a falling-out? A fight over a boy? I've got all kinds of plausible scenarios, but I don't really think any of that's true. I think it's more likely Claire copied her book, got caught, and killed her."

"Really? Even though she's Claire Woodward?"

Stephanie glanced toward the stairs like she was afraid Claire would walk in, then leaned closer to

Megan again. "The thing is, she has a history of plagiarism. Back when we were in a writing group together in Sacramento, she got caught lifting whole sections from other books and saying it was her own work. I don't know how she thought she'd get away with it—romance readers are voracious and recognize passages and sentences and phrases like you wouldn't believe—but she tried. And it was stupid, right? But she was young and mortified when she got caught, and swore she'd never do anything like it again."

"Wow. Holy cow. Did you believe her?"

Stephanie shrugged. "She never did it again in anything the group critiqued, anyway. Believe me, we were looking."

"Was she a good writer, if she wasn't relying on other people's stuff like that?"

"Good enough, anyway. I mean, look who she became. Unless she's somehow got other people secretly doing all the heavy lifting, but I *never* would have introduced Bláthnaid to her if I thought she was still doing that kind of thing. But now I have to wonder, you know?"

"Yeah. Jeez. Wow." Megan shook her head, remembered her mocha, and took another sip. "Do you think that's more likely than the other way around?"

Stephanie made a face. "I don't know. It would have been really, really dumb of Bláthnaid to copy Claire's work, because there's no way she could ever get away with it, but this whole writing gig, it's a real crapshoot, do you know that?"

"Claire was telling me most writers don't even make ten grand a book."

"Right. And people who want to write for a living, we're a little crazy. You have to be. You learn by doing, so basically for a long time you've got a second unpaid job that you sacrifice your lunch hour or television time or nights out with your friends for." She waved a hand. "And nobody's making us do it. I'm not trying to say 'oh woe is us,' but you really do have to be kind of obsessive to have a shot at getting traditionally published, much less making a living. Sometimes people try to take shortcuts, so . . . yeah. I could see her just hoping she would somehow get away with it, and going for it. But look, I mean, obviously we've all been gossiping about this like mad for the past couple days, but maybe don't bring it up with Sadhbh? She can't even look at the idea that Bláthnaid could have done something wrong."

"Well, even if she did, she certainly didn't deserve to end up dead for it."

Color flushed Stephanie's face and tears glittered in her eyes for a moment, making Megan feel like a heel. "Sorry. That was really insensitive."

"No, you're right, though. I didn't mean to sound like I was blaming her."

"You didn't. It's just all awful." Megan picked her coffee up again as Adrian came back downstairs, with Juliet and Sadhbh in his wake.

Sadhbh stopped dead a few steps away from the table as she recognized Megan. "What are you doing here? Sounding us out for that cow Claire?"

Juliet, sounding very much like a mother, said, "Sadhbh!"

Megan only shook her head and stood, though. "No, I just wanted to see how you all were doing. I know we don't know each other, but I'd see you working here often enough to feel sort of connected."

"That and she's the one that found Bláthnaid's body," Adrian said.

Megan hid a wince as the women's gazes all snapped from him to her. Sadhbh's voice cracked. "Really?"

"I was here when she was found, yes." Clearly letting Adrian know that had not been a good idea, but it was too late now.

"What was it like?" Sadhbh reached toward Juliet without seeming to realize it, and the older woman took her hand to hold it firmly. "Did she look . . . scared?"

"She looked dead," Megan said as gently as she could. "Even if I had a better answer, and I don't, that's enough, Sadhbh. It's really all you need to know."

The girl—young woman, really—shuddered, then began to cry. Juliet pulled her closer and exchanged a weary, sad look over her head with Stephanie, then Megan herself. "I know, chicken," she said unhappily. "I know. Let it out."

Sadhbh, between heaving sobs, said, "It doesn't help," and Juliet's eyes closed in sad sympathy. Adrian curled in on himself uncomfortably, as if he was trying to pull away from the rush of emotion without being too obvious about it.

Megan, sorry to have made things worse, murmured, "I'll leave you alone," and went upstairs to stand in line so she could pay for her coffee. Just as she got to the till, Juliet came up and hesitated at her side. Megan paid, got out of line, and tilted her head toward the front door. Juliet nodded and Megan followed her out, curiosity itching down her spine. "Everything okay?"

"It's desperate in there," Juliet said. "It's always busy, but it's been mental since the . . . event. Are you working with the guards, then?"

Megan shook her head, then, eyeing the sky, gestured toward the alley so they would be protected from the almost-certain oncoming rainfall. Wind shivered through the little tunnel, but it was better than on the street. "I really did stop by to check in on everybody. How are you doing?"

"Not well," Juliet said with businesslike briskness. "Bláthnaid was the age of my own son and it's hard to think of a child that age dying. I'd say I'll feel better once they catch the killer, but I don't think I will. It doesn't do her any good, or the rest of us with a hole in our hearts where she was."

"You don't think catching them would be justice?"

"What's justice?" Juliet asked bitterly. "It's more just for a killer to be caught and imprisoned than to go free, but none of it brings back the dead."

"You sound like you were close," Megan said cautiously.

"She dated my son for a while, so I would have known her well enough. I brought her in to the group when she said she wanted to be a writer, and she brought Sadhbh along."

"Was she any good?"

"She had talent," Juliet said after a moment's consideration. "It helps to have talent. It helps more to have discipline."

"Did she?"

Juliet shrugged. "She came to our writing sessions regularly, and didn't have to be scolded into working like some of the others do, so I'd say so."

Megan's eyebrows rose. "Dare I ask?"

"Stephanie, mostly. She's years behind on the last book in her series and will find anything else to do. She worked with Bláthnaid a lot, even before Ms. Famous Romance Novelist started mentoring her."

"You don't like her very much, do you?"

"Claire? I wouldn't, no. She wants everything her way."

Megan shook her head. "I barely know her, so I'm not arguing, but she hasn't come across that way to me."

"Ah, no, but she wants something from you, doesn't she now. Megan Malone, the murder driver. You're a whole book unto yourself."

"That's what she said, too." Megan made a face. "I don't want to be anybody's story."

"Most people don't. Sometimes we don't get a choice."

"Like poor Bláthnaid." Megan sighed. "If Stephanie was working with her before Claire, would she know who was really plagiarizing whom?"

"If she does, she hasn't told us, but I assume she'll have told the guards." Juliet gave Megan another brief, assessing look. "Where's that tall one?"

"Doing his job, I imagine. I'm really not working with him." Never mind that Paul wasn't on the case anymore either. Megan didn't think any of the writing group needed to know that, and if they did, she certainly didn't need to be the one who told them. "I take it you'd be just as happy if it was Ms. Woodward."

"I'd be happy if none of this had ever happened," Juliet said sharply. "If it has to have, I'd as soon the perpetrator was someone I already disliked, sure enough."

"I suppose that makes sense. Look, I know it's unlikely, but if there's anything I can do . . ."

"Make sure that detective does his job."

There wasn't much point in saying that was out of her control. Megan only nodded. "I hope it all gets sorted out soon. Is Sadhbh okay?"

"Not even a little." Juliet glanced back toward the building. "I'd better get back. The words won't write themselves, and they gossip more if I'm not there."

Megan smiled. "Adrian said you were the taskmaster of the group."

A little to her surprise, Juliet returned the smile. "Someone has to be. I'm sure we'll see you later, Ms. Malone."

"Oh, you can call me Megan," she said, but Juliet was already around the corner and gone.

CHAPTER 8

Jelena was home already, sprawled lazily on the couch with the air of a woman who had done a good day's work, when Megan arrived. The dogs jumped down and rushed to greet her, sticking their noses in her hands and knees as she bent to greet them. Then she looked up at Jelena with a smile. "It smells amazing in here. Did you cook?"

"Pierogi. I wanted something warm and comforting."

Megan's stomach rumbled. "I didn't even know I was hungry and I'm now prepared to eat my body weight in pierogi. Everything ready for the parade?"

"We're out of time, so I hope so. Did you solve the mystery yet?"

Megan laughed. "No. I ended up talking to the writers, but I don't think I got anything usef—well, no, apparently Claire has a history of plagiarism, so that's interesting."

"O szlag!!" Jelena sat up, blurting a Polish phrase that Megan had learned roughly meant "holy crap." "Did you tell Paul?" She tucked her legs in so Megan would have room to join her.

"Paul," Megan said with a drawl for dramatic effect, "is off the case. I'll sit as soon as I've changed. I don't want to get my uniform covered in dog hair."

Most of that was lost under Jelena's "Holy *shit*, what?" and, unsurprisingly, she followed her to the bedroom. "What happened?"

"He mentioned Claire had been against Niamh's casting in the movie to his . . . chief," Megan said, trying to get the word right and doubting she had, "and she saw it as a conflict of interest and took him off."

Jelena sat on the bed, eyes wide with dismay, interest, and then alarm. "Wait. This doesn't mean *you're* allowed to investigate, Megan!"

"I know!" Megan hung her uniform up and grinned sheepishly at Jelena as she pulled on a T-shirt and loose pants. "I've been telling myself that all day. I'm trying, I swear!"

"If you spend tomorrow chasing a murderer instead of me, I will not be responsible for what happens," Jelena warned her.

Megan lifted her hands in surrender. "I promised I'd help carry stuff and squish through the crowd to get whatever last-minute thing somebody forgot. I'll be there."

"Better be." Jelena lifted her chin toward the

kitchen. "Everything's ready for dinner, if you want to eat."

"I do not deserve a woman as magnificent as you are."

"No one deserves anyone," Jelena said with a one-shouldered shrug. "But sometimes we're lucky enough to be with them anyway."

"I can't decide if that's incredibly romantic or just incredibly Polish of you."

Jelena grinned as they went into the kitchen. "Why not both? Oh no, pierogi is not for puppies," she added as the dogs danced around them across the kitchen floor. "Sauerkraut will make you smell bad."

"Sauerkraut makes me smell bad, too," Megan said cheerfully. "I eat it anyway."

"Yes, but you're an adult human being who can make decisions on your own. Dogs are about as smart as toddlers and adults make choices for toddlers all the time."

Megan laughed. "Fair. Thank you for dinner." She kissed Jelena's shoulder and they sat down to eat with the dogs under the table, doing their best to convince them that they'd never been fed in their entire puppy lives. "You cooked. I'll clean up. Find something fluffy to watch for a while and then we should have an early night. You have a long day tomorrow."

"Which *you* are going to help me with," Jelena said with satisfaction. "Or else."

"Or else," Megan agreed.

* * *

Despite Megan's objections, Jelena's enthusiasm somehow extended to getting up and going to the gym before the parade, so they'd not only worked out, showered, and eaten before she was meant to be at the parade staging grounds, but were a solid forty minutes early.

Megan, who generally avoided city centre on parade day, said, "Oh my God," involuntarily as they came around the corner onto Parnell Square East. A seething mass of people, noise, and color filled the street past the Rotunda Hospital, with floats crowding next to one another as bagpipe-carrying men in kilts squeezed by acrobats in flamboyant costumes. Drums thumped arrhythmically from one end of the road to the other, with other instruments answering them. Voices rose in laughter, frustration, and occasional panic while people ran back and forth trying to get last-minute emergencies sorted out. "Can I change my mind?"

Jelena, with a smile, said, "No. We need your strong back," and dragged her up the street toward the Polish float.

"And my weak mind?"

"And your pretty face," Jelena said, which didn't answer the question at all. Megan laughed and, when introduced, greeted the float committee people she didn't know, and said hi to the handful she did.

"Jelena, this is wonderful. You've all done an amazing job." She circled around the float—the theme was Polish heritage—and laughed as she discovered recognizable-to-her symbols like oversized cardboard pierogi and kielbasa sausages tucked between replica art and architecture she knew very little about. Several people on the float were wearing traditional clothing in bright, beautiful colors, and one of the women wore what Jelena murmured was a wedding gown, hand-painted with sprays of brilliantly colored flowers. "Everybody's so beautiful," Megan whispered back, and Jelena tossed her hair.

"Of course. All Polish women are."

"The men aren't bad either!"

Jelena wrinkled her nose. "Eesh. Men. Here, this is Megan," she said to one of the others, then fell into rapid Polish that Megan didn't have a hope of understanding. "She's strong," Jelena finished in English. "She'll help carry the banners."

"She doesn't look at all Polish," the woman said critically.

"Neither does your mother, now hush."

The woman barked laughter, gestured, and Megan, who really *didn't* look at all Polish, followed obediently to be caught up in the surge of forward motion when the parade finally began to move. People tapped her on the shoulder, switching places with her often or sending her to help someone else, while Jelena's choir group fell in just behind the leading banner and sang traditional songs that had whole sections of the parade audience joining in on, as they traveled slowly through the streets.

Somebody had told Megan once that a full quarter of Dublin's population and tens of thousands of people from all around the country turned out for the parade and celebrations in the city. She'd believed it in principle, but walking down O'Connell Street, seeing the crowds from the parade's point of view, taking in all the leprechaun hats, and the smiles on green and orange and white painted faces, it *felt* like half a million people were there, all celebrating the country she'd chosen to call her own. Tears kept dripping down her cheeks, despite her smile, and at some point as she traded duties with another banner-carrier, Jelena stopped to hug her and whisper, "Thank you," in her ear.

"I wouldn't have missed it for the world," Megan said with absolute sincerity. "Thank you for letting me be part of it. Polska górą," she said cautiously, trying to get the accent right.

Jelena burst into a delighted laugh. "Up with Poland!" she agreed in English. "You've been practicing."

"Trying to impress my girlfriend," Megan explained and Jelena laughed again.

"It's working. G'wan now," she said, sounding very Irish herself for a moment, "go climb up on the back of the float for a few minutes so you can see everything. It's worth it."

"Are you sure?" Megan, reassured, scrambled off to do that, and for a few minutes watched not just the cheering crowds, but the floats ahead of and behind them, admiring the craftsmanship and creativity that had gone into their creation. She got down again semi-reluctantly, all too aware that they'd only walked half the parade's route so far, and went back to her duties with a light heart.

By the time they reached the other end at St. Stephen's Green, her feet were killing her and she was hungry enough to gnaw her own arm off. Jelena met her at the back of the float with a kiss and an order to go find some food while they got the float back to its resting place before tomorrow's deconstruction.

"Are you sure?" Megan asked again. "I promised I'd help."

"We're all just going to be yelling at each other in Polish for three hours," Jelena promised. "Go get some food and we'll meet at the George later?"

"Right. Are Niamh and Paul coming?"

"Yes, although we're supposed to not expect to recognize Niamh."

Megan laughed. "We'd better not be able to recognize Paul either, or all the tabloids will have pictures of him stepping out on her with some other woman."

"He wouldn't dare." Jelena stole another kiss and hurried off, shouting, as promised, in Polish. Megan watched until she'd disappeared into the disintegrating parade, then, smiling, went the other way herself. The gathered crowd was trying to disperse, but almost literally had nowhere to go, with bodies crashing up against one another and people muttering or shrugging it off, as was their wont. There was a festival food market at Collins Barracks that Megan was dying to try, but that was a half-hour walk when there *weren't* hundreds of thousands of people trying to move through the street simultaneously.

On the other hand, there was a not-entirely-terrible burrito place—Dublin was not a great city for Mexican or even Tex-Mex—less than ten minutes away, and while it would probably be packed, it would be faster than almost anywhere else. Megan cut through the crowd as best she could, and ended up in a long line outside of the restaurant. The staff were clearly prepared, though, and someone came out to take orders from the people in line so in theory, their food would be ready by the time they got inside. Megan had a bellyful of burrito faster than she expected and enough time to go home, play some fetch with the dogs, and change clothes before it was late enough to head out to the bar.

A cryptic text message arrived from Niamh just before she headed out the door: **dress up. no, more than that. dress up the MOST.**

Megan blinked at it, went back into the bedroom, and put on the gold pants suit she wore to drive Orla's richest client, an over-the-top, but ultimately rather kind woman who always demanded Megan drive her, and paid outrageous amounts to get her way. She'd had her hair down, but put it up, and did her best with her makeup, then added long, drippy green earrings and sent a selfie back to Niamh. **Will this do?**

Perfection! came back. **See you later!**

"Well, perfection is pretty good," Megan said to Dip, who wagged his tail hopefully. "Dinner," she said, mock-severely. "Nothing fancy, just kibbles. And then you two need to go out to the garden, because Jelena and I won't be home until all hours of the night. I know, I know. I'm the worst dog parent in the history of dog parents. Okay, maybe I'll give you a T-R-E-A-T to warm your little doggy hearts while you're in the literal, but not metaphorical, doghouse."

Thong, whom Megan was fairly certain was smarter than Dip, started wagging her tail at the spelled-out word and trotted to their food dish, where she sat politely and thumped her tail a few more times. Megan laughed and fed them, then put them out with some of the longer-lasting dog bones, and caught a very crowded tram back to St. Stephen's Green.

The city was still going strong at ten PM, and would be for hours yet, with celebrants out in their green and orange, an abundance of over-sized, glittering shamrock glasses on display, along with Irish flags worn like capes, silly hats, and plenty of people simply glammed up for the evening, as Megan herself was. The George, Dublin's oldest gay bar, had a queue that stretched down past a convenience store locally known as Gay Spar. Megan, who'd gotten there before the rest of her group, took up the duty of standing in line beneath the pride flags the until everybody else arrived.

She didn't see the other three until they were almost on top of her. Niamh wore a bobbed red wig and sunglasses, even though it had been dark for hours. Jelena, who rarely wore heels, was in them, making her almost as tall as Paul, who had traded his usual skinny suit for looser layers, giving them all semi-unrecognizable profiles. Megan croaked a greeting to Niamh and Paul, but they were both grinning like fools, watching her take Jelena in.

They had *clearly* conspired on Jelena's outfit for the night, because she'd borrowed the burgundy Prada ensemble from Niamh, and now smoothed her hand over her bared stomach nervously as Megan said, "Oh my God," faintly.

Niamh, all but dancing with smugness, elbowed Jelena and said, "See?! I told you!"

"It's not too short?" Jelena tugged the Peter Pan–collared crop top down a little, to absolutely no avail.

"It is *not* too short," Megan said, still faintly. "It's just shorter than it is on Niamh." What was a rib-length crop top on Niamh hit Jelena just below the breasts, and the high-waisted trousers rode lower, revealing her well-toned tummy. The hems brushed her ankles instead of falling all the way over her toes, so her strappy high heels were visible. "Oh my God, Jelena."

"See?" Niamh tossed her short-cropped hair triumphantly. "You two are absolutely gorgeous." She said it as Irish-ly as she could, *gaar-gis*, and Paul shook his head.

"All three of you are. I am literally the luckiest man in Dublin tonight, and some gobshite is going to have a go at me for being a waster out with three beautiful women."

"You're doing all right for yourself," Megan promised him absently, but stepped forward to embrace Jelena and mumbled, "You look amazing," against her shoulder. "And very tall."

Jelena laughed and hugged her back. "You look fantastic, too."

"Thanks to Niamh," Megan said. "I mean, I looked fine before, but not good enough to go out with you."

"All of this is thanks to Niamh," Paul said. "She

dressed everybody tonight, including me. Apparently I'm to be taken to task for the deplorable state of my shoes."

Everyone looked at his shoes, which were leather, slightly scuffed, and overall went well with the casual layers he wore. "They're not shiny," Niamh said with a sniff, but winked. "And now I'm going to be responsible for getting us through the door faster, but don't get used to leaning on my star power for fabulousness. C'mere to me now." She waltzed up to the bouncer with the three of them as her entourage, pulled down her sunglasses, and smiled.

Megan, who had seen this happen before, was still astonished when the guy's own smile exploded across his face and he waved them in without a word. She murmured, "It's good to be the queen," at Niamh's back as they went in, and Niamh threw a blinding grin back over her shoulder.

"It is, so!"

A moment later they were fully immersed in the club's pulsing music, and any hope of conversation disappeared as they took to the dance floor. After a bit, Paul signaled he was going for drinks, and the women stayed together until he'd stood at the bar for them for a while. Then Niamh tilted her head that direction, and they filtered off together, shouting praise for the DJ in each other's ears.

Megan bounced against a tall man, yelled an apology, then looked up to see it was Adrian Tchaikovsky blinking down at her in surprise. "Hey! Adrian!"

"Megan! What are you doing here?"

"Dancing!"

"Fair, fair, us too."

A little to Megan's surprise, a man about Adrian's own age stepped away from the bar and pressed up to his side as he handed Adrian a drink. Then she kicked herself for her own biases. Just because Stephanie had mentioned Adrian asking Bláthnaid out wasn't a barrier to him dating a guy. Megan herself should know that better than most. Adrian's friend waved his own drink at Megan and bellowed, "Hi! My sister's the DJ, isn't she brilliant?" over the music.

"She is!" Megan bellowed back. "We were just talking about that!"

The music cut out as a song ended, and over the cries of disapproval, a woman's amplified voice said, "Ah, stop yer moaning. I'm only taking a minute to say I want a shout-out for that tall lad over there. Adrian, won't you wave for the crowd?"

Adrian flinched guiltily and turned toward the DJ's booth as if afraid he'd done something wrong. "Everybody give it up for this lad!" the DJ shouted. "A total hero, proper sound, he is. A load of you know about my ex."

The boos and hisses that rose from the crowd made the club sound like a pantomime audience for a moment. "That's right," the DJ went on. "Right bastard, he is. I've still got the bruises. Anyway, so's I got out, didn't I? But we had a storage shed in the back garden for my gear and I couldn't take it with me at the time and the fecker, he changed the locks. But this lad here, he's my brother's new boyfriend—good job, Brody. Anyways, he and a couple other lads went on over to my old place just this last Monday night in the wee hours of the morning, so they did. They went over the fence like proper robbers, broke the lock on the door on the way out with my stuff, and that's why I'm here playing for you tonight! Let's hear it for Adrian!"

A genuine, heartfelt roar of approval went up from the audience as the music started again, and Adrian, smiling with embarrassed pride, turned back from the applause to find Megan now accompanied by Detective Paul Bourke.

CHAPTER 9

Adrian went so pale Megan thought he might actually pass out. She put a hand under his elbow, but his color rushed back, a horrible, guilty tomato-red blush. Paul, blasély handing drinks to the women he'd come in with, said, "So that breaking and entering, that would be what you were actually doing Monday night when Bláthnaid died, would it now?"

The young man with Adrian—Brody, apparently—actually stepped in front of him protectively, which, given that he was barely taller than Megan, and Adrian easily cleared six feet, was pretty cute. "He didn't do anything wrong!"

"He absolutely did." Paul sounded to Megan like he was trying not to laugh, but Adrian looked like he was about to wet himself.

"That bastard was never gonna give Chloe her gear back—"

"Brody," Adrian hissed, "he's a guard."

Brody paled as dramatically as Adrian had, then puffed up even more, his jaw thrust out as he glared up at Paul. "So's why're you harassing Adrian, who's only after doing what the guards should do in the first place? What good are yis if my sister and all the wans like her are left barely able to get out of a bad place safely because nobody will take it seriously when she says she's being hurt? Wh—"

"All I want to know," Paul said mildly, "is if this is what you were doing between four and eight AM on the Tuesday morning, Mr. Tchaikovsky."

"Yeah, he was," Brody said belligerently, and Adrian sagged.

"We were up half the night planning it," he admitted. "And we may have the drink taken. It seemed like a good idea, so we went ahead and did it."

"It was a good idea!" Brody folded his arms and glared at Paul while Niamh pulled her sunglasses down a quarter inch so she could make wide eyes at Jelena and Megan. Megan shook her head fractionally, trying to keep Niamh from drawing attention to them, and the film star's mouth quirked. Megan didn't dare look at Jelena to see the expression of exasperation she was certain graced the tall woman's face.

Paul ignored them, his eyebrows lifted as he said, "Can your accomplices speak to your presence, Mr. Tchaikovsky? Are they a reliable alibi?"

Adrian, having clearly given up all hope of getting away with it, drooped more. "My mate Robbo's got half the heist on video, he was that pleased with us."

"I'll want to see that footage," Paul said firmly, and Brody seemed to finally get the idea that this could be serious.

"You're never going after him for this, are ye," he demanded incredulously. "It was my sister's own stuff they got back for her!"

Paul finally transferred his gaze to him. "What I'm doing, Mr. . . . ?"

"Doyle," he said stiffly.

"Mr. Doyle," he continued. "What I'm doing is trying to establish your boyfriend's innocence in a murder. If there's video footage of him elsewhere at the time of the murder, regardless of what that footage may show itself, it's an extremely important piece of evidence in clearing his name. As for the rest of it, I would personally expect that footage to disappear in the near future, as to not make it easy for your sister's ex, should he want to press charges."

Brody Doyle mumbled, "Oh," and then, "*Oh*," with increased understanding as Adrian stared disbelievingly at Paul, then said, "Thanks. Thanks very much. Thanks *very* much, Detective Bourke."

"Just get me some time-stamped stills from that video," Bourke drawled. "Good night, Mr. Tchaikovsky."

Adrian took Brody's hand and absolutely fled into the depths of the club, leaving Bourke to finally look around at his own companions. His gaze landed on Jelena, and Megan followed it to find Jelena looking at *her* with an expression of weary resignation. "You just can't help it, can you."

"I didn't do anything!" Megan protested. "I didn't do anything at all this time!"

"And neither did I," Paul said with a sigh. "This will make Detective Reese look good."

"Well." Niamh looked between them brightly. "Should we dance, or did you want to crawl the club in hopes of securing another alibi for your case?"

Megan and Paul both said, "It's not our case!" and their girlfriends exchanged glances.

"So they'll be looking for alibis," Jelena said. "You want to dance?"

Niamh tossed her hair, threw back her drink, and dragged Jelena out onto the dance floor, leaving Paul and Megan behind with a burst of objecting laughter. "I think they don't trust us!"

"I think they do," Paul said in amusement, and then, after a moment's pause, added, "Do you think any of the rest of them are here?"

Megan said, "No," firmly, then screwed up her face. "We could look . . ."

"It would practically disappoint them if we didn't, right?" Paul nodded toward the dance floor, where Jelena, her drink lifted in one hand, spun Niamh dramatically with the other.

Megan, more firmly, said, "No. No, nope, nyet, nein, nei, non, níl, no. I am not screwing up St. Patrick's Day with my girlfriend, not even for the sake of solving a murder."

"Well, you threw the Irish in there, so I guess I can't argue. What was the *nai* one?"

"Norwegian," Megan said as she pulled him out onto the dance floor. "That and *da mi*, which means *mine*, are the only words I know in Norwegian. Learned 'em from a toddler."

Paul laughed. "I guess that and 'where's the toilet' could get you quite a ways." The rest of any possible conversation was swallowed by dancing, until the bartenders announced the last call to a packed floor of revelers, who let out a collective groan of disappointment.

Megan, footsore and happy, said, "I'll get the last round," and returned several minutes later with drinks for everyone, then shouted an agreement to a largely-incoherent toast of general goodwill amongst her friends. They spilled out onto the street with hundreds of others who were reluctantly heading home.

Niamh, forgetting to adjust her volume, bellowed, "I hate to bring down the craic," then looked abashed and lowered her voice now that there was no music to compete with. "Sorry. I hate to bring down the fun, but I got up at about four in the morning yesterday to go to London and haven't slept since. You all can go on and party without me, but I have to stagger home."

"You have to call a taxi," Paul said. "I can't even think about you walking that far in those heels. Any of you," he said, glancing around at their feet. "I don't know how you can even dance in them."

Niamh snickered. "That's why we drink, so we can't feel our feet."

Jelena lifted one of hers and circled it. "I guess I didn't drink enough, then. Think we can get a taxi?"

"Lemme see." Megan stepped up to the curb and gave a piercing, New York–style cab whistle. A number of people in the crowd flinched and looked her way, but no taxis magically appeared.

Niamh held her phone up. "Much as I admire

your American enthusiasm, the taxi app works just fine. We'll have one in five minutes."

"Show-off." Megan hugged her, but stayed on the curb, trying to hail a taxi. "We only have to go up to Rathmines. It's barely over a mile; there must be somebody going that way."

"There is," Jelena said after a moment, lifting her own phone. "Got one on the app."

"Hmph. Don't you long for the days of standing around on the curb, trying to hail a taxi, getting soaked by drivers hitting puddles as they went by?"

All three of the others and a bystander said, "No!" and Megan laughed as she came back up off the side of the street.

"Yeah, okay, neither do I, honestly. But I don't know—nostalgia."

"Nostalgia for bad things is silly." Jelena kissed her, then turned to hug Niamh as their taxi pulled up. "Thank you for lending me the outfit. I'll have it cleaned and return it to you."

"I literally have more arriving every week," Niamh said. "Keep it, and I'll borrow it back for a night if I need it." She climbed in the taxi, Paul on her tail, before Jelena could object, and Megan let out a delighted hoot.

"I'll take you to Paris for a very nice dinner in that outfit," she offered.

Jelena shook her head. "With this much belly hanging out I'd be afraid to eat anything!"

"I'll also bring you a large, shapeless hoodie to wear over it when you're self-conscious," Megan promised, and Jelena smiled.

"That, maybe. There's our taxi." The trip home

only took a few minutes, and after a brief debate in the doorway about whether the dogs should be left to sleep undisturbed outside, the discussion was settled by Dip's hopeful whine at the back door. Megan went to let him in and Thong followed in his wake, although she was clearly more interested in curling up on her inside dog bed than investigating them after their absence.

Dip, however, spun like a whirligig, bouncing off their shins and occasionally being obviously uncertain as to whether he was greeting them or chasing his own tail. After getting nothing more than a sleepy pat on the head and some vague praise for his efforts, he went to join Thong in bed, which sounded like a good idea to Megan.

"Well," she mumbled aloud to herself as she hung up her clothes, "maybe not *their* bed."

"Hmm?"

"Nothing, just going to bed seems like a good idea and I'm tired or tipsy enough to be talking aloud to myself."

"You were already doing that when I moved in, regardless of how much sleep you'd had," Jelena said with a smile.

"Right. I remember thinking at least I wouldn't be talking to *myself*, if I kept the dogs . . ." Megan crawled into bed and flopped down with an *oof*. "I'll be asleep and snoring in ninety seconds. Any last words?"

"Thank you." Jelena came to bed, too, and pulled Megan into an embrace. "I was afraid the murder would keep you busy all day, but you spent it with me after all."

"I promised," Megan murmured. "I'm sorry I'd given you reasonable grounds for doubt. It was a lot of fun, too."

"More fun than solving a murder?"

Megan laughed. "C'mon now, you're trying to get me in trouble. Different fun!"

Jelena's grin was audible. "I'll take it. Sleep now, bejb."

"Too late, I already am." In about half a minute, that was true, and Megan didn't wake up again until Thong put her cold nose in Megan's hand at the side of the bed and whined.

She breathed a laugh and touched her finger to her lips. Thong, at least, had a pretty good idea of what the *shh* motion meant, and wagged her tail with enthusiasm, but said nothing else. Megan crept out of bed, checking the time—a little after seven in the morning—and slipped into the living room, whispering, "Good pup, let's let Jelena sleep, she had a big day yesterday and has another choir performance today," as she closed the bedroom door.

The dogs scampered around relatively quietly, rushing for the door, then demanding to be let back in to eat. Megan checked the time, got their leashes on them, and took them for a brisk walk in the early-morning mist. "It'll burn off," she informed them, more out of hope than confidence. "Should we go over to Baked and get something nice for Yella for breakfast? Or the Orange Tree? Yeah, the Orange Tree, maybe, huh? Good idea."

Jelena was right. She absolutely talked to the dogs as a pretense of not talking to herself. "This is why people get cats," she told the dogs, then laughed. "Or dogs, I guess." A few minutes later, armed with croissants, scones, and a variety of other pastries from the bakery, they went home again, just in time to find Jelena emerging from the bedroom.

"Oh. Oh, I think maybe we should have St. Patrick's Day every day. First I get you all to myself, then I get breakfast delivered to me. I like this."

"I forgot coffee. Should I go back out and get some?"

"I'll make do without, this time." Jelena sat at the table, her feet tucked up under her, and went through the breakfast options happily. Megan's phone buzzed and she ignored it resolutely until Jelena, softly amused, said, "You'd better look. You'll explode, otherwise."

"I will not," Megan said with dignity. "Whoever it is can wait until after breakfast." It buzzed again and she wrinkled her face, mumbled, "Just to see who it is," and took a quick look. "Orla. Okay, no, I can't answer, she'll ask me to work. And she knows it, or else she'd be calling. Croissants! No work!"

"Scones for me." Jelena rose to heat a couple in the microwave while Megan smeared jam on one of the croissants and, having made a huge mess doing that, made an even worse one as she ate it, flakes going everywhere.

"I'll never understand how people eat these elegantly," she said around the crumbs, "but I love them."

"Well, that's not how," Jelena said cheerfully. "Scones are easier."

"But they invite the butter-jam-cream debate," Megan said with a sad shake of her head, then laughed as Jelena decisively put those things on her scone in that order. "Or maybe there's no debate."

"There is one," Jelena admitted. "Just not for me. Lucky I'm Polish and we don't have to follow British scone-eating rules. And you're both Irish and American, so you don't either. Twice as much as I don't."

"Next time I'll have a rebellious scone," Megan promised, but for the time being had another croissant. "What time do you need to be there for the performance?"

"We're on at two, assuming everything is running on time." Jelena sounded skeptical. "We're not supposed to be later than half one."

"So you'll be there at one-fifteen and won't perform until three," Megan guessed.

Jelena made a face. "If we're lucky. I don't know how close to on time the grandstand stage performances run, but . . ."

"They're Irish," Megan finished with a sympathetic smile. "All right. I'll probably come over with you and hang out, if that's okay."

"You're not going to call Orla?" Jelena's eyebrows rose.

"I'm trying very hard not to," Megan promised and Jelena laughed.

"Dziękuję, bejb. I appreciate it."

Megan, half under her breath, echoed, "Jen-*koo*yeh," trying to get the pronunciation right, and Jelena applauded her lightly.

"I'll have you speaking enough to bring you home for a visit soon. 'Thank you,' 'please,' 'where is the toilet' and 'Jelena is very beautiful' should get you through."

"Jelena jest bardzo ładna," Megan said with more confidence than she'd repeated "thank you," and Jelena laughed again.

"Oh, very good. You've been practicing. All right." She pushed her breakfast dishes away. "I'm going to shower and get ready, and you can pretend you haven't called Orla when I get back."

"What if she calls me?"

"Then you'll remind her you took the weekend off," Jelena said firmly.

Megan flicked a salute. "Ma'am, yes, ma'am! I'll clean up the breakfast stuff, too."

"You're a star." Jelena dropped a kiss on her head as she went by and Megan tied up, stepping over the dogs when necessary. Her phone rang as she got the last of the dishes done and she approached it gingerly, picking up to say, "This is Megan," when she saw Orla's name on the screen.

"I'd triple your rates," Orla said.

Megan laughed. "Extra money won't do me any good if Jelena's drowned me in the canal. Then I'd really be the murder driver."

"Sure and murder driver isn't the same as murdered driver," Orla muttered. "She's desperate for you, is Ms. Woodward. She wants you to meet her editor."

"Why on earth would she want me to do that?"

"I've no idea, but if you drove her this afternoon I'd say you'd learn," Orla said slyly.

Megan, grateful for the fact it was a voice-only call, gritted her teeth and kicked her feet with stymied impatience before saying, "I'm sure you're right, but I'm still not going to," in a bright, cheerful voice.

"You're a hard one, Megan Malone." Orla hung up in an obvious sulk. Megan kicked her feet again, making the dogs bark, then sat on the floor to let them climb on her as she checked the time, then rang Paul.

The alarm in his voice when he picked up made her remember that she only called when somebody was dead, and she said, "No, no, nobody's dead, sorry!" hastily. "I was just wondering if you were going spare not working on this thing like I a—uh. I mean, not that I was working on it anyway." She grimaced at Thong, who decided it was an expression of dominance and fell over to expose her belly. Dip jumped on her and the kitchen was suddenly a blur of excited small dog enthusiasm, with yaps and ridiculous little growls interspersed with the sound of toenails on tile.

Paul, after a judicious and somehow amused silence on his end, said, "Is everything all right there?"

"Just the dogs going mad," Megan said weakly. "My fault, I set them off."

"All right." He waited a beat, then sighed. "I don't like being taken off a case, no. The chief isn't wrong, but I still don't like it. There's a sense of obligation to see it through."

"Exactly! I'm sure Detective Doogan or whoever it was—"

"Dervla. Detective Garda Dervla Reese."

"Right—her—will do fine, but . . ." Megan groaned and tilted over. "But I'm not a guard and

I should stay in my lane. All right. I'll just keep telling myself that. How's Niamh this morning?"

Paul chuckled. "Still sleeping, last I saw. If she's awake before half three I'll eat my hat."

"Lifestyles of the rich and famous, huh?"

"I don't know if I'll ever get used to it. C'mere to me, are you well, Megan? You're less in the news thanks to the holiday, but it might rise up again."

"I'm honestly trying to keep my head down," Megan said with a shrug, then considered that she'd tilted herself all the way to the floor, and chuckled. "Literally. I'm lying on the floor as we speak."

"Well, give the dogs a rub for me and tell them herself says hello."

"Do we mean Niamh or their mother, by 'herself'?"

Bourke laughed. "I meant Abhaile." He'd adopted the stray Jack Russell that Megan had found with her two newborn puppies, and as far as Megan could tell, the little dog seemed glad to be shut of her offspring. Puppies, as it turned out, were a lot of work. "Go on now and drown your sorrows with Jelena. I'm sure whatever you've planned for the day is better than investigating murders."

"Right. Right, yes, it definitely is. Look, will we text if we're still in town at dinnertime?"

"Not unless you've already made reservations. It's mental out there and it's only just gone nine."

"That's the tourists," Megan said cheerfully. "Never catch an Irishman or woman out reveling this early, unless they haven't gone to bed yet."

"There's a fair few of those, too," Bourke said

rather less cheerfully. "G'wan then, I'll talk to you later."

"I'm sure you will." Megan put the phone away and called the dogs back to her, giving them the promised rubs before going back to the bedroom to fall on her face until Jelena was out of the shower. "I turned Orla down. All yours for the day, just like I promised."

"There may be hope for you yet. Go shower and we can walk to city centre if it's not raining."

"My phone says it's not supposed to."

Jelena laughed. "And what does the actual weather outside the door say?"

Megan got up to steal a kiss on her way to the shower. "It didn't rain on us earlier, but that's meaningless. We'll bring umbrellas."

"And wellies. The choir will be uroczy, which means adorable in our raincoats and boots."

CHAPTER 10

The choir was, in fact, adorable in their wellies and raincoats, at least as far as Megan was concerned. They were also far better protected from the sudden midafternoon downpour than the audience was: The portable stage setup on O'Connell had a roof, at least, whereas the open-air audience had a scattering of umbrellas and a largely offended attitude, as if the idea it might rain hadn't occurred to anybody. Given the country's literary penchant for dark humor, Megan found the Irish people resolutely optimistic about the potential for good weather, and always thought it was funny when they were betrayed by it being reliably Irish instead.

Of course, it might have been easier to see the humor when she was one of the few carrying an umbrella. She shared its rainbow cheer with the people next to her, which was the best she could do, and fumbled it to applaud when the choir finished up, only half an hour later than they'd been expected to.

"Practically on time, by Irish standards," Megan breathed as she squeezed back out of the crowd. A group off to one side crowded together, singing the Polish anthem, which the choir had ended with, and Megan had the ridiculous urge to stop and hug them. She did stop a moment to listen, then turned away as she thought someone called her name.

Because there were a hundred thousand people on the streets, and it was so very likely that one of them would be looking for her. But after a moment, Claire Woodward's semi-distinctive American accent cut across the crowd again, and Megan's stomach twisted in a combination of delight and oncoming dismay. A moment later Claire barged up to her, breathless and pink-cheeked. "I did see you! I hoped I might, after you said your girlfriend was performing with the Polish part of the parade!"

"The parade was yesterday," Megan said uncertainly, but Claire waved a hand.

"I extrapolated that she might be with the choir here today, so I thought I'd see if I could find you. No wonder you couldn't drive for me."

"I took this weekend off eight months ago." Megan tried not to let it sound like an apology.

"Of course you did. I'm just a pushy American. Speaking of which, let me introduce you to Derek." Claire looked around, locating a slender white man about her own height threading his way through the crowd. "Derek, this is Megan the murder dr—"

"Megan Malone," Megan said loudly. "I drive limos for a living."

Derek had thinning brown hair and a nice, if slightly rueful, smile as he offered his hand. "So I've heard. Nice to meet you, Ms. Malone. Derek Jacobson. I'm Claire's editor."

"You just flew in, right?"

"I was in Cork for a few days, with plans to meet Claire here for a book signing at Eason." He nodded toward the enormous bookstore just down the street from where they stood. "I came up earlier than expected."

"Right. Is it the publicist who flew in last night, then?" Megan glanced at Claire, who nodded.

"Kiki Rogers, yes. She's been talking to the press and the publishing house all day, on about three hours of sleep. I don't know what I'd do without her."

"It'll be fine," Derek said, in what sounded like a well-repeated reassurance. "Kiki knows what she's doing."

"You'll come to the signing, won't you?" Claire put her hand on Megan's upper arm, sending a chill of discomfort across Megan's neck. It was obviously intended to be a friendly, welcoming gesture, a very American thing to do. Megan had been in Ireland too long, maybe. She managed a smile and shrugged, which had the effect of helping to shake Claire's hand off.

"When is it?"

"In just a couple of hours! Six PM at Eason's. It would be so nice to have a friendly face there, with all this going on."

"I'll check with Jelena," Megan said cautiously. "We may have plans."

"Oh, bring her, too, please? I'd love to meet her!"

"I'll see," Megan said, still cagily. "I hope it goes well, whether we make it or not."

"Here." Derek offered a business card. "Old-fashioned in the day of QR codes, I know, but if you decide to come, call me and we'll get you through the door."

Megan blinked at the card, then smiled. "Thanks. If you'll excuse me now, though, I have to go congratulate my girlfriend." She smiled and made her escape through the crowd, mumbling, "Good Megan. Good job. Jelena will be happy," at her impulse to turn back and hang out with the writer and her editor. Not that she could even report anything she learned back to Paul, so there was definitely no reason to do so.

"Nothing except my own insatiable curiosity," she muttered, then tried to wipe the encounter from her mind as she got around to the back of the stage just before Jelena's choir swarmed out, all smiles and laughter. Megan lifted her hand in applause and a few of the women she knew curtsied or bowed.

Jelena beamed when she saw her and pulled Megan into a hug. "I couldn't see you in the crowd! I even looked for the umbrella, but there were too many like yours!"

"There weren't even that many umbrellas at all!" Megan protested, but Jelena wasn't wrong: The style of umbrella she carried was both popular and easily available at a shop in the GPO Arcade, only a minute's walk from the festival stage's location. "You were all great. You sounded wonderful."

"I thought we were pitchy," someone said with a sniff on her way by, but Jelena made a face at her, and, when she was gone, murmured, "Anna wanted the solo that Maja got and has been bitchy ever since. Ignore her, we were great."

"You were," Megan said happily. "Are you starving? We could go up to Cutie Waiter's and have crêpes or something."

Jelena laughed. "You know that's not what it's called, right?"

"I do, but there's that one waiter and he's really cute."

"They're all cute," Jelena said. "I think they have to pass a cute test to work there. And I *am* starving, so I hope you made a reservation?"

"No, but I can call now if you want." Megan took her phone out as they went against the flow of the crowd, working their way to Abbey Street, where the Luas tracks meant there weren't quite as many people clogging the entire street. They weren't the only ones walking along the tracks, though, and everybody eventually scooted out of the way when an impatient Luas driver honked from two blocks away to inform them the tram was on approach.

"They think I'm ridiculous for calling when I'm a five-minute walk away," Megan said as she hung up, "but they've also got a table they can hold for us. Score one for the pushy American."

"Partly I think I should scold you and partly I'm glad we'll have a seat," Jelena said wryly. "I'm so hungry."

"I should have brought you one of the leftover

croissants," Megan said apologetically, but a few minutes later they were at Lemon Jelly, a glass-fronted café on a stretch of pedestrianized street between a large shopping center and the river. The owner waved a greeting as they walked up, calling, "Welcome back, ask Peter for your table!"

"Thank you!" They went inside, both smiling, and the tall, handsome young man Megan referred to as Cutie Waiter showed them to a table still damp from being wiped down. He and Jelena exchanged a few sentences in Polish before he said, "Apple juice with ginger?" to Megan, who spread her hands.

"You know me so well! And a Jervis Way, please."

"You never change," he informed her solemnly, but nodded at Jelena. "This one, she's trickier."

"Tricky enough to need a menu," she said apologetically. "And a coffee, please."

He offered the menu with a promise to be back in a few minutes, and Jelena made a visible effort not to chew her own arm off after she ordered. "Tell me something to distract me."

Megan winced. "I ran into Claire Woodward right after your performance?"

Jelena's eyebrows rose. "Well, that's a distraction, all right. What happened?"

"She invited us to her book signing at Eason's at six."

"Ooh." Jelena, obviously despite herself, looked intrigued. "I've never been to a book signing. I'm always too nervous to meet anybody famous. I don't know what to say." She sat forward, suddenly intrigued. "Like, how did you get to be friends with Niamh? I know you met because you were hired as her driver, but I'd have been terrified to even talk to her! I still am sometimes!"

"And yet here you are, borrowing her clothes," Megan said with a grin. "I met her, I swear I'd only been in Ireland for like five minutes, honestly, but I drove her to that awards show, do you remember? The one where she went viral?"

Jelena's eyes widened. "Oh, yes. Right, yes, I knew you'd driven her to that, but how did you get to be friends?"

"I was right there when she eviscerated that guy." Megan cast a dreamy smile at the café's industrial-style, open-to-the-pipes ceiling. Niamh's Afro-Caribbean heritage was still the source of a lot of media commentary about her "authenticity" as an Irish film star, but that evening she'd been subjected to a particularly condescending series of questions by an entertainment-TV talking head. Rather than sit back and take it, she'd politely obliterated the guy, but while the networks had cut away, people filming the interaction with their phones sure hadn't. She'd utterly upstaged the awards ceremony, and her already rising star had gone meteoric. "God, she was great. Anyway, I told her so when she got back in the car, even if as the help I should have kept my mouth shut. She laughed—you know that huge belly laugh of hers? And then burst into tears, the poor woman. I drove a couple blocks away and then crawled over the seat to give her a hug. Super-professional of me, I know."

"I never would have dared," Jelena said, astonished.

Megan shrugged. "I don't know, it just seemed like the only decent thing to do, and you're decent, so probably you would have. Anyway, we brought the car back and went to the pub and got plastered on what may have been the last night of Niamh O'Sullivan's life when everybody in Ireland didn't know her face. They sure did by morning."

"You're just like this," Jelena said with a crooked smile. "You can't help getting involved."

"I'm really trying not to be involved in the case, though, Yella. I really am."

"I know. Oh, good, food." They both fell silent while they devoured their crêpes, although Jelena slowed down near the end of hers and sighed contentedly. "All right. We'll go to the book signing. You can teach me how to be brave with famous strangers."

"Claire's not nearly as famous as Niamh and you're okay with Nee."

"But I wasn't when I met her! I was too scared to talk!"

"Well, all you have to say is 'Hi, nice to meet you,' and you'll probably be fine. Do you want dessert?"

"I do. I'm still perishing." Jelena finished her crêpes and Cutie Waiter came over to take their dessert orders, then brought them each a slice of cake nearly as big as Megan's head. Jelena announced, "I can't eat all of that," but still managed to do a more thorough job than Megan did on hers, and eyed what was left thoughtfully. "If I waited twenty minutes I could probably finish it."

Megan checked the time and grinned. "We have an hour before the book signing and it's a ten-minute walk away. We can wait twenty minutes if you want."

"I think I'd better go for a longer walk instead. Maybe even go buy a copy of one of Claire's books." Jelena scowled. "Or not, since she didn't want Niamh in her movie."

"That's right, Irish girls stick together." Megan offered a fist bump and Jelena knocked her knuckles against Megan's, chuckling.

"Not that I'm Irish."

"You've lived here a lot longer than I have. Close enough." Megan got up to pay the bill, then met Jelena at the door so they could have a wander around the Henry Street shopping area before heading back down O'Connell Street to the bookstore.

"Oh," Jelena said in dismay, as they approached. A line snaked out the door and around the block, filled with people—mostly women—holding one or two Claire Woodward books, most of which looked well-read and well-loved. "Oh. We should have come to stand in line!"

Megan, feeling almost guilty, took Derek's card out of her pocket and mumbled, "I could—I could call her editor. He said he'd get us past the queue, if I called,"

"Oh, you should do that, then," Jelena said firmly. "Because I'm not standing in that line for a woman who didn't want Niamh for the role."

"I like how petty we all are." Megan put Derek's number into her phone and called, not entirely surprised when a woman answered. "Hi, this is Megan Malone with Leprechaun Limos. I'm Claire Woodward's dri—"

"Brilliant, you're here. Are you outside? Can you go around to the Abbey Street entrance? I'll meet you there. I'm Aoife."

"Aoife. Great, sure, we'll be there in a minute." Megan hung up, her eyebrows rising. "They were expecting me to call."

"Good. Let's go be petty." Jelena smiled so sharply Megan wasn't sure she was kidding. They circled around to the side of the Eason's building, where the line petered out just before the side entrance. A young woman in well-cut business clothes and a press badge stood in the doorway, clearly keeping an eye out for them. She smiled professionally when Megan waved uncertainly, and gestured them toward her.

"Megan Malone? And Jelena? Grand, if you could come with me, please? I'm Aoife, I'm with Kiki Rogers in the publisher's publicity department? Grand, just this way, please." She led them in past the ground-floor coffee shop and Jelena squeaked at the book-signing setup that took over the entire front half of the bookstore.

An enormous snaking queue wound around the floor. The first few people in it stood a few feet away from a long table that had a stack of Claire's books on it, and a backdrop of posters with her name, picture, and biography behind it. Claire wasn't there yet, but it also wasn't quite six. Derek Jacobson, though, stood off to one side of the table with a petite white woman who could have been anywhere from forty-five to sixty. She was sleekly coiffed in a chignon, business suit, and heels so high they made Megan's feet hurt to look at. "Ms. Rogers, this is Ms. Malone with Leprechaun Limos, and her associate Jelena Nowak. Ms. Malone, this is Ms. Rogers with publicity. May I take your coats, ladies?"

Jelena shrugged her coat off, murmuring, "I didn't know anyone knew my last name," to Megan, who pulled a little face of confusion as she handed her coat over, too.

"Great to meet you." Kiki Rogers had a strong New York accent, a firm grip, and a glint in gray-blue eyes that said she'd wrestle a tiger to the mat if she had to. Up close, Megan thought she was probably in her early fifties, and that she might get along well with Orla. "Please, call me Kiki. Claire's delighted you joined us today. We're all looking forward to this. Can Aoife get you coffee? Water? Makeup?"

Megan's eyebrows rose. "Makeup?"

"For the photos," Kiki replied. "The lighting in here isn't flattering to anyone, and a little concealer and lippy go a long way toward hiding the sins of a late night or a long day."

"No," Jelena said firmly. "I'm fine."

"You're already wearing makeup," Kiki said pleasantly. "I like the blue. I think you'll be happy with the results, Ms. Malone, if you'll come this way for just a moment?"

"Why do I need makeup?" Megan went behind the promotional posters with a sense of faint surreality and found herself being powdered, concealed, and lipsticked while a smiling woman told her what nice skin she had. "Thanks? I use moisturizer sometimes? What's going on?"

"Don't worry," Kiki said cheerfully. "Nobody expects you to sign any books yet."

"What? Why would I sign any books ever at all?"

"Oh, excellent," Kiki said, regarding her as the makeup woman stepped away, "you really do have great skin. Terrific, thanks so much for being so obliging, it makes my life so much easier, all right, so Claire will be introduced in a minute here and there'll be the usual round of applause and everything, and then we're going to bring you out before the press gets a chance to start digging into this murder business—"

"Press? What press?"

"Just a few people. The *Irish Times*, the AP, Talk-Tally, you know, the usual."

"TalkTally has people in Dublin?" Megan shook her head, trying to step back and recalibrate. The social news network carried—or made up—all the latest gossip, while keeping people on-site with best-of lists, feel-good videos, and quizzes, most of which were cribbed from other locations on the internet. Megan wouldn't have thought there was enough celebrity gossip in Dublin to make it worthwhile.

"TalkTally has people everywhere. Derek, if you could let Claire know Ms. Malone is ready?"

"She's on her way," Derek said from the other side of the promotional posters. A moment later, Megan caught a glimpse of Claire and heard the applause, some calls of *I love you, Ms. Woodward!* and at least one person in tears. Claire extended her thanks for everyone's attendance, and Megan felt a hand in the small of her back, pressuring her to go out.

She balked, confusion burgeoning toward anger. "What is going *on*? Why do I need to go out there?"

Kiki Rogers appeared at her side with a tension-ridden shark's smile fixed in place. "Because we need you here to announce Claire's new murder driver mystery series based on you, Ms. Malone."

CHAPTER 11

"*What?*" Megan's voice cracked on the question as she found herself caught between doing the polite thing of not causing a scene, and the very real burst of outrage and horror that shot through her. "What? Excuse me? No! I don't think so!"

Kiki's smile went even more strained and Megan upwardly revised her age to closer to sixty. "Claire said you talked about this."

"Claire said somebody should write a series based on me and I said that was a terrible idea!" Megan wasn't sure they'd even had that much of a discussion, but she was fairly confident that had been her side of the conversation, anyway.

"Ms. Malone..." Cords stood out in Kiki Rogers's neck before she pressed her eyes closed, took a visibly deep breath, and exhaled again. When she opened her eyes, it was with an equally visible effort to retain some degree of calm. "I'm sorry. Claire was very clear about having spoken to you and having gotten your approval for this project."

"Claire was very misleading, by which I mean, she lied."

A hint of frustration flashed in Kiki's eyes again, making Megan wonder if Claire lying about easily-verifiable things was habitual. "I realize I'm putting you on the spot here, Megan, but I'm in a bind. I've got a PR disaster on my hands and I'm desperate to distract from it. You're an amazing distraction and I'd really, really appreciate your help."

"You're trying to keep Claire's career from imploding by blowing up my life instead," Megan hissed. "That's not me helping, that's me being the sacrificial lamb!"

All pretense of friendliness disappeared as Kiki's shark smile snapped back into place. "I'm going to blow up your life whether you help me or not, Ms. Malone. You can't actually stop her from writing a series about a taxi driver who gets caught up in murder mysteries. If you go out there right now you might be able to do some damage control, but otherwise, we direct the narrative and *believe* me, Ms. Malone, I can make it sound like this was all your idea. You fight me on this and any word of protest you leak will be attributed to sour grapes, not getting what you think is enough money, losing control of your image, a million things, Megan. I will be the shit in your sunshine sandwich."

Hot anger flashed through Megan, scalding her

face. She kept her hands from turning to fists with effort, but her pulse was so fast in her throat she thought she might be sick from it. She had no doubt the publicist meant every word she said, and that she could follow through on her threats. Maybe not as effectively as she threatened, but effectively enough. Claire Woodward was both rich and famous, and Megan was neither. Fights balanced that way didn't tend to go well for the little guy.

The idea of pulling Niamh in scattered through her mind for about half a heartbeat, and bounced out again. The last thing Niamh needed was to publicly defend a friend who got into a fracas with the writer who'd already blacklisted her from a leading role.

There wasn't anything Megan could even *say*. "This isn't over" might have been true, but its clichéd melodrama robbed it of any teeth. Maybe she wasn't stuck for good, but she was stuck for the moment, and Kiki was right: If she went out there, she could at least try to control how it went, whereas if she didn't, she was entirely at Claire and Kiki's mercy.

And if she did, Detective Bourke, his boss, and Jelena were all going to pull a full-on *Murder on the Orient Express* on her. Nobody would ever be convicted of her murder, and she wouldn't even blame them.

Megan turned away from Kiki Rogers, plastered a smile on her face, and walked out in front of the promotional backdrop as they called her name.

* * *

Claire was talking, some gushing introduction Megan could barely hear through the blood rushing in her ears. Something about her friend and inspiration for her new series. Something about tragedy turning into opportunity, which Megan thought was a misstep in marketing terms, but she was hardly going to keep Claire from shooting herself in the foot, if that's what happened. She didn't dare look toward Jelena, because it wasn't the foot Jelena was going to want to shoot anybody in.

Hundreds of fans stood behind a thin row of journalists, most of the former ducking their heads to talk to each other or texting and taking pictures. One of the journalists said, "How do you feel about having your life commercialized, Ms. Malone?"

Megan, probably too honestly, said, "Pretty lousy, actually," which got a startled laugh from both the journalist and the crowd, and a shocked look from Claire. "I never agreed to any such thing, but I was just told I couldn't do anything about it, and that it was better for me to play along than have my name smeared by the publisher's publicity department, so here I am." Megan shrugged.

Claire's expression turned to horror, then lurched toward a forced smile as even more phones were raised for photographs, and the journalist raised his eyebrows at her. "Any comment, Ms. Woodward?"

"Well, of course I'm not *commercializing* Megan's life," she said in a bright, strained tone. "I'm fictionalizing the idea of it. I won't, of course, be taking real incidents from her life. That would be rude!"

"Really?" Megan's own smile became slightly

less forced as she started to enjoy turning the tables on the writer. "Then how come you grilled me for case details when we first met?"

Claire snapped, "Professional curiosity! I'm appalled my publicist would allow you to think I was going ahead with a project you hadn't approved—" By then, the entire gathered room of autograph-seekers had their phones out, lifted, with lights and sometimes flashes indicating they were probably filming. Megan had a sudden sinking sensation of solidarity with Detective Bourke. This must be a little bit what it felt like to be dating Niamh.

Or worse, maybe it was what it was like to *be* Niamh. Megan had a shivering thought about going viral, then pulled herself back to the moment, not wanting to lose control of a situation she'd perhaps gained the upper hand in. Another reporter, clearly more interested in Megan than Claire right now, said, "How *do* you keep getting involved in these situations, Ms. Malone?"

Megan shrugged. "Sheer bad luck. But really, I wouldn't want to make this all about me, so I'm going to step away and let Claire start her si—"

"How many murders have you been involved with?" another reporter asked.

Megan squinted at that one. "Are you from TalkTally? Are you going to do a 'Top Ten Murder Driver Murders' list or something? Because you're going to have to do your own research on that, or at least steal it from somebody else who's already put the work in."

A ripple of snarky appreciation ran through the crowd, and the first journalist, who at least saw an opportunity when it arose, turned his attention back to Claire. "Speaking of which, Ms. Woodward, what can you say in response to the recent plagiarism accusations that have come along with Bláthnaid O'Leary's murder?"

Claire blanched, fumbling for an answer as her publicist swept out from behind the backdrop, gave Megan a look of pure rage, then slapped a professional smile into place as she called, "I'm very sorry, gentlemen, but we only have ninety minutes for the book signing and we can't leave Claire's fans disappointed. Perhaps there'll be time later to discuss current events if you want to wait."

The younger Irish woman who'd been helping her came out with several security guards, and the reporters exchanged glances, then reluctantly closed up shop. Jelena slid her hand into Megan's and hurried her out the side doors before the journalists caught up, glanced up and down Abbey Street, and scurried into a small vegetarian restaurant a few doors away. "Oh my God, Megan."

"I'm sorry!" Megan dropped into one of the chairs near the door, then stood again as Jelena gestured further back into the restaurant, away from the front windows. "I didn't know they were going to do that!"

"Obviously. You should have seen your face." Jelena got her around the back corner where the restaurant increased in width, then glanced toward the front. "You stay. I'll get us some tea or something." She went to the buffet counter, which smelled good enough to make Megan's stomach rumble even though they'd eaten less than two hours earlier, and came back a few minutes later with brewing tea. "You turned it around on them, though. Are you all right?"

"I don't think so." Megan poured weak tea—she didn't care, she didn't like it anyway—and wrapped her hands around the cup, letting the heat sting her palms. "I bet Irish Twitter's gonna be all over that. I'm sorry," she said again after a moment. "That didn't . . . I had no idea that was going to happen."

Jelena snorted. "I know, bejb. You wouldn't have gone if you'd known. You certainly wouldn't have brought me."

"Oh, God." Megan met her eyes. "Was anybody taking pictures of you?"

"Oh, no, I think you had their full attention." Jelena smiled crookedly. "Especially that PR woman. You should have seen her face when you started talking. I've never seen anybody turn that color before."

"She told me I could help control the narrative if I went out." Megan bared her teeth, but didn't imagine it was a smile. "So I tried." She lifted the teacup, blowing on the hot liquid even though she didn't intend to drink any. "Well, one way or another that should end her wanting me to drive her anywhere. I'm all yours for the weekend." Her phone rang as she said that, and Jelena's eyebrows rose.

"I'll bet you a month's rent that's Orla."

"That is not a bet I'll take." Megan got the phone out, turned it so Jelena could see that it was, indeed, Orla's name on the ID, and answered with, "Dare I ask?"

"Will I be renaming us to Murder Driver Incorporated, then?" Orla demanded. "The lads say you're trending, whatever that means, and that so are we."

"I want stake in the company if you're naming it after me," Megan said with a flash of a grin, then held the phone away from her ear to avoid Orla's screech of outrage. "Are we booked for the rest of the year yet?"

"The phone's gone mad," Orla admitted grimly. "Half of them want you to drive them and the other half want interviews. D'yis know any press, Megan, because you might want to get ahead of this."

"That's what I was trying to do! And the only—" Megan gave a rough laugh. "The only person in the press that I know at all is Aibhilín Ní Gallachóir, and she covers sports, not—I don't even know what this is. Local interest?"

"I'd say it's more than local," Orla muttered. "Some of these calls are coming in from America. Ring yer wan, Megan. She got a boost from that golfing murder you were caught up in and she'll give you the ear you need."

"She doesn't like me at all!"

"She'll like the publicity." Orla hung up and Megan put the phone down, shaking her head.

"I don't think that could possibly help. I don't want *more* attention!" Her phone rang again, Niamh's picture coming up this time. Megan stared at it. Jelena reached across the table and accepted the call, which came up with a video image of Paul and Niamh squished together in-frame.

"Told you she'd take a vone call," Niamh said triumphantly as Paul spread his hands in acceptance.

"Jelena took it," Megan objected, but Niamh smiled.

"I win anyway. Hi, Yella, where are you?"

Jelena put her hand over the camera lens and waved.

"Hi! Where *are* you?" Niamh asked again, the inflection making it a different question.

"Govinda's on Abbey Street."

"Oh, god, they're good. You can eat your body weight in curry for like ten quid. Anyway, hi, Megan, you're trending. I want to star in the TV series, okay?"

"What? What TV series? Is there a TV series now?" Megan heard panic rising in her voice and actually took a sip of her tea to try to quell it. It distracted her, anyway, and she shuddered. "God, that's awful."

"No, but if there *is* one, I want to star in it. Prestige TV, right? Short seasons with a clever fecking storyline that I win a load of Emmys for. Favorite Chris can play Paul."

Paul gave her a startled look. "None of the Chrises look anything like me."

"I don't look anything like Megan either. How about a Gleeson?"

"Bloody hell." Paul sat back, visibly starstruck at the idea. "Can you imagine!"

"Oh my God, you two!"

"I don't want anybody playing me," Jelena said in a strained voice. "That sounds terrible."

"Right? What she said! You two are losing your minds!"

"Domhnall's done a load of television," Paul mumbled, obviously looking at his own phone. "Some of it in Dublin!"

"Paul! You do not have your eye on the ball here!"

He looked up from his phone guiltily, then squinted at Megan through Niamh's phone. "The Irish don't play baseball, Megan."

"But you knew what I meant!"

"It'll all blow over as soon as Woodward's out of town," Niamh promised, then pursed her lips and cast an innocent gaze upward before fluttering her eyelashes at Megan. "But if it *doesn't*, and there's a TV show . . ."

"Yes, yes, you can play me, as far as I'm concerned! You and Domhnall, my good buddy Domhn—wait, who's going to play you?"

"Oh." Niamh's eyebrows drew down thoughtfully. "Ah, flip, that's a good point. Would I want to be you or would I want to be my own self in special guest appearances?"

"*Megan*!" Jelena looked appalled and Megan made an apologetic face at her.

"No TV shows," she promised. "Or books, I hope. I just wanted to get out of there, Paul."

"No, I know, we were only ringing to see if you were all right. It's not often you see a friend trending," Paul replied.

"I didn't even know you did much social media."

Niamh waved guiltily. "That was me. I saw it from my stealth account and I promise not to boost it from the main one. Unless you want that TV series, in which case I'll ask who's going to make it so I can sta—"

"Do! Not!"

Niamh laughed. "I wouldn't, love. Look, do you need a lift home now that you're famous? I can make Paul drive over to get you."

"Oh, you can, can you?" Bourke sounded amused, but nodded even before Niamh gave him a soppy puppy-dog look. "Sure I can so, if you need."

Megan shook her head. "I think a taxi app will get us there in one piece, if people start losing their minds on the Luas or something. Which they won't," she promised Jelena. "Niamh's right. This will all blow over as soon as the case is solved." She gave Paul a tight glance. "Any news on that?"

"I wouldn't know. Reese is keeping it close to her chest." His eyebrows rose and he shrugged. "And I can feel the urge to tell you everything I do know rising in me, so it's as well I know nothing."

All three of the woman mumbled, "Jon Snow," under their breath, and Bourke's expression sagged.

"I'm surrounded by madwomen."

"I haven't even seen the show," Jelena protested. "I've just read that line on T-shirts."

"We're going home," Megan told her phone. "If you guys want to come over . . . ?"

"Lads," Niamh said with a click of her tongue. "If you *lads* want to come over. You'll never be properly Irish if you keep saying *guys*, Megan."

Megan snorted. "Are you *lads* coming over, or what?"

"I've got another press thing in the morning," Niamh said apologetically. "I'm flying to Paris in a couple of hours, and Paul's driving me to the airport. Keep me in the loop, yeah? I can get my PR firm to do you a solid if you need a hand, Megan, all right?"

"Thank you." Megan pressed her hand over her heart. "Thanks, Nee, I really appreciate it. I'll let you know."

"All right. Safe home, you two." Niamh blew a kiss and Bourke waved as she hung up.

"You're not really going to need her PR firm, are you?" Jelena asked nervously.

"I can't imagine so. Everybody will lose interest and we can go back to normal by morning."

Jelena eyed her and Megan crinkled her face guiltily as she pulled up a taxi app. "All right, not by morning, but soon, all right? I promise."

"All right." Jelena caught her hands and held them hard for a moment. "All right. Let's go home for some peace and quiet until this all blows over, bejb."

CHAPTER 12

Peace and quiet lasted until somebody turned the news on at the gym the next morning.

Megan hated the litany of bad news first thing in the morning anyway, so had already left her treadmill to ask if the channel could be changed when a cheerful brunette from the Dublin entertainment scene came on with a picture of the book signing in the corner above her head. "And if you haven't been keeping up with all the goss, international bestseller Claire Woodward has been in Dublin this week ahead of a book signing. Earlier this week she was accused of plagiarism by a local writer whose tragic death wracked Dublin's literary scene, and an obvious attempt to redirect by announcing a new series based on local limo driver Megan Malone went terribly wrong. You can watch that here on exclusive footage obtained by *All the Goss* after last night's fiasco."

The photo in the corner zoomed in, taking over the screen, and to Megan's absolute horror, she came up in shaky phone camera footage, obviously taken from the front of the line at the previous evening's book signing. Megan spread her hands over her mouth, staring in dismay as the Megan on screen, looking a lot more composed than she'd felt, threw a couple of one-liners while Claire Woodward, half in the video, went through a series of truly desperate expressions before even trying to get herself under control.

"Jaysus, it's herself!" One of the other gym rats came forward, grinning hugely as he looked between the screen and Megan. "It's yourself, yeah?"

Megan, hands still over her mouth, nodded as several other people gathered around, watching the screen and bouncing their gazes toward Megan. "Here, let us get a snap," somebody said, pulling her phone out. "Lookit me, going to the same gym as the murder driver! Deadly!"

"Oh God, no." Megan held her hand in front of her face, trying to block the selfie, and the young woman pouted, although not seriously.

"C'mon now, don't be like that, I'd get cred all over me socials with a snap of you!" She put her phone away, though, and no one else took theirs out. The short video on the TV screen folded away to reveal the entertainment reporter again, and the woman chattered on cheerfully about unexpected twists to the holiday weekend, which segued into another topic.

"Is she legit, does this really keep happening to you?" the first gym rat asked. "Is there gonna be a TV show?"

Megan groaned. "No. There's not going to be books either, I hope. Look, I gotta get back to my workout, or . . . something." Maybe she needed to flee back to the house, and actually stay there for real until this all settled.

"Yeh, no, sorry, that wasn't cool, I just never met a real celebrity before."

"I am *not* a celebrity."

He grinned almost sympathetically. "You're literally on celebrity TV, love."

That was hard to argue with. Megan made a face and he went back to the weight room, where several of the lifters gave all pretense of working out and gathered to talk, glancing toward her often enough to make it clear what their topic of conversation was. Jelena finished her cardio and came over, wiping a towel across her forehead, and studied the men a moment. "This must be what it's like for Niamh all the time."

"Except it's worse for her, but yeah. I wonder if Orla's right and I should ring Aibhilín Ní Gallachóir to—I don't know what," Megan ended, baffled. "I don't feel like I've got a 'my side of the story' that needs to be told, or anything."

"Then I wouldn't call her," Jelena said decisively. "She'll eat you alive, even if you're not a sports story. We'll go home and you—" she drew the word out, clearly thinking about it, then exhaled noisily. "You'll put on a baseball cap and big sunglasses like Niamh does, and take the dogs for a long, long walk so you feel normal again, and then we'll go out to the pub for a bit and come home and I'll cook dinner for you."

"That sounds wonderful," Megan admitted. "Thanks, bejb."

Jelena's smile lit up. "If all the Polish you ever learn is endearments, that'll do. C'mere to me, let's go home and shower, and after that the dogs will love you for the walk."

"The dogs love me anyway. I don't think I own a baseball cap either."

"I do. You can borrow it. And my cat-eye sunglasses."

"Oh, no. Those look a lot better on you than they do on me."

"Exactly," Jelena said, as if bringing the conversation to a thunderous conclusion. Megan laughed and they left the gym, eyeing the sky and debating whether that was a high fog that would burn off, or a low mist that wouldn't. "Time will tell," Jelena said philosophically.

Enough of it had burned off by the time Megan left the house bedecked in Jelena's sunglasses and baseball cap and with the dogs on their leads, that it seemed like the day might turn beautiful. Jelena tossed a bottle of sunblock at her as she left, and Megan, catching it, said, "I don't burn!"

"It's still better for your skin. Have a good walk."

At the word, the dogs, who obviously already knew they were going for a walk, since they were outside on their leashes, began to dance around so frantically that Megan had to unwind herself from the tangle they made before she could take a step. "Stop! Stop! If you want to *go* for a walk, you have to let me move my legs! Sit," she said more firmly, and they both did, tails thumping while their gazes rested guiltily on her.

"All right, all is forgiven," Megan said as she got loose. "Do you want to walk up and see if Brian and Ms. Kettle are home? We haven't seen them in a while, huh? Yeah? Okay."

Several minutes later, actually at Brian's front door, Megan remembered he had a standing class on Saturday mornings, and that even on St. Patrick's Day weekend, was unlikely to be home. She knocked anyway, and after a minute Ms. Kettle, Brian's enormous, long-haired Angora cat, came to the window beside the door and stared at them, but there was no further movement from inside. "Next time," she told Ms. Kettle, and said, "All right, we'll go the other way," to the dogs. "Down to the Iveagh Gardens, maybe. Ooh, maybe even all the way over to the food festival thingy in the barracks, yeah? That sounds good. Not too much to eat if we go there, though. We don't want to spoil Jelena's dinner for us."

The mist had cleared entirely by the time they'd meandered two kilometers at a 'two dogs interested in sniffing everything' pace, but even so, they had to wait a few minutes for the gardens to open. The entrance was tucked between buildings, easy to miss, and shadowed enough that the cold March sunshine didn't have much effect in warming the space. Megan and the handful of other early risers—by Irish standards, anyway; the gardens opened at ten on bank holidays—were audibly glad when the gates opened and they could stretch their legs and warm up with another walk.

Dogs weren't supposed to be let off-leash there, but a few other dog-walkers let their animals run

while Dip and Thong strained at their leashes hopefully. "Sorry," Megan mumbled to them. "I'm a
rules-following sort of person." Dip gave her a dubious look and she said, "Yeah, no, I don't *know*
how a rules-follower keeps ending up adjacent to
murders, but imagine if I was a chaos goblin. I'd
probably be out committing the murders instead
or something. We wouldn't want that, so you stay
on the leash."

The trees hadn't started to leaf up yet, and the
sun poured down brilliantly enough that Megan
was glad for both the cap's brim and the borrowed
sunglasses as she took the dogs through the minia-
ture maze in the garden's most southerly corner.
Thong tried leaving through a break in the bushes
and got offended when Megan picked her up to
carry her out along the same winding trail they'd
come in through. All was forgiven when Megan
put her down again, though, so they made their
way around the garden's perimeter, Megan leaning against trees with her face turned upward when
the dogs wanted to have a good sniff around.

A woman said, "Aww, they're lovely, may I pet
them?"

"Sure, they're friendly." Megan opened her eyes
with a smile, saying, "Dip might ju—oh! Sadhbh?"

The dark-haired girl crouching to greet the
dogs was unmistakably Sadhbh, Bláthnaid's best
friend. She flinched in confusion as Megan asked
her name, then stared blankly as she rose. Megan,
strangely embarrassed, said, "I'm sorry, of course
you wouldn't remember me, I'm—"

"Claire Woodward's driver." Bitterness twisted

Sadhbh's pretty face as she backed a few steps away. Thong edged forward, tail wagging hopefully. "I didn't recognize you at first. But you're all over the news, aren't you. Capitalizing on my friend's death."

"I—" Megan, taken aback, swallowed the impulse to defend herself. Sadhbh was both young and in mourning, and it was arguably better to lash out at strangers than the people mourning with her. "I work for Leprechaun Limos, yes. Megan Malone."

"The murder driver." Sarcasm dripped with every syllable. "I guess Bláthnaid dying is good for business."

Megan also checked the impulse to admit it was, saying, "I'm so sorry, Ms. . . . Flanagan, right?"

"Oh, now I'm Ms. Flanagan, am I?"

"I remembered your first name first," Megan said, still keeping her tone apologetic. "You had to spell it out for the police detective, so I remembered it." She hesitated. "If you want to sit with the dogs for a few minutes, I'll back off. They can be pretty comforting."

Sadhbh's chin quivered and she tensed it, yanking her gaze toward the garden's distant archery field. "I'm grand."

Thong, obviously not believing her any more than Megan did, inched closer yet, lay down, and put her head on Sadhbh's foot to peer up at her with enormous, sympathetic eyes. The girl looked down like she couldn't help herself, and gave an awful blurt of sob-ridden laughter. Then she crouched again, and Thong sat up to lean into her knees. Dip hurried in, too, and Sadhbh thumped onto her butt, curling over the dogs as they crawled into her lap. Megan offered her the leashes, and she slid them over her arm while Megan backed off, as promised.

The poor kid looked wrecked, by Megan's estimation. She guessed the funeral had been the day before, since Irish funerals often took place within a day or two, but the combination of the suspicious circumstances of Bláthnaid's death and a midweek bank holiday might mean it hadn't even been held yet. She pulled up RIP.ie, which she thought was a humorously macabre URL, and checked for Bláthnaid's death notice.

The funeral wasn't scheduled until Monday, a full week after the girl's death. That would be hard on everyone in its own right, and her heart went out to the family. The site obviously didn't say *murdered horribly and found in a closet*, and it occurred to Megan that for the first time in one of these messes, she actually didn't know what Bláthnaid had died of. Detective Dervla Reese certainly wasn't going to tell her, and asking Sadhbh seemed like a bad move. She poked at the internet a little, but all she could find were three-day-old references claiming the cause of death was not yet known. She wrote a text saying **Do we know what killed Bláthnaid yet?** added a nervous-looking emoji, and sent it to Paul, who responded almost instantly with **being murdered.**

Megan could envision his sour expression as he'd sent that, and was about to text an apology when another message came through. **I couldn't tell you if I did know, but if I had a good imagination I might think she'd been strangled with a non-fibrous scarf or something else soft.**

"Oh, wow. I didn't know," Megan breathed to the phone. She didn't remember seeing any marks on Bláthnaid's neck that would suggest strangulation. Then again, there'd been a lot of screaming and panicking at the time, and she had neither looked at the girl very carefully, nor had the training to determine that kind of cause of death anyway.

But she thought almost anybody could strangle someone with a scarf. It would take a certain amount of strength or time, and the willingness to go through with it for as long as it took, but throats were fragile and humans, generally speaking, were strong. Adrian had an alibi, but Megan didn't know if any of the others had alibis that could be verified. Claire hadn't thought her whereabouts could be, for example. Presumably, the guards had been to the B and B to check their security tapes, if there were any, but Megan bet she could get some mileage out of her new murder driver fame and—

And do *nothing*. Going over to Claire's B and B and nosing around was *exactly* the kind of thing she wasn't supposed to be considering. Megan really didn't want to be a cop. She just hated not *knowing*.

Sadhbh reluctantly put the dogs out of her lap and got to her feet, approaching Megan to offer her the leashes as she mumbled, "Thanks. Sorry for being a cow."

"You've had a terrible week," Megan said gently. "It's all right. Look, you've been sitting on cold concrete for ten minutes. Can I buy you a coffee to warm you up?"

Sadhbh sniffed. "That'd be grand, actually, yeah. Your dogs are nice. Purebreds, are they?"

"I think so. They were strays that I accidentally adopted." Megan gestured toward the park entrance, but they went around the long way toward it instead of cutting across the damp grass. "Should I ask how you're holding up?"

The girl gave another one of those wet laughs. "Not well. Not well at all. Jules keeps ringing to check on me and it's kind of her and all, but I wish she'd text like a normal person."

"Us old people are very annoying that way."

Sadhbh's laugh was a little less wet that time. "I saw you texting a minute ago."

Megan, as solemnly as she could, said, "Just trying to stay hip and relevant," and Sadhbh laughed properly.

"Yeh, cool mac daddy-o, that's you. I think she's checking in so much because she's afraid somebody will say she did it, because of the whole thing with Bláthnaid and Aaron."

"Aaron. That's Juliet's son, right? I heard something about that," Megan admitted. "What's your take on it?"

Sadhbh gave her a sideways look and kept quiet long enough Megan thought she might not answer, but finally shook her head. "Look, Bláthnaid was my mate and I don't want to say anything that puts her in a bad light."

"I'm not a guard, Sadhbh. There's no one for me to tell."

She got another skeptical look, and held her hands up as best she could without pulling the dogs back from their end-of-leash explorations. "Honestly, I'm not working with the guards. The one I even know isn't on the case anymore."

Sadhbh's shoulders hunched and fell. "Yeah, I met the new guard. She's kinda fit."

So was Paul Bourke, which led Megan to conclude that what Sadhbh meant was that Dervla Reese was also in her age range. "If you say so. I've never met her."

Apparently those were the magic words, because Sadhbh let out a huge burst of air as they left the garden. "Bláthnaid didn't handle it well when she and Aaron broke up, all right? I never said it in so many words to her face, but she went a little mental and stalkery. And Jules is fierce protective of her kids, to the point that I'd say there's not a soul good enough for any of them on the whole of the planet, but if there was, it wasn't Bláthnaid for Aaron. She and Jules got along well enough when they were dating, but as soon as it was over . . ." Sadhbh shook her head. "And then Bláthnaid went off and really did mess up his career. They're saying he'll have to go to London or America to start over and him only our age. And he's a good bloke, like. He wouldn't be the type going around blaming things on his crazy ex, except . . ."

"Except in this case she really went a little crazy," Megan said. Sadhbh nodded and Megan, carefully, said, "How long ago was this?"

"Four months? Five? Yeah, five, because they broke up when university was starting again and Bláthnaid barged on set just before Halloween."

Megan held her breath. "Okay, I have a horrible thought that you can shoot down, but . . . was the breakup affecting her in other ways? Like, was school going okay for her? Was her writing?"

"She was mad to get good grades so she never stopped studying, but she'd almost stopped writ—" Sadhbh paled, clearly seeing where Megan's thoughts were going. "No. No, she wouldn't have. No, she'd have never copied that cow's work, she'd never have submitted it as her own, no matter how bad the writing was going. That was her own work, I'd swear to it, and somehow Claire Woodward got it published first!" Spots of color stood out in her cheeks and her eyes were bright with anger. "Bláthnaid didn't plagiarize that story!"

"Had you seen any of it in progress?" Megan asked as gently as she could.

"No, but her class would have!" For all the strength of Sadhbh's protestation, she didn't sound much like she believed it. Much less defensively, she mumbled, "Bláthnaid didn't like to show much of her work to people while she was in the middle of it. Said it made her lose confidence, like."

They'd passed two coffee shops, neither of which were open because it was Saturday morning, and were most of the way to Grafton Street by then. Megan nodded toward a small café just across the Luas line from where they were. "How about These Hands? We could sit down outside with the dogs."

"They're good, too. I like their lattes." They went across the street and Sadhbh took the dogs while Megan went in to order. When she came out again, Thong was in Sadhbh's lap and looking smug about it while Dip lay forlornly at her feet. Sadhbh herself looked more like Dip, and all but whispered, "I don't like to think she could have copied Claire's work," at the dog in her lap. "But you're not wrong. She was in a state all last autumn, and maybe she got desperate. I don't know."

"Did you tell the guards any of this?"

Sadhbh shook her head. "I haven't even let myself *think* any of this."

"It's hard," Megan said with genuine sympathy. "It's always hard, when we think we know someone and it turns out maybe we're wrong about some things, and it's even harder when they're not there to explain themselves anymore. I really am sorry for your loss, Sadhbh."

The barista came out with their coffees and two dark chocolate brownies, the latter of which made Sadhbh's eyes shine. "Ah, you shouldn't have."

"I totally should have." Megan lifted her cup toward Sadhbh's, offering a toast. "To Bláthnaid."

Sadhbh's eyes went wetter and she touched her cup to Megan's. "To Bláthnaid. Thanks. You should come with us tonight," she blurted. "We're doing a literary pub crawl. It was supposed to be the last thing we did with Claire before she got out of our hair—" She managed to look innocent when Megan coughed on a laugh, and corrected herself. "Before she left on tour. The extra tickets are all paid for, so you should come instead."

Megan grimaced. "My girlfriend's cooking me dinner tonight . . ."

"Invite her along, we have four extra tickets now, without Claire and her entourage." As Megan's eyebrows rose, Sadhbh added, "Her editor and publicist," in explanation.

"Oh, God, if that publicist is going to be there I absolutely can't. She'll shiv me."

"That's what I'm saying, she won't be. G'wan, ring your girlfriend and ask if she wants to come along." Sadhbh looked almost as pitiful as Dip, all sad eyes and hope.

Megan groaned and rang Jelena with the invitation, and could essentially hear the look Jelena gave her. "Are you investigating, Megan?"

"I'm not! I just ran into Sadhbh and she invited me along."

"Let me talk to her." Jelena sounded dangerous and Megan, nervously, handed the phone over.

Sadhbh's eyebrows went up and she took the phone with a cautious, "Hello? Yes. Oh. Yeah, thanks, yeah, it . . . sucks. Um. No? I don't think so? Oh, come on. Have you ever done one before like? Then it'll be fun. We've loads of extra tickets and it'll be worse if we don't have people to . . . yeh. Yeh, grand, it starts at the Duke at half seven. Brilliant, we'll see you there!" She handed the phone back to Megan with an air of triumph. "She said she was taking you to a pub this afternoon anyway, so why not."

"Yella?" Megan lifted the phone back to her ear, checking to see if Jelena was still there, although the connection said it was still open.

"I can't even claim you gave the phone to her to let her try to talk me into it," Jelena said, audibly bemused. "I asked to talk to her. But she's right that it would be very bad to have only the few of them there, when their friend is dead, so we'll go,

Megan. But dinner first, bejb. I am not going pub-crawling on an empty stomach."

"I'll come home and eat right now if you want me to."

"It's half eleven, Megan."

"I will shop for you and come home to admire you cooking."

Jelena laughed. "Better. See you in a while, skarbie."

CHAPTER 13

"There will be no investigating," Jelena whispered as they slipped through the doors at the Duke. She'd said it at least four times, but Megan laughed again anyway, whispering, "I promise!" back. The old pub, just past its second century in business, was wood panelled inside and out, and Megan liked to imagine that at least some of the old, dark floor planks had been supporting feet and absorbing spilled beer for the whole two hundred years.

The barman waved them upstairs for the pub crawl tour, where, a little to Megan's relief, Stephanie Burgis was already waiting. She looked up from her phone as they came in, smiled brightly, and gestured for them to join her at a table near a four-pane sash window. "Sadhbh said you were coming. I'm so glad you did. Hi, I'm Stephanie." She offered Jelena her hand and repeated, "I'm really glad you came," just as Jelena blurted, "I love your books!"

Stephanie's smile blossomed for real. "Oh, gosh, thank you. Thanks so much. I'm sorry the last one is so late."

"Me, too, but I bet you're even sorrier, so I won't be an arse about it," Jelena said clumsily, but Stephanie's smile went rueful and thankful all at once.

"Thanks. I appreciate it. And I appreciate you coming. This is going to be weird and hard anyway, but at least if we have more or less the right number of people it won't also feel pathetic. The crowds are mental," she added with a gesture at the street below.

Megan, despite having just come in from that street, stepped to the window and looked out at a sea of people, many of them still wearing leprechaun hats and other over-the-top St. Patrick's Day adornments. Laughter and shouting rose to sail indistinguishably through the single-pane glass, and Megan, watching the flow and ebb, thought it was astonishing more fights didn't break out with so many people trying to push through such small spaces. "This is why I usually stay out of city centre on the holiday weekend. And it's going to be much worse in a couple of hours!"

"We won't mind then, because we'll be drunk," Jelena said with a grin.

"Last time I got drunk you still made me get up at six in the morning to go to the gym, so no way."

"Which part, the getting drunk or the going to the gym?"

"I threw up on the elliptical, Jelena!"

"You were *very* drunk," Jelena conceded. "Probably we should not have gone to the gym."

"You two are cute," Stephanie announced. "I think Adrian and Jules are planning to do the self-guided literary pub crawl after the official one, if they don't think they've drunk enough. Maybe you should go with them."

"Jaysus," Megan said, not entirely meaning to go all Irish on it, but hearing herself fall into the accent anyway, "that'll be a crawl indeed."

"We'll see," Jelena said in the superior tone of a woman who knew she could hold her alcohol.

"What'll we see?" Adrian came in a few steps ahead of Juliet, who was dressed more somberly than Megan might have expected for a pub crawl. The tall young man sidled over to Megan and mumbled, "I sent that file to the detective," and she resisted the urge to give him an encouraging pat on top of the head.

"Good, I'm sure he appreciates that. Don't forget to lose it from the cloud."

Adrian said, "Shite," and took his phone out immediately. Megan nodded a greeting to Juliet, who nodded in return, glanced at Jelena, and sat without interacting more with either of them. She'd brought a half pint of Guinness up with her, and started drinking it as soon as the foam rose. "Sadhbh just texted," Adrian said without looking up from his phone. "She's running a few minutes late."

Megan felt her eyebrows rise in surprise and Stephanie smirked. "No, she's not so late as most Irish would notice or care, but I'm American and Juliet's one of the few who are a stickler for time, so Sadhbh tries to tell us if she's going to be late. She must not be more than out of the shower, though, because she doesn't usually bother if it's less than fifteen minutes or so."

"Isn't she going to miss it, then? This actually has a start time, doesn't it?"

"There's four or five pubs on the tour," Stephanie said wryly. "She can catch up."

An older man with a spring in his step and a bowler with the brim turned up came through the door, proclaiming "Welcome to Dublin's literary pub tour," in such an "Oirish" accent that Megan slapped a hand over her mouth to mute her giggle. The guy winked at her and she laughed out loud behind her hand, unable to stop herself.

"A local, then, are ye?" he asked.

"I'm *not*," she protested, hearing how very American she sounded and he laughed, himself.

"Been here a while, have ye?"

"Five years now." Megan had heard actors do that accent on American TV, and after being stunned to realize that a number of those actors were actually Irish-born, had finally come to realize that they were being asked to use it. It was what Americans thought the Irish accent sounded like, broadened to the point of caricature. She'd never heard it *in* Ireland, though, and was compelled to ask, "Do you have to practice that a lot?"

The guide grinned. "Not anymore. You wouldn't all be wise to me, would you? I could use me real accent."

Megan was halfway saying, "I think we're all local," when Claire Woodward walked in.

* * *

Megan spun away from the door like she'd been caught stealing cookies from the jar and stared wide-eyed at Jelena. "What's she doing here?"

Jelena bugged her eyes in return, then clutched Megan's hand like they were in a haunted house as everyone noticed Claire's arrival. Megan peeked back over her shoulder, almost hiding behind Jelena. Claire had her editor Derek in her wake, but not, to Megan's relief, the publicist Kiki. "I'm not late, am I?"

The guide, obviously sensing tension in the sudden complete silence, turned to the door, looked around the group, and said, "I'm happy to take your drink orders before we get started," and fled.

Adrian, clearly only half paying attention, glanced up from his phone, saying, "I'll have a—" and sagged as the guide hurried downstairs. Then he saw who'd come in, and with a spectacular lack of tact that Megan wholeheartedly appreciated, said, "What the hell are you doing here?"

Hurt surprise colored Claire's cheeks as she looked from one writer to another, then noticed Megan and reddened further. "The pub crawl is tonight?"

"Yeah, but—" Adrian shut up as abruptly as he'd spoken, as if realizing he was taking point on an argument he wasn't prepared to have.

Claire, in a small voice, said, "Should I go?"

Stephanie, hastily and in a strained tone, said, "No, don't be silly. You should stay."

A bright, relieved smile swept Claire's face as Derek, still behind her, made a semi-valiant attempt to disguise the skepticism that curdled his own expression. Megan glanced around at everybody else, watching social niceties win out over their own preferences and discomfort. It was *hard* to tell someone they weren't welcome, no matter how true that was, and so no one said anything to contradict Stephanie. Jelena breathed, "Oh dear," barely loudly enough for even Megan to hear.

"She has to know they're just being polite, right?" Megan whispered back, muffling the words in Jelena's shoulder.

Jelena shrugged and nodded, but also whispered, "Not my circus," which made Megan cough with laughter and mumble, "Nie moje malpy," in her badly-accented Polish. Jelena gave her a tiny, sparkly-eyed smile, and Megan bit her lower lip to keep from smiling back. She hadn't thought the phrase—*not my circus, not my monkeys*—was actually Polish when she'd first heard it attributed, but Jelena had assured her it really was regularly used in Poland.

Part of her almost admired Claire's audacity. There were people who genuinely didn't know how to read social cues, but Megan didn't think Claire was one of them. It seemed more like she was accustomed to bulldozing her way to what she wanted, just as had been suggested days earlier. Once she got it, *how* she got it no longer mattered, and neither—clearly—did the comfort of those around her. She trilled, "I'm so excited to be doing this! The pub, the pint, and the poet, right? Isn't that what they say about Dublin?"

Juliet turned away from her to look daggers at Stephanie, who winced apologetically and dropped her gaze. Adrian had his head bent over his phone again, texting rapidly. Megan whispered, "Wanna take a bet on whether Sadhbh shows up?" to Jelena.

"I'd take a bet on whether Sadhbh is going to stab her," Jelena said, almost evenly. "I think maybe we should go, Megan."

"And miss all the fun?"

Jelena twisted to give her a hard look over her shoulder and Megan, much like Stephanie had done, winced. "I'm sure it'll be all right, but we can go if you want to."

As she spoke, Claire bore down on them with a smile that appeared to be entirely sincere. She offered Jelena her hand, saying, "Hi, I'm Claire. You must be Jelena. Megan's told me all about you."

Megan felt her own eyebrows go up as Jelena's did, although Yella shook Claire's hand politely and said, "I've heard a lot about you, too," in neutral tones.

"Well, we hit it off, didn't we, Megan? No hard feelings about yesterday," Claire said airily. "Kiki was furious, but I talked her down. She hadn't understood the substance of our conversation."

"Really." Megan's voice cracked. "She seemed pretty confident she understood."

"Oh, no, obviously she didn't. I absolutely never said you were on board with me writing books about you."

Derek Jacobson lowered his gaze like he was keeping himself from speaking, and Claire, having had her attention drawn to him, said, "Oh, Jelena, this is my editor, Derek. I didn't know you were coming on the pub crawl with us!"

Derek said, "Jelena," in a soft voice, shaking her hand when she offered it. "A pleasure. I apologize for crashing the party."

"Oh," Jelena said in a too-sweet tone, "don't worry, we crashed it, too. We were invited because so many people were expected to not attend."

Claire, with evident sincerity, blinked around the group gathered in the small room and said, "Oh? Who's not coming?" Her face fell. "I mean, besides poor Bláthnaid, of course. I don't see Sadhbh either, though—oh, is she feeling all right?"

Megan, watching Derek's expression roll from cordial apology to barely disguised exasperation that touched on anger before he pulled it back to a stiff smile, decided she was probably right, and Claire's failure to read social cues was deliberate. Or at least, Derek thought it was, too. Megan shook her head at Claire. "Sadhbh is just running a little late, that's all. How did the book signing go?"

Claire's jaw tensed, although she put a smile on. "Oh, fantastically. Everyone's very excited for the new series. I really want to talk to you more about that."

Jelena murmured, "I imagine so," just as Sadhbh came in.

The young woman stopped dead at the door, her voice rising. "What's *she* doing here?"

Claire turned toward her with a motherly smile. "I couldn't miss the pub crawl, and everyone assured me I was welcome."

Furious color climbed Sadhbh's cheeks. "How do you know I wasn't talking about *her*?" She pointed at Megan, who felt a pang of actual guilt that subsided into amusement as pure astonishment crossed Claire's face. Apparently, it hadn't occurred to her that anyone else could be worthy of an emphasized pronoun. Sadhbh stalked into the room, clearly prepared to throw a wobbly, but the tour guide came in a step or two behind her and with a theatrical announcement, cut off all further drama except for his own. Megan nursed a single-shot whiskey while he regaled them with stories about Dublin-as-it-was in Joyce's era, and about the man himself. She hadn't known that he'd invented the word *quark*, which had eventually been applied to quantum physics, and added it mentally to her own list of tidbits to tell tourists about. Some twenty minutes into his lecture, he herded them out of the Duke and down the street toward the next pub, never really breaking from his storytelling.

Rather than listen too carefully, Megan watched the group, and when Claire's editor fell a few steps behind, slowed her own pace to walk with him for a minute. "Can I ask you something? Did Claire tell *you* I was okay with the whole murder driver mystery series, too?"

A look of pain crossed his face before he nodded. "I'm afraid Kiki is right. There's nothing you can do about it if she decides to, but Claire had been emphatic about your enthusiasm for the project."

"Does she do that a lot?"

"Create a narrative that suits her and change it without any apparent awareness or concern that she's being duplicitous? I'm afraid so."

" 'Duplicitous,' " Megan said with a thread of admiration. "I'm not sure I've ever actually heard anyone use that word out loud before."

Jacobson gave her a quick smile. "Occasionally one wishes to show off one's editorial credentials by pulling out a ten-dollar word."

"I can't blame you!" Megan hesitated, glancing toward Claire, before asking, "Does that mean I shouldn't take anything she says at face value?"

Derek inhaled and exhaled slowly through his nose, clearly giving himself time to think. "If it's self-serving, especially if it'll make her look good, she certainly means it in the moment. If it's something like you agreeing to be part of this project, something that can be empirically challenged, she'll pretend she never said that. I think she might even believe it."

"So . . . no. You sort of can't trust anything she says."

"Unfortunately, her books sell very, very well," Derek said, almost under his breath.

Megan, suddenly mindful that this could only be called investigating, said, "Thanks," and squished through the crowd to catch up with Jelena, who gave her a wry look.

"Learn anything interesting?"

"Maybe, yeah, and I'm not sure if it's something that would come up with the guards. I think Claire lies a lot, but I'm not sure it's the kind of lying you notice until it's happened to you regularly. Her editor says she does that kind of thing like yesterday all the time, where she told everybody I wanted a series written about me and then just pretended she never said anything like that when I called her on it. So now I'm wondering what else wasn't true."

"Megan." Jelena sighed. "You're hopeless, aren't you."

"I just think I should tell Paul so he can tell Detective Reese."

"And that's all? You're not going to follow up on it?"

"No?"

"Try to sound more convincing, Megan."

"It just made me wonder if she really was in her B and B room the morning of the murder. I know, I know, I know! That's something the Garda can check on! It's not a me job!" Megan smiled brightly, hoping to earn a little forgiveness, and Jelena wrinkled her nose.

"All right, fine. Text Paul. But try to leave it alone after that, Megan. I don't like all of this."

"I know." Megan's voice dropped in apology. "I'm sorry. I just hate not—"

"Solving the mystery," Jelena said. "I know. Go text Paul, and then please leave it alone, or I want to go home."

"Fair," Megan said. "Totally fair. Thank you, Jelena."

"Tomorrow you cook dinner for *me*," Jelena said firmly, and Megan, feeling like she'd been forgiven, smiled.

"Absolutely." They reached the next pub and Megan paused outside the door, saying, "I'll just text Paul and be in in a minute."

Jelena nodded and went in with the others, the guide's cheerful voice regaling them with a story about James Joyce that Megan suspected was entirely fictional. She sent Paul a text: **Reese should know Claire may be a pathological liar** and wasn't surprised when he rang her a minute later, his voice rising in incredulous challenge as he said, "And how do you know this, that Reese should know it?"

Megan glanced at the pub like she was afraid Claire would suddenly appear, and shouldered her way through the crowd to move a little farther away from the door. Even outdoors, alcohol could be smelled on the air, and even though it was early yet, there were obviously a number of thoroughly inebriated people already on the streets. She muttered, "This is why I stay out of city centre on holidays," and stepped into the alley nearby to try to get out of the throngs of people.

"Where are you?"

"Doing the literary pub crawl on Grafton Street."

"On the holiday weekend? You're mad."

"That seems extremely likely. Anyway, Reese should know that apparently Claire will do a one-eighty on any topic if the coverage or conversation isn't playing out the way she expects it to. All the time, according to her editor. So I'm not sure she's said anything trustworthy this week."

"And how am I to tell Reese I came by this information?"

"You're a detective," Megan said. "You deduced it. You knew my side of the story, you heard hers, you figured it out."

"You've a devious mind, Megan Malone."

"I really don't think I do!" Megan wailed.

"Maybe not," Bourke said, like he was relenting. "How's Jelena taking you being out with this crew tonight?"

"She's here, too. Sadhbh talked her into it, not me."

"Ah, grand so. All right, then, have fun, the two of you. Raise a glass to Brendan Behan for me."

"I'll give the quare fellow my best," Megan promised, and hung up to go into the pub before she was missed.

CHAPTER 14

Judging from the number of shot glasses and empty pints on the table where the pub crawl group was meeting, Megan hadn't been missed at all. Even Jelena had a half pint glass in one hand, although unlike most of the others, hers only had a sip or two taken from it. Claire had a whole line of overturned shots in front of her, and Derek was making a neat stack of what Megan hoped were not all his own empties. She felt ill just looking at the six glasses.

Juliet didn't seem to be partaking heavily, so Megan sidled over to her and murmured, "Was there a drinking challenge?"

"I think Sadhbh's trying to kill Claire through alcohol poisoning," Juliet murmured back, clearly only half kidding. "I don't know which of them will drop first, though, as Claire's taking shots but

Sadhbh's half her weight. We're like to have to bring them both in for stomach pumping."

"Oh look at the time," Megan muttered, and Juliet laughed.

"You should run now while you still can," she agreed. "What are you even doing here tonight? I know Sadhbh invited you, but . . ."

"Jelena and I were going out to a pub tonight anyway, and we'd never done the literary crawl before, so why not?"

"You're not investigating, then, Ms. Murder Driver?"

"I'm not." Megan waited a judicious beat. "Although if you've got any good goss to share . . ."

Juliet chuckled. "No, although I heard Adrian's been cleared of suspicion. It's mad, thinking there's guards looking into you and trying to decide you might have done it. It's easy enough for me. I don't get up until half eight if I can help it and my husband is in and out of the bedroom all morning, so he can verify I was sleeping, but for Stephanie, like, she's up to run at six every morning, and Bláthnaid dead between six and eight, they're saying."

"I'm usually at the gym then myself," Megan said, as if she had to present an alibi, too. "Does Stephanie have someone to clear her name?"

"Her neighbor's dog always barks when she leaves and comes home again, and it did that morning, so there's that, but I'm sure I wouldn't know if there's more," Juliet said with the prissiness of a woman who wanted to be pressed for details.

"Sure, are you?" Megan asked with what she hoped was the right note of interest.

Juliet immediately leaned closer. "You didn't hear it from me, but she's caught a lot of hell from her editor for introducing her to a plagiarizer, and she's in trouble already because she's so late with the last book in her series."

Megan took a heartbeat to try to fit that in with Stephanie's early-morning jogging habit, then filed it under a new tab, mentally, and said, "Oh yeah? But that couldn't have happened fast enough to be motive. The plagiarism was only discovered Sunday night, right? And Bláthnaid was dead by Monday morning." Megan hesitated. "Where was she before she died, does anybody know?"

"I imagine the guards do," Juliet said tartly. "The one detective is your friend, isn't he? Why don't you ask him?"

"Because I'm not a guard," Megan replied, trying not to sound as tart in return. She wanted to know, though. Not enough to ask Paul, but enough to glance around at the others and wonder if any of them knew where Bláthnaid had been before she died. Sadhbh was the most likely, probably, but if Megan didn't talk to her soon, she would be too obliterated to form a sentence. Jelena hadn't drunk more than another sip of her Guinness, but Claire was slamming another shot as the tour guide told them about the writers who had frequented the pub, and Stephanie clutched a glass of wine like it was a lifeline. Of all of them, Adrian looked most like he was out for a normal night at the pub, listening with half an ear while looking at something on his phone. "Does Sadhbh always drink that much?"

"I wouldn't be in the habit of going down the pub with twentysomethings, so I wouldn't know."

Megan laughed. "Yeah, no, I guess not, me either. 'Scuze me, I'm gonna go . . ." She left Jules's side, approaching Sadhbh as she finished a beer with a grimace. "You doing okay?"

"Feckin' grand." Sadhbh waved toward a barman like she wanted another drink, but Megan, watching, saw how the guy's gaze managed to skip right over her with the ease of long practice.

Sadhbh muttered a curse, but Megan said, "Wait," before the younger woman could head for the bar. "I wanted to ask you, although if you'd rather I didn't—"

"It's about Bláthnaid, then." Sadhbh made a short motion, enough of an invitation that Megan hurried on before she could change her mind.

"You're roommates, right? Did she come home Sunday night after she left the café?"

"Housemate, and you're asking where she was all night and whether I saw her before she died." Sadhbh curled her lip. "She came home, aye, and sobbed her eyes out and went to bed sick with grief. I never saw her again, and no, she wasn't one to get up early. The gardaí asked me all this. I've no idea why she was out before sunrise and no one's seen her phone since she died."

"The guards would be able to find out who called her, I think," Megan said. "If anybody did."

Sadhbh shrugged hugely. "Maybe, but I'm not a guard, so I don't know."

"Can you think of anybody who might have? Her ex, maybe?"

Sadhbh shot a look toward Juliet. "Wouldn't that be gas. Not a chance, though."

"Why's that?"

"Because if he'd killed Bláthnaid, he'd have rung his mam and Jules would have made sure they never found the body."

Megan gave a startled laugh, loud enough to draw attention from even the tour guide. "You think?"

"I'm dead certain. Dots her t's and crosses her i's, does Jules. She'd never let Aaron get away with a messy murder." Sadhbh blanched and hunched her shoulders. "Jesus, get away with you, making me talk about my friend like that. What kind of arsehole are you?"

"Apparently the kind that can't let it go no matter how many times she says she's going to," Megan said softly. "Sorry. Next round's on me, if you like."

"Fuck off with you."

Megan breathed, "Fair," and slipped past Claire to Jelena's side, to murmur, "How are we holding up?"

"*We*," Jelena said, clearly meaning herself, "are fine. How are *we* doing with not investigating?"

"Poorly."

Jelena's mouth pursed. "I can't decide if I should give you credit for admitting that or just go home now because you're not keeping out of it."

"Can I just talk to Claire a bit first?" Megan made hopeful eyes and Jelena groaned.

"You've been spending too much time with the

dogs. All right, go on, but only because I've never heard any of this part of Irish history."

"You're a star," Megan whispered, and scooted away again to interrupt Claire before her next shot. "You okay?"

"Of course! Out partying with my besties on St. Patrick's Day weekend in Dublin itself! How could I not be?" Claire slurred most of her s's in that, and gestured at one of her untouched shots. "Want one? I'm beginning to think I should shlow, *sssssl*ow, down."

"Oooh, no, I have to . . ." Megan couldn't think of an excuse, so ended up smiling lopsidedly. "Not get drunk. I have to not get drunk."

"How come?"

"Because I don't like it."

"Oh." Claire made a moue. "Okay, I guesh. I'll just have to finish 'em myshelf." She giggled. "Myshelf. I like that. Self. My *self*."

"How come you want to get drunk?"

"Ireland! Shaint Patrick's Day! Tradition, right?"

"Stereotype, anyway." Of course, given the number of people in the pub and on the streets, Megan understood where the stereotype had come from. To be fair, though, an audibly distinct number of those people were tourists, their accents or language giving them away. "The thing I like best about St. Patrick's Day is how the Irish collectively concluded that God understands about it, so they're allowed to break Lent."

Claire gasped rather dramatically and spoke with the emphasized clarity of a drunk trying not to sound drunk. "I did not know that. I never thought about Lent and St. Patrick's Day before. Oh, how terrific. An understanding with God. We should all be so lucky." She brandished her last shot. "To an understanding with God! And on to the next pub!" She slammed the drink and headed for the door, regardless, it appeared, of what anyone else was going to do.

Jelena gave Megan a look that clearly said "this one is on you," so Megan followed Claire out the door, thinking that Sadhbh had fallen behind in the run for alcohol poisoning. Claire's walk was unsteady and she kept reaching for the wall, although there were enough people on the street that she manhandled a couple of them on her quest for stability. Megan caught up, helped her get to the wall, and said, "Maybe we should wait here for a minute for the rest of the tour."

"Yeah. I don't feel so good."

"You just had at least six shots. I wouldn't have made it to the door."

Claire giggled, then wobbled. "Woo, it's really shitting me. Hitting! Me. But, you know, niters are rotworious for drinking. Ooh, no, that was wrong. Niters are wortor, no. Wri. Ters. *Writers.* Are notorious. For drinking. Do you think . . ." She leaned close to Megan, misjudged the distance, and clobbered her head against Megan's. "Ooh. That hurt. There are two of you. Are there two of you? Two drurder miders. Miders. Driders."

Megan, unable to help herself, said, "Murder drivers," through the thud of pain in her head.

"*That.*" Claire pointed dramatically at Megan's mouth. "That. Those words. That you said. Muuu-urrrrder. Driiiivers. Oh, there's only one now."

She moved her hands together like she was squishing two Megan heads into the same space, and nearly squished the one real Megan head. Megan moved back, avoiding contact as Claire visibly searched her memory for what she'd been saying.

Derek Jacobson came out, his eyebrows furled worriedly as he caught a glimpse of Megan and Claire leaning on the wall. "Everything okay?"

"Honestly, I think Claire should go home. Whatever she's been drinking hit her like a truck."

"*Nope!*" Claire shook her head vigorously, although she could clearly not focus after doing so: Megan watched her eyes swirl around so wildly they looked like they were working independently of one another. "Nah, I'm great! I wanna do the next pub! And the one affer that! Aaaaan . . . then maybe I should sleep."

Megan frowned in concern at Derek. "There's only two pubs left on the tour, I think, but they're not even going to let her in, in this condition."

"Nah! I'm a happy drunk! It'll be . . ." Claire leaned in again and Megan backed off, barely avoiding another collision of skulls. "It'll be *grand sho*," Claire pronounced happily. "That's what the Irish shay when things are . . ." She giggled again. "Grand sho. Right?"

"It is," Megan said under her breath. "It's also what they say when everything's falling apart."

Derek, a bit grimly, said, "Grand so," and Megan flashed him a rueful smile.

"Just like that, yeah."

"I'll get her home," Derek said, clearly reluctant. "Can I get a taxi here?"

"No, you'll have to walk back down to Dawson

or up to . . ." Megan waved her hand in a circle, meaning to indicate that there were a number of surrounding streets where a taxi could be picked up, but the pedestrianized Grafton itself was a lost cause. "I can walk you down to the nearest taxi rank, or call—ugh. Hang on. Let me go . . ." She left them without finishing the sentence, meeting Jelena as she came out of the pub with the others. "Claire's totally legless. I'm going to walk her and Derek down to where they can catch a cab, if that's okay?"

Jelena glanced down the street where Claire was slowly sliding down the wall and her face creased with worry. "Jesus, is she okay?"

"I don't really think she is, no. I'd feel better if she threw up."

Jelena gave Megan a canny look. "You'd feel better if you drove her home yourself."

"I would," Megan admitted, "but I don't have a car and it'd take longer to go back up to Rathmines and get one than it will to walk her to Dawson or College Green for a taxi."

"All right." Jelena kissed her, then lifted her chin as a directive. "Go get her home safe, bejb. I suppose I wouldn't love you as much if you were able to just leave desperate messes alone."

"I'll try to be back soon enough to finish the crawl," Megan promised. "Thank you, Yella."

Jelena wrinkled her nose and kissed Megan again. "You've been very good about not wrecking the weekend with your murder. I can give you this."

Megan, helplessly, said, "It's not *my* murder!" but, having been released to be of use, hurried back to Derek and Claire. The rest of the group had gathered around them, including the tour guide, who had the look of a man this had happened to many, many times before. "Go on up to next pub," Megan advised when she reached them. "Derek and I will get Claire home."

Claire, from her seat on the pavement stones, said, "Nooooo," but made no actual effort to rise. Megan had said *legless* without meaning it literally, but it appeared to be alarmingly accurate right now. Adrian stepped in to give Claire a hand up, letting Megan and Derek get under her arms for support.

"Jaysus," Adrian said quietly. "Are you sure you don't want my help? I'm bigger than the both of you put together."

Derek shot Megan an assessing glance, then grimaced in a way that suggested it was meant to be a smile. "Maybe not quite bigger than the both of us. No, we've got her now. Thanks, though."

Adrian said, "All right," dubiously, but joined the others in trailing uncertainly after the tour guide, who was chatting up his story like the world might end if he didn't sell it well enough. Jelena lifted her phone toward Megan, mouthing *text me*, and Megan gave her a thumbs-up before she and Derek maneuvered Claire toward the Dame Street taxi rank.

"But I don' *wanna* go," Claire said, pathetically enough that despite everything, Megan's heart went out to her.

"You'll want to barf all over a pub floor even less," she said, hoping that was true. "C'mon, Claire, it's just a few minutes' walk and it'll do you

good to get the air." Although even the air outdoors carried the scent of alcohol, there was that
much drinking and partying going on, and Megan
thought they could do with a little more crispness
and a little less lingering cigarette smoke. Claire
managed to get her feet going in a more or less
steady walk, and they made it to the main street
within several minutes.

"I should let you go back," Derek said with obvious reluctance. "Getting her home isn't your job."

Megan screwed up her face. He was right, but
bringing Claire home herself—or helping to, at
least—gave her an excuse to . . . not *investigate*, per
se. She could just . . . ask a little, maybe. "Tell you
what," she said, feeling guilty at taking the opportunity, "why don't you go back and finish the pub
crawl? I live in Dublin, after all. I can do it any
time."

Some of her guilt faded as Derek's face lit with
sheepish hope. "Really? She's not your respon-
sibi—"

"She's her own responsibility," Megan interrupted dryly, "and she's langered, but neither of
us are going to abandon her to sleep on the street,
so yeah, go on so. I'll get the driver or somebody at
the B and B to help me get her out of the car, if we
have to."

Derek looked so grateful it bordered on embar-
rassing. "Thanks. Man, thank you so much. I've
never been to Dublin before and this week has
been absolute shit and nothing like I hoped."

Megan felt her grin turn sympathetic. "Yeah,
no, none of this would be on my top ten highlights
to do in Dublin either. Look, yeah, go on with you,

have fun, all right? And remember I was nice to you when she comes and pitches that murder driver series again."

A laugh caught Derek off guard. "I'll do that. Thanks, Ms. Malone."

"You're welcome, Mr. Jacobson." Megan lifted her hand, hailing a taxi, and between the two of them they got Claire, mumbling in protest, into the car. Megan crawled in after her, gave the address, and waved at Derek, who turned and went back up the street as they drove off.

The driver eyed them both in the mirror. "It's a hundred fifty quid if she vomits in my car."

Megan sighed. "If she vomits I'll not only pay it, I'll clean it myself. I drive, myself, but I don't have my car tonight."

He visibly relaxed at her solidarity, then eyed Claire again. "Early for it, yeah?"

"She was really putting the time in," Megan agreed. "Busy night so far?"

"Not too bad, but it's early yet. The week's been mental, though, with all the tourists." They chatted idly about driving the whole way to Claire's B and B, and to Megan's huge relief, Claire moaned a few times, interjected herself somewhat incoherently into the conversation a couple of other times, but didn't lose her lunch. The driver voluntarily helped Megan get her out of the car, and the proprietor of the B and B helped her get Claire up the stairs into her room, although she turned to Megan worriedly when the door was closed behind her.

"Is she all right, then? I know it's been a terrible week for her." The woman's eyebrows drew down and she studied Megan with growing suspicion. "You're the one the news has been on about."

"I am," Megan said wearily. "I think she's all right. She just drank a lot really fast this evening. Probably trying to put it all out of her mind."

The proprietor sighed, heading for the stairs. "I'd like to, too. There've been calls asking about her, whether she's a model guest or a hellion. She's grand," she added preemptively, clearly expecting Megan to ask. "Polite, prepaid, doesn't need new towels or sheets every day. Nothing to complain about."

"Was she here Monday morning?" Megan knew she shouldn't ask, but the opportunity was right there. Jelena couldn't possibly expect her *not* to ask, under the circumstances.

Obviously Jelena could, and should, expect her not to. So could, and would, Paul.

Megan breathed, "Oh well," hopefully inaudibly, as the proprietor gave her a sharp look when they entered the lobby.

"You *are* the one they're talking about. The murder driver who gets all caught up in investigations. I'd assume she was here," she said with a sniff. "She's not an early riser, that one. Comes down for breakfast, but not until just before it closes."

Megan's heart clenched. "There's no security tapes to be sure she was here?"

The woman scoffed. "Tapes? No. There's cameras that we keep an eye on during the day, but we close the front desk around ten unless a new arrival is coming in late."

"So it's possible no one saw her come in Sunday night?"

"I'd say likely. The guards asked this," she added. "What are you, some kind of private investigator?"

"Pretty sure I'm just a busybody," Megan murmured. "Might anyone have seen her in the morning?"

"The girls are in the kitchen from five, though, getting breakfast ready for all those damn Americans who want to be up and out the door at the crack of dawn."

"So someone might have seen her if she left and came back between then and nine or so?"

"After half six other guests might have, and the desk is manned from seven," the proprietor said with a shrug. "Before then, I'd say the girls are too busy in the kitchen to notice or care. The guards asked all of this, too. No one saw her coming or going, and she was in her slippers when she came down for breakfast at half-nine."

"You know what time she came for breakfast?"

"It's written down on the ledger. Breakfast is from half six to ten and she's never down before half nine. I'd say she's not out of bed until five minutes before that."

Megan nodded, then screwed her face up and blurted, "I'm sorry, I have to ask to satisfy my own curiosity. Is there a back door she could slip out?"

"It's alarmed. Would you like to go try it to make sure? The guards did."

Megan ducked her head. "No, thanks. Sorry."

"Well, you wouldn't be the murder driver if you weren't like this, and now here's me getting to tell everyone I talked to a real live local celebrity."

"Just don't tell the guards or they'll have my head."

To her surprise, the proprietor's eyes sparkled. "Not popular among them, are you? Well, there, that's my bit of gossip that nobody else knows. Now, if you don't mind, I could lock up if you weren't here."

Megan laughed. "Right. Sorry. Thanks for your time, and good night." She left, texting Jelena to say she'd gotten Claire home safe, and asking if they were still at the third pub.

We're on to the fourth now and everybody's langered. Jelena said. **Might as well go home. I'll see you there**. It ended with a heart emoji. Megan sent a kiss in response and, not being in a hurry, caught a bus back to Rathmines, met Jelena at their door with another kiss, and took the dogs for a walk before the night closed in on them.

Her phone rang bafflingly early the next morning, with Paul Bourke's name coming up on the screen. Megan fumbled it to her ear, mumbling, "Yeah? Paul? Everything okay?"

"It's not. Claire Woodward is dead, and you were the last person seen with her, Megan."

CHAPTER 15

Megan's stomach dropped, a sick sensation that didn't seem like it should be entirely possible when she was lying down. She sat up, which didn't help, and croaked, "What?" as adrenaline burned through her, both waking her and making the sickness in her belly more pronounced.

"Claire's dead," Paul repeated.

"There is no way you should be telling me that," Megan said, still hoarsely. "What the—what happened?"

"Heh. You're right about that. I don't know yet. I only know because Dervla rang me to ask what my friend the murder driver had been up to last night. Why were you with Claire, Megan?" His voice cracked in frustration and Megan put a hand over her face, trying to steady herself.

"I didn't mean to be with her. Sadhbh invited Jelena and me to a pub crawl that nobody expected

Claire to show up to, but she did, and she got utterly legless and I brought her home so her editor could have one not-lousy night in Dublin."

"Megan?" Jelena curled around her hips sleepily, her voice rough with concern. "What's wrong, bejb?"

"Claire's dead."

Jelena went white and jolted out of bed, staring down at Megan. "*What?*"

"I don't know. Paul's on the phone, he's telling me . . . it's barely seven." Megan's heart thudded around her chest, swimming in sickness as she tried to think. "Why does anybody even know this yet?"

"Because Claire was supposed to be on a six AM radio interview," Paul said grimly. "When she didn't answer, her editor went to check on her, and she was dead."

"Oh my God." Megan sank off the side of the bed, pulling her knees up as she sat on the floor. Jelena stayed on her feet, still pale as she wrapped her arms around herself tightly. "I, uh. I talked to the B and B proprietor for a couple minutes, then got on a bus and came home. Jelena was here, and . . . I guess the bus security cameras can be checked? I didn't kill her, Paul."

He snapped, "Well, obviously not," which twisted Megan's heart a little more, wringing a small, shaky laugh out of her.

"Thanks."

"It looks terrible, though, Megan. Jesus, I never thought I'd be glad to be off a case, but—"

"Oh God no." Megan's heart twisted again,

sending cold through her hands. "You'd lose your career if you were still on the case. Oh my God." Somehow the idea of a thing that hadn't happened cut deeper than the reality of Claire's death. She took a deep breath, trying to shake shock off, then took another one as the dogs ran into the bedroom, clearly worried about their humans. "I—do I need to come down to the station? Oh, no, I can't, you'll get in trouble for telling me." Dip climbed into her lap, licking her face, and she smiled weakly at the little animal, but put her hand up toward Jelena, searching for support.

It was a long moment or two before Jelena's hand found hers, long enough that Megan looked up to find deep lines of distress drawn in Jelena's face. After a few seconds, Jelena released her hand and left the room. Dip, obviously expecting breakfast, abandoned Megan without a second thought and trotted after Yella, leaving Thong to sit uncertainly beside the door, looking between Megan and potential breakfast. Then food rattled in the bowl and she looked apologetic, but darted toward the kitchen. Megan laughed, although it sounded more like a cough, and Paul said, "Are you okay?"

"Jelena's mad."

"This isn't your fault, Megan."

"No, but if I hadn't taken the job . . ."

"You didn't know Claire Woodward was involved with Bláthnaid O'Leary when you took the job. And even Jelena said you could, should, keep on driving her."

"Is this the argument you're going to make to your boss?"

Bourke chuckled, a short, rough sound a lot like Megan's own laugh a moment earlier. "Something like it, yeah. She took me off this case. I don't see how she can be mad at me for the situation. I know," he added before Megan could say anything, "that won't stop her being livid."

"Should I expect Detective Reese to show up here?"

"I'd say so."

"I'll try to act surprised."

She could almost hear Paul's wince. "Don't. People aren't as good at acting surprised as they think they are, and it'll make you look bad."

"Telling her you told me is going to make *you* look bad!"

"I'm an adult, Megan. I'll take my lumps."

Megan sighed. "All right. I'm sorry to get you into this. Again. Deeper. More. Whatever."

"You do keep life interesting, Megan Malone. Go on and talk to Yella. Good luck." Paul hung up and Megan dropped her forehead against her knees, trying to take stock. Her thoughts skittered and slid around instead, coming up against the idea that Claire Woodward was dead and bouncing off it, as if it was too improbable to really consider. She couldn't do anything about it. She might be able to reassure Jelena, somehow. Megan got up, feeling much stiffer and older than she had when she'd gone to bed, and went out to the kitchen.

Jelena sat at the table, one of yesterday's scones open and melting with butter on a plate in front of her. Her fingertips were on the edge of the table, and her gaze was low, fixed on the scone. Megan gingerly sat down across from her, like if she moved carefully enough, she wouldn't draw Jelena's attention, or at least, her ire. When Jelena didn't say anything, Megan pulled in a breath to speak.

Jelena shook her head once, sharply. Megan exhaled again and knotted her fingers in her lap, watching Jelena through her eyelashes, so she could see if she looked up without seeming like she was staring. Jelena did, eventually, look up, once all the butter was soaked so far into the scone it no longer appeared to have been buttered. "What happened?"

"I don't know yet."

"You don't *know*," Jelena snapped. "You don't *know*, Megan. There is no *yet*. You aren't *supposed* to know."

"Right. Yeah. No. I don't know. Sorry." Megan cast her gaze further down, staring at the table instead of Jelena's anger. "I'm sorry, Yella."

"For what?"

Megan lifted her eyes, surprised. "For getting involved in all of this when I promised I wouldn't."

"*Are* you?"

"I—" Megan frowned, trying to find the right answer. "Yeah. I am. I'm sorry any of this happened at all and I'm sorry I took a job driving somebody who knew enough to ask for the murder driver. I'm sorry I've screwed up our holiday weekend. I—" She broke off with a helpless shrug. "I'm trying not to be involved, but things keep falling in my lap and I don't know how to stop them."

As soon as she said that, it occurred to her that

Bláthnaid had literally fallen in their laps, and she winced all over, trying not to find any bleak humor in it.

Clearly, Jelena didn't see any humor in it at all. "I don't know how you stop them either, and that's what upsets me. I know I agreed to go out last night, but, *Megan* . . ."

"I know," Megan said helplessly. "I know, Yella. Would it be better if Derek had brought her home and I hadn't been the last one to see her before she died?"

"Yes! No! I don't know! She'd still be dead and you would still be—*involved*!"

"Do you want me to quit driving?"

Jelena stared at her, clearly taken aback. "You need a job, Megan."

"I know, but this one seems to keep getting me in trouble and I've got my military retirement. It'd see me through for a little while, while I found something else, maybe."

"You like your job."

"I like you more!"

Jelena at least smiled at that, ducking her head and breaking eye contact a moment before looking back up. "That's good, at least. Megan, I—I don't know. I wouldn't have thought to ask that."

"You didn't ask. I did. I don't know, Yella. Maybe I could get a taxi."

Jelena's lip curled a little. "You would already drive a taxi if that's what you wanted to do. You like the big, fancy cars and the rich tourists."

"I'm less keen on the dead people."

"Are you, though?"

Guilt surged through Megan and she looked

away, trying to find an answer to that. Jelena, less angrily now, said, "I'm sure you'd prefer it if there weren't any, but you love getting involved once it happens, Megan. And Paul gets a kick out of it, too."

Megan's eyebrows crinkled dubiously. "I'm a pain in his arse."

"Professionally, yes, but you're interesting, and you keep being helpful." Jelena sighed and put her face in her hands. "But this can't keep happening, Megan."

"I *genuinely* don't see how it can," Megan said helplessly. "It'd been ages since the last one. It *can't* keep happening, it's insane. I'm sorry, Yella."

"I know. But sorry doesn't change it. If it happens again, Megan . . ." Jelena looked up, her eyes unhappy. "Murders and—and *infamy*, is that the word? Is not what I want to live with."

"I know. I know, Jelena." Megan reached across the table, hoping Jelena would take her hand. "I don't see how it can keep happening. It'll be okay." The doorbell rang, startling them both and sending the dogs into a frenzy of excited barks. Megan said their names sharply and they backed off from the door to sit and watch hopefully while Megan went to open it.

A woman who looked like she hadn't had enough sleep recently stood outside the door, her expression focused and intent. "Megan Malone? I'm Detective Garda Dervla Reese. I have some questions for you."

Megan felt herself go through a series of complex expressions, a moment's honest surprise drowned under the panic of remembering to try

not to *act* surprised, then a sweep of tiredness and
guilt rolling over her before she gave up. The detective was younger than Megan expected, in her
late twenties or very early thirties at most, with
pale freckled skin and thick, curling red hair wres-
tled into a tight, smooth bun. Megan, impulsively,
said, "Do all detective gardaí have to have red
hair?" and regretted it immediately as Reese's face
stiffened. "Sorry," Megan mumbled. "That was stupid. Come on in."

"Thanks." Reese stepped in, eyed the dogs and
the entire apartment with equal suspicion, then
turned to Megan. "Do you know why I'm here?"

"I assume it has something to do with Bláthnaid
O'Leary's case. I know you're the detective who
took over." Megan sat down on the couch, rubbing
her face, then gestured for Reese to sit, if she
wanted. "Can I get you tea or coffee?"

A hint of desperation crossed Reese's freckled
face, but she shook her head. Behind her, in the
kitchen, Jelena got up to make tea, and Megan
shot her a grateful smile past the detective, then
focused on Reese again. "What can I do for you,
Detective?"

"Claire Woodward was found dead this morning."

Even hearing them for the second time didn't
prepare Megan for the blunt words. Sickness rose
in her belly again and her hands went cold before
a shudder rolled over her whole body. "What—
happened?"

"I was hoping you could tell me. I understand
you were the last person to see her alive."

Megan shook her head, genuinely afraid she

would be sick. "The B and B proprietor and I helped her into her room last night at about . . . nine? She was drunk as a skunk. I came home after that. On the bus. Jelena was here when I got home, and . . . I went for a walk with the dogs," she said, remembering. "And came home again."

Jelena, bringing the detective a mug of tea, nodded, then sat down beside Megan, sliding her hand into hers. "What happened, Detective?"

"How drunk is 'drunk as a skunk'?" Reese took an obviously grateful sip of the tea, but put the mug down again to take notes.

"Totally legless," Megan said. "Literally. She could barely walk. She was slamming shots at the pub last night. We were on a pub crawl, the literary one, and she said she was celebrating the holiday like the locals do."

Reese's expression soured and Megan sighed. "Her words, more or less. Not mine. But I don't think she was drunk enough for it to kill her. She would have had to keep drinking at the B and B. Were there any bottles in her room?"

"I'll be asking the questions, Ms. Malone."

"Right." Megan closed her eyes. "Sorry. Is— Jesus."

Reese, almost beneath her breath, said, "Jesus is almost certainly not," which warmed Megan to her unreasonably. "You've quite a reputation amongst the guards, Ms. Malone."

Megan's eyebrows lifted. "Oh, I bet I do. Are the odds for or against me?"

"Depends on the betting pool. There's one that's got money on you being a very clever serial killer, but nobody's put much into it. You might take yourself down to Ladbrokes and put some money on yourself, though. I hear they're paying out on you. What was your relationship with the deceased, Ms. Malone?"

"Uh." Megan knew the chat was to soften her up so a question like that would take her off guard, and to her mild irritation, it worked. "She was a client of my employer's car company. I drove her a couple of times after she asked for me specifically."

"And she did that because . . . ?"

Megan sighed. "Because I'm the murder driver, and she wanted to base a book series on me."

"Which you . . . ?"

"Didn't want."

"So would you characterize your relationship as contentious?"

"I would barely categorize it as a relationship at all, Detective. I embarrassed her in public when she said I was on board with the idea of being the inspiration for her new series, but otherwise we got along all right, I'd say."

"So why did you kill her?"

Megan blinked, then blinked again. "I didn't. Does that—uh, does that work?"

The detective shrugged. "Sometimes. Not usually with the smart ones."

"I . . . thanks. I think."

"Would you have done?"

Megan's eyebrows were going to take up permanent lodgment in her hairline. "No."

"Even though she banjaxed your friend's career?"

Megan stared at Reese blankly a moment, then shook herself. "You mean Niamh? No, I . . ." The absurdity of the question caught up to her and a question pinched her eyebrows. "What good would that even do? No, that would be stupid. Are you going to ask Detective Bourke if *he* killed Claire, too, beca—oh my god," she said faintly, as Reese's eyebrows lifted fractionally. "Oh my God, you are."

"It's motivation," Reese replied. "That's my job, Ms. Malone."

"Yeah, but he's a guard!"

"I'm sure I don't have to tell you how many murders are committed by police officers, Ms. Malone."

"No." Megan sat back, rubbing her face. "No, I guess not."

"And yourself, Ms. Nowak?" Reese turned her attention to Jelena, who straightened in uncomfortable surprise. "What was your relationship to the deceased?"

"I only met her for the first time last night." Jelena sounded defensive and angry. Reese's eyebrows rose farther and she took a note. Jelena's shoulders hunched and her hand tightened on Megan's.

"And how did you feel about her?"

"I didn't like the idea of her," Jelena said sharply. "Partly because of Niamh, but more because she asked for Megan as a driver and I hate all of this."

Guilt sluiced through Megan as she dropped her gaze, wishing there was more she could do to reassure Jelena. The detective took more notes, mostly without taking her attention from Jelena. "So you wouldn't be sorry that she's dead."

"Oh, yes, I am. I'm sorry for her friends, her

family, and her fans, but right now I'm especially sorry for us, for me, because her death means Megan's in this even deeper than before and that's the *last* thing I want." Jelena's pretty face contorted with frustrated anger. "I do not want a life of murders and investigations, Detective. Even if I despised Claire Woodward, I wouldn't make my own life worse by killing her." Her hand trembled in Megan's, unhappiness in every line of her body.

A faint smile twitched at Reese's mouth. "Killing people usually makes the killer's life worse."

Jelena curled a scathing lip. "You know what I mean."

"I do. All right." Reese stood with a sigh. "The truth is, neither of you are much under suspicion, although it doesn't look good that you were the last one to see her, Ms. Malone. That said, stay in the country, answer your phones, and generally," she said, fixing Megan with a glare, "stay out of it."

"No one believes me when I say I'm trying to," Megan all but wailed. The dogs, worried, came over to lean against her leg and eye Reese warily.

"That'd be because you've been neck-deep in half-a-dozen deaths in three years and legitimately solved a few cases," Reese said dryly. "The supe can't decide whether to hire you or run you out of the country."

Jelena said, "*Neither*," with such emphasis that even Reese chuckled as she departed, her almost-untouched mug of tea left behind on the coffee table.

In the silence the detective's absence caused, Megan said, "At least I kept Paul's name out of it? I mean, that he told me before she showed up?" as if someone—probably not Jelena—would give her absolution for that.

"I don't *care* if you keep Paul out of it! I want you to keep yourself out of it, and—" Jelena rose, got Reese's tea mug, and stomped into the kitchen with it, half yelling, "*that's* clearly not going to happen!" as she went.

"What? No, I'm not going to investigate," Megan protested, following her. "Jelena, I—"

"Of *course* you are!" Jelena spun toward her, splashing tea, and swore as it hit her pajamas and the floor. The dogs rushed to lick it up, and Jelena let them, her hands clenched in fists of frustration. "Of course you are, Megan. Because you can't stand not knowing what happened to her, because the guards will probably figure it out, but they might not give you all the details, even if Paul's inclined to tell you too much. Because people like to talk to you and they're not afraid to the way they are with the guards, because you can't help asking questions, because you want to help people, because what kind of terrible person would *I* be if I said no, don't try to help these people who lost their friend and who decided to trust you and your big, open American smile and heart? Because this is going to be on the news, that the woman who was going to write the murder driver stories is dead now and the murder driver herself is the last one to have seen her alive! Of course you're going to investigate, Megan!"

"I . . ." The apologetic little sound was all Megan could manage. She came forward, walking in the cold tea and feeling warm dog tongues trying to clean it off her feet as she opened her arms, hoping Jelena would accept the offering of an embrace. After a heartbeat or two, Jelena sighed and stepped into the hug, knotting her arms around Megan, who mumbled, "I'm sorry, Yella."

"So am I, but I'm not going to change who you are, so you should go wash your feet and go figure this out so it can be behind us, Megan. I want this to be behind us."

Megan whispered, "Okay," into Jelena's hair, and went to do as she was told.

CHAPTER 16

She was at Accents Café a few minutes before it opened, pacing the covered alley beside it and wishing she'd eaten before leaving the house, although she fully intended to eat at the café. She looked around the corner just before nine and Liam, the short-haired, sandy-blond barista, slid her a grin as he let her in early. "Shh, don't tell."

"I won't. Thanks very much. What time do you get in to work, if you're opening?"

"Half eight, usually." Liam made her a mocha without her asking, putting a dish of chocolate chips on the coffee tray, so she could make it as chocolatey as she wanted, and heated up the scone she usually ordered.

Megan tapped her debit card to pay for it with a smile of thanks. "I love being a regular. Is that when the first person is always in?"

"Unless the owners come in earlier, but usually.

There are security cameras," he said, nodding to one in the corner. "But they were off Sunday night."

"Is that normal?"

"It's not." Liam sighed as he put her mocha on the tray and went to get the scone out of the oven. "Know where the switches for it are?"

Cold certainty gripped Megan's guts. "In the make-out corner?"

To her surprise, Liam laughed out loud. "Is that what you call it? Yeah, though. Where they write. Their 'office.' "

Megan smiled sheepishly as she stirred chips into her mocha. "It's a stupid name for it. It's the best-lit corner of the whole downstairs. But yeah, that's what Jelena and I call it."

"I knew exactly what you meant, though, didn't I? The one couch is set into that nook, so yeah, I get it, it's as private as anything down there is. But yeah," he said more seriously. "The cameras and the café music controls are down there."

"So it'd be really easy for anybody who knew that to turn them off." Megan sat on the arm of one of the couches, sipping her mocha and groaning appreciatively before looking toward the downstairs. "But wouldn't you have noticed if they were turned off before you closed up for the night?"

Liam shook his head. "I'd say no? Not if we were busy closing up. We don't usually check them to make sure the café is empty, we just walk the place."

"You told the guards all this, right?"

"I'd say all three of us did and the owner, too.

We were a wreck on Monday. I'm still not great."
The fact that he said *great* instead of *grand* told
Megan how rattled he still was. "Is that tall guard
of yours not doing his job, then? He was thorough
enough on the Monday."

"No, it's nothing to do with him," Megan admitted, then hesitated, unsure of how much she
should say. Then with a shrug, she said, "It'll be on
the news anyway, I guess. Claire Woodward was
found dead this morning."

"Janey Mac!" Liam took an actual step backward, a hand clutched over his heart. "She never
was!"

"She was. And I was the last one to see her, so
now I feel sort of invested in figuring out what's
going on."

"Jaysus! Give me your card like. Your debit card."
He took the sale of Megan's coffee and scone off
the register, saying, "You need a treat after that
shock. Are you all right?"

"Aw, no, you don't have to . . ." Megan got cash
from her wallet and put the whole cost of both
scone and coffee into the tip jar over the sounds of
Liam's protest, then sat down to eat. "Thanks very
much. Do you get into the closet when you're closing up?"

"We're always after getting into it in the middle
of the day," Liam admitted. "There's not enough
room to get it all out at night and have it ready for
morning, so we use up what's left from the night
before and then go into the closet around ten and
six, usually."

"So somebody could in theory hide in the

closet, if they knew it was there, and they might not get caught."

Liam's eyebrows rose. "Could, but then what? Why was herself here hours before opening anyway? Lured here, was she?"

"Is the door alarmed? Like, could it be opened from the inside during off hours to let somebody in?"

"Could, but it was locked when I got here Monday morning."

"Any keys missing?"

Liam examined her briefly. "You've a killer's mind, haven't you?"

"You're the one proposing Bláthnaid was lured here," Megan pointed out, then fell silent a few minutes while he made drinks for incoming customers and she ate her scone. In a quiet moment, she abandoned the scone and her drink to examine the door lock, which looked entirely standard. The glass-fronted café never had metal sheeting pulled down in front of it, so that wouldn't be a barrier to illegal entry, and she'd never noticed an extra chain or other additional security on the door. "Do you have to actually lock it up behind you or does it lock when it closes?"

"We'd lock it up, but . . ." Liam frowned at the door a moment. "It would lock itself, but not with the dead bolt, if it was just left to its own devices. Sometimes we forget the dead bolt and have a bad moment in the morning, but I didn't open Monday, so I wouldn't know if that happened. I wouldn't know that anyone would remember, anyway, given . . ."

"Given what happened next," Megan agreed grimly. "Still, who opened? I can at least ask."

"Anie. I was in at ten 'cause I've a morning class on Mondays."

"I'll ask her. Thanks." Megan went downstairs with her coffee and scone, her thoughts bouncing from one place to another. She felt as if she'd been keeping all her ideas about the investigation stuffed down deep, and now that she was allowed, for lack of a better word, to focus on them, they were all boiling to the surface, jumbling up with one another.

No one was in the make-out/office corner yet, so she knelt on the couch's wide arm and studied the switches and buttons hidden behind a stereo on a shelf in the wall. They were—a little unfortunately, maybe—clearly labeled: cameras, music, building alarm. The cameras and alarm required keys, but the silver slots looked sort of generic, as if something like a standard luggage key would turn them. Megan expected the keys probably weren't *that* generic, but also felt like she could maybe go buy some kind of low-grade security system and get a key that would fit.

Which was not, she thought, a normal kind of thing to carry around. You had to plan in advance to need that, unless you were just generally the sort of person who went around looking for opportunities to break into places or kill people.

Claire Woodward really hadn't struck Megan as that kind of person, but she'd also freely confessed that writers did all sorts of things most people would consider unusual, at best. She took out her

phone, texted Paul with **Did Claire have any security keys in her belongings?** and wondered which of
them would be in more trouble if he answered.

Of course, if *she* had gone to the trouble of securing a key to turn off cameras, lure somebody to
their death, and lock up behind her, Megan herself would have dropped the key in the rubbish
bin just outside the café with the confidence that
by the time anybody thought of looking for such a
thing, it would be buried in the tons of trash collected daily by the city.

Possibly, Megan thought, possibly Paul was right.
Maybe she did have a devious mind. She'd have
done the same with a stolen door key, although
she assumed that would have been noticed as missing sooner. The guards would have followed up on
that, probably. Megan resisted the temptation to
text Paul and ask about that, too. She sat down on
the couch, scowling blankly across the lower floor
of the café and letting her thoughts skitter where
they wanted to.

No one had *seen* Claire at the bed-and-breakfast
on Sunday night or Monday morning, not until
breakfast time. It was possible she'd never come
back. She could have hidden in the café, called
Bláthnaid in the morning, killed her on the
premises, and stuffed her in the closet, although
Megan could hardly imagine the effort necessary
to get a literal deadweight adult into a closet several feet off the ground. She wouldn't want to do
it, not without help, whether that help was a ramp
or another person.

She finished her coffee, went back upstairs, and
asked if she could look in the storage rooms. Liam

gave her an amused glance—he looked like an adult kid humoring their weird parent—and lent her the key. Megan went and poked around in both the upstairs and downstairs rooms, but while she found brooms and cleaning equipment, not even her most creative ideas could turn those things into an easy way to get a dead body into a closet.

Anie, the barista who had actually found Bláthnaid's body, had come in by the time Megan was done with the storage rooms. Liam had clearly caught her up on what Megan was doing, and she came over with her hands knotted in front of her stomach. "Can I help?"

Megan took a breath to say no, then had a terrible idea. "You're about Blathnaid's size. Want to pretend to be dead and see if I can shove you in that closet?"

Anie's eyes widened. "Em. Really?"

"I was just wondering if I could do it alone," Megan explained. "I'm fitter than Claire, but it's more a question of if anybody could than me, specifically."

"Em. All right." Anie grimaced uncertainly, then nodded with greater confidence. "Yeah, all right. Try not to knock me silly."

"You're already silly," Liam said on his way by. Anie made a face at him and Megan grinned at them both, then went to open and examine the cupboard.

It was certainly deep enough to fit someone in, although the supplies piled up made finding a place to tuck a body awkward. Megan stood on the couch, rearranging the closet's interior until she thought she could fold Anie up into it, then gestured to the girl. "Let's see, you wouldn't be on this couch, because she was strangled from behind. It'd probably be easiest to kill you at the door, so let's do that. Maybe I'd put something around your neck when you came in and then drag you across the floor with that, getting you closer to where I wanted to hide the body. Are there any scuff marks?"

"Millions," Anie said drolly. "Are you going to drag me, then?"

"No, we'll just assume you're dead at the step here." The area the closet was above was a single step up from the rest of the ground floor, so Megan stood on that and gestured for Anie to turn around. By then, several customers were watching, but without banishing them from the café entirely, or at least downstairs, Megan didn't know what to do about that.

Liam, obviously recognizing the problem, said, "Free drinks for everybody who goes downstairs right now," and exactly nobody left.

Megan, despite herself, chuckled. "Look, at least don't film this, okay? I'm already in enough trouble."

At least one person put their phone away, and Anie turned her back to Megan, who said, "Okay, you're dead now and probably you weigh more than I expected, so you'll probably fall down," and Anie, obligingly, did. Or lay down, at least, which was close enough. "All right, go as limp as you can. You don't want to be helping me at all."

Anie, from the floor, said, "I'm not sure I want to be doing this at all!" but waited patiently for

Megan to roll her into a fireman's carry. "Really?" Anie said, her head dangling around Megan's ribs. "Is this what you think she did?"

"Not really," Megan admitted. "I know how to get somebody off the floor with a fireman's carry. I bet our perpetrator actually grabbed Bláthnaid under the arms and dragged her. You think I should do that?"

Anie sighed. "See if you can get me in there like this, first, and then we'll see."

An inappropriate cheer went up in the café when Megan stuffed Anie into the closet. Anie lifted her head, eyeing the people watching. "Really? I'm dead and you're cheering me getting stuck in the cupboard? That wasn't too bad," she added to Megan, who nodded.

"Easier than I expected." She got down from the couch she'd stepped up onto, giving Anie room to escape the closet. "I think it'd be a lot harder if I had you under the armpits."

"Well, I'm invested now, aren't I." Anie went back and dropped onto the step so Megan could try picking her up again.

It went much worse the second time, Anie's arms flopping upward and allowing her to slither loose as Megan tried to get her under the armpits, then around the chest. On the third try, Megan managed to squish her sufficiently hard against her own chest to haul her a few steps backward, but Anie's heels caught on the edge of the step. Megan lost her grip and went over backward, scraping her hip and back on the wooden coffee table between the couches. The audience hissed in sympathy as Megan screwed her face up against

the deep, dull pain and tried to breathe deeply
enough to not snarl at the people who worriedly
asked if she was okay. After a few minutes, the ache
faded enough for her to get up muttering, "Right.
Let's try that again," and Anie went limp again.

It took a good twenty minutes of wrangling to
decide it wasn't *impossible*, but that it was incredibly
difficult to get somebody into the closet that way.
Anie, who had been knocked around quite a lot by
then, said, "It'd be easier with a dead person who
didn't care you were bruising the shite out of her,
but *ow*."

Megan, mortified, said, "I'm sorry, we'll stop,"
just as Liam came over.

"Let me get her legs and see if that works."

A minute later they had Anie tucked neatly in
the closet, and Megan collapsed into the couch to
another round of ill-considered applause. "And
I'm fit," she said, breathing heavily. "I'd hate to try
that if I wasn't."

"Do you think it took two people?" Anie climbed
out of the cupboard again and straightened her
clothes while the café patrons reluctantly went back
to their own business.

Megan spread her hands. "I think if it did,
maybe the second person is the one who killed
Claire. But I don't know how to figure out who
that person is, and I doubt the guards would take
it well if I rang and asked if they'd considered that
an accomplice to Bláthnaid's murder is the primary killer in Claire's death. For one thing, I'd
hope they've already thought of that. Oh. Was the
door dead-bolted Monday morning?"

Anie, who'd sat on the opposite couch, straightened as if she'd been given a shock. "It wasn't! I forgot about it in the madness, but it gave me a bad moment, thinking we hadn't locked up properly the night before." Her eyes widened. "Do you think the killer hid in here all night?"

"They might have done. I still don't know why Bláthnaid would be here at six or seven in the morning, though. The café doesn't open until nine. If *you* were trying to lure somebody to a secluded location to kill them, you wouldn't choose a city centre street and a closed building, would you?"

"I'd lure them somewhere they thought was safe," Anie said thoughtfully. "Like, I wouldn't say, 'Hey, meet me at O'Connell Bridge so I can push you over the railing,' would I? I'd suggest somewhere safe. The café is safe enough, even if it wasn't open."

"Is anything else along here open that early?" Megan shook her head before she was finished asking. There were a couple of nearby hotels, but six AM breakfasts were unlikely anywhere in Dublin. "Maybe she thought the café would be open early for some reason?"

"Ms. Woodward did keep getting after us about opening early," Anie said dubiously as she got up to go back to work. "She liked to write early, she said, and wanted to soak up the ambiance like."

"Huh. The landlord at her B and B said she never showed up for breakfast before half nine." Megan had assumed Claire was sleeping in, but maybe she got up early to write and didn't make it down to breakfast until it was almost over because of that.

Or maybe Claire said whatever came to her mind

at the time, and didn't worry about whether it was at all consistent. Her editor certainly felt she did. Megan checked her wallet and found Derek Jacobson's card. Maybe he knew something about her writing schedule. Pinning anything down would help. She rang, not entirely expecting him to pick up on an unfamiliar number when his client had just died, but to her surprise, he did, saying, "Derek Jacobson," in a low unhappy voice.

"Mr. Jacobson, hi, this is Megan Malone, f—"

"The murder driver," he agreed, although Megan had been going to say "from Leprechaun Limos." "I take it you've heard the news."

"The guards talked to me this morning," Megan said. "I'm sorry for your loss, Derek."

"Kiki's over the moon," he said grimly. "All the publicity without having to deal with Claire being a diva."

"Oh, wow, that's awful."

"Kiki's a real piece of work. What can I do for you, Megan?"

"I know this is a stupid question under the circumstances, but do you know if Claire was in the habit of writing early in the day?"

"Yeah." She could hear him shift, like he took a seat. "She said she felt better about herself if she got some words early on in the day. She would stay in bed and write on her laptop until she got hungry, or get up and go to a café if she was afraid she'd fall back asleep."

"Do you think . . ." Megan sighed, hearing her own question, and found herself reluctant to ask it.

"Probably," Derek said. "Go ahead, ask."

"Do you think she might have convinced Bláth-

naid that Accents was opening early, and gotten
her to come there?"

"So you think she did it." Derek sounded tired.

"I don't know anymore. I'm just trying to figure
out why Bláthnaid would be at Accents that early.
Irish people wouldn't assume it was open yet. Like,
ever." Megan finally finished the last of her mocha,
which had just enough warmth left to justify drinking it.

"Is there anywhere to sit around there? Maybe . . .
maybe Claire wanted to talk and it was somewhere
she knew they both knew?"

Megan made a skeptical face. "There's the sidewalk. Dublin's not great for public seating, and by
'not great' I mean 'terrible,' but that's a good
thought." She stood and went to the door, looking
up the street. "There might be a couple of benches
on the other side of the Grafton Hotel. There used
to be. Let me go look. Yeah," she said, less than a
minute's walk later. "There are still benches. That
would be something, at least. It may not be *the* answer, but at least it's *a* possible answer. Thanks.
Look, how are you doing? This has been an awful
week for you."

"Well, I'm wishing I hadn't stayed out at the
pubs last night, as if I could have changed anything by being the one who brought her home."

"Yeah," Megan said sympathetically. "Do they
know what happened yet?"

"Nothing official," Derek said. "From the way
she was drinking last night, they'd have said alcohol poisoning, but I didn't think that could just
kill somebody like that."

"It's like any other one-off bad reaction to a

drug." Megan pulled her hand over her face. "Jesus. God, I shouldn't have left her alone last night. I knew she was langered."

"How many drunk friends have we all tucked into bed and left alone?" Derek said. "It's not your fault, Ms. Malone. You didn't make her do a dozen shots in forty minutes."

"A dozen?" Megan asked, horrified. "I only saw about six shot glasses."

"She was drinking doubles."

"Oh. Oh no. My God. Are they doing an autopsy?"

"They are. This afternoon. I'm told that's fast, but she was already in the news and they want to stay ahead of . . . whatever happens."

Megan nodded, forgetting he couldn't see her. "If there's anything I can do . . ."

"I'll call," Derek said. "If there's nothing else, I have a lot of things to attend to right now."

"No, that's ever—oh, wait! This is a weird question, but do you know if she had any security keys, for accessing, like, electric boxes or anything?"

Derek sighed heavily. "Not that I know about. Why?"

"Just trying to put some pieces together. Thanks for your time, Mr. Jacobson. I'll talk to you later." Megan hung up and went back up the street toward Accents. An American woman called her name as she reached the door, and Stephanie Burgis waved from the corner. Megan held the door, waiting for her, and they went in together, Stephanie smiling ruefully as they went to the counter.

"Morning. I can't believe I'm up, after all that drinking last night, but it was fun. I'm sorry you missed the end. Did you pour Claire into bed?"

"I did," Megan said slowly, watching the other American carefully. "And this morning the coroner's office poured her into a body bag."

CHAPTER 17

Color flushed Stephanie's face, burning her ears red and then draining so fast she was left mottled with white and pink. She reached for the counter, her hands visibly trembling as she stared at Megan. "What?"

"Claire Woodward is dead," Megan said. "She died sometime last night after I left her at the B and B."

Stephanie staggered away from the counter, backing up until she ran into the arm of a couch, where she sat, despite the fact that somebody was already in the seat. The kid said, "Hey!" and she whispered, "Sorry," without moving, and after a baffled, angry look at Megan, the kid scooted to the other half of the couch. Stephanie slid into the now empty seat, her gaze still huge and shocked on Megan. "What happened?"

"Nobody knows yet, but maybe alcohol poisoning. She drank a lot last night."

"Oh my God." Stephanie put her face in her hands, shaking, then took her phone out and sent a message before dropping the phone into the couch beside her. "How horrible. What an awful coincidence. Jesus. How could this happen twice in a week?" She looked up sharply. "How do you deal with this?"

Megan sat across from her, avoiding another dirty look from the kid they'd displaced. "Do you really think it's a coincidence?"

Stephanie's color fluctuated even more, running hot and cold. "Isn't it? It has to be. It can't be—I mean, who would kill her? How would they kill her? Why? Poor Bláthnaid's already dead. Whichever of them copied the other, it hardly matters anymore, does it?"

"Does it have to be related?" Megan asked beneath the sound of the coffee foamer-thing. The café was full of such ordinary noises—people chatting, the drinks being made, laughter, a playlist of decades-old music, and occasionally, when it fell quiet enough, even the sound of somebody typing on their computer nearby. It seemed so normal, as if lives weren't ending and being turned upside down all around it.

Stephanie gave Megan a bleak look. "I guess it doesn't *have* to be related, but it seems like it probably is, doesn't it? Maybe it was her editor." She sagged into the couch. "He's been in Ireland all week, right? Maybe he killed Bláthnaid when he found out she'd plagiarized Claire, or worse, when he found out Claire had plagiarized *her*, and then killed Claire because she found out or something."

"I think he was in Cork, yeah. I hadn't considered him as a possibility," Megan admitted. "He wasn't here Sunday night. But Claire was a cash cow, wasn't she? You wouldn't kill your moneymaker. You'd just ride it out and hope it all got forgotten, wouldn't you?"

"I wouldn't know," Stephanie said bitterly. "My editor's furious I introduced her to a plagiarizer, and I've got until Friday to turn my draft in or they're canceling my contract and I'll have to pay back the advance. That's the opposite of being the moneymaker."

"Oh, no," Megan said in real dismay. "I'm sorry. Is there any chance you'll finish it?"

"I had a breakthrough last week," Stephanie said, her tone still acid. "Right before all this happened. I mentioned it to Claire because she offered to brainstorm and I didn't want to, and I was going to talk about it on Sunday when we were doing our weekly brag, but the whole thing happened with Bláthnaid and Claire's books and it all went to hell. That's why I'm here so early today. I've got to get it done, so I came over to work as soon as I could."

"Oh good! I'm glad you had the breakthrough. Was she hard to brainstorm with?"

Stephanie curled her lip. "If she came up with a good idea you *had* to do it her way. It was the only way. Otherwise it was all Sturm und Drang about how you were making the worst choices."

"Juliet said something about that. Her way was the only right way to write a book?"

"Yeah. And she's read my whole series, so she had ideas." Stephanie stressed the last word all the way into sarcasm. "And I was stupid and got drawn into it and started telling her what I was doing and she got weird about it because I guess it wasn't what she would do, so I had to shut that whole thing down and then the next day Bláthnaid was dead and by Wednesday I had this new deadline and I'm fucked, so I am." She fell silent abruptly, pressed her eyes closed, then said, "Sorry," though her teeth.

Megan smiled a little. "It's all right. Ranting at somebody who's on the outside helps, sometimes."

Stephanie's phone blew up with messages as Megan spoke. She picked it up, glanced at the screen, then turned it to Megan so she could see the suddenly-scrolling responses to what was obviously Stephanie's chat group announcement that Claire Woodward had died. Shock and horror ran through the answers, and then a video call—*vone call*, Megan thought, thinking of Niamh's insistence on the phrase with brief amusement—popped up and faces began to appear. Stephanie turned the phone back to herself, answering the vone call and gesturing Megan over to join the picture.

Sadhbh's expression contorted with surprise when Megan came on-screen. "What's she doing there?"

"I came by the café early today," Megan said with a shrug. "Are you all okay?"

"Savage," Sadhbh said, and although her tone

emphasized the word's usual meaning, Megan figured she meant it in the uniquely Dublin manner that meant *brilliant.* "Claire being dead is the best news I've had all week."

Juliet, audibly shocked, said, "Sadhbh!" and the girl shrugged defiantly.

"What? Do you really expect me to care? She can feck off into the sea for all I care. Let her burn. What happened, anyway?"

"Nobody knows yet for sure," Megan said. "She drank a lot last night."

"So did I," Sadhbh said dismissively. "I'm not dead of it. Will we get together to raise a glass, anyway? To good riddance?"

"Sadhbh, she might have been *murdered,*" Stephanie said in horror.

"Yeah, well, so was my best friend, so sorry if I don't give a shit. Come on with yis," she said, looking at the other faces on the call. "Adrian, don't tell me you're in bits."

"No, but I wouldn't like to speak ill of the dead," he said uncomfortably.

"If you don't want to be spoken ill of when you're dead, you shouldn't be a—what'd you call her, Megan? A heinous bitch when you're alive. Look, if you need somebody to crack the whip so you get your words done, I'll come over to Accents, Steph, I've no classes until later, but don't think I'll be there to talk about how sad it all is."

"That would be grand, I'm desperate altogether," Stephanie said, sounding very Irish, and all at once everyone left the call with an urgency that made Megan feel they'd all be at the café almost immediately. She went back to slump in the seat she'd left, fingertips steepled in front of her nose. Stephanie frowned at her across the coffee table. "Are you all right?"

"Fine. The guards haven't talked to you yet, obviously. I was just thinking they'd want to talk to all of you."

Shock crossed Stephanie's face. "They will? Why?"

"At least two of you have motives that even I know about, and for all I know there could be others. Like Juliet's son's career. Maybe Claire knew he'd gotten in trouble on set because of Bláthnaid, and she obviously knows people in the film industry. She could have spread stories about him being hard to work with, and ruin his chances in the States, too. For example."

Stephanie grimaced. "I guess. Although, no."

"Why not?"

"Juliet would make sure the body was buried six feet deep, not dead in a hotel room. Juliet," Stephanie said with finality, "is *meticulous*."

Megan couldn't help laughing. "That's what Sadhbh said, too. But what about a crime of opportunity? She saw the chance to get Claire sick drunk last night and ran with it, but how would she get rid of the body then?"

"You can't be sure somebody will die of alcohol poisoning," Stephanie pointed out. "Juliet would never leave it to chance."

"Or would she, just to fool everybody, if you all think she's too careful to do that?"

Stephanie visibly considered that before shaking her head. "Too risky, but even more, it would annoy her sense of sense of tidiness. Juliet is a no-loose-ends kind of person."

Megan chuckled. "Okay. What about Adrian? He's got an alibi for Monday morning, but is there any reason he'd have it in for Claire?"

"So you're saying Sadhbh and I are the two you've got motives for," Stephanie said. "What's my motive?"

"Professional envy, and she's screwed things up for you by getting you involved in a plagiarism scandal, regardless of whether she or Bláthnaid was the guilty part."

Stephanie blushed. "How does killing her help me with that?"

"Maybe it doesn't, but people don't commit murders just to help themselves. I think they mostly don't, in fact. Most murders aren't premeditated."

"I guess that's true." Stephanie turned her attention to her bag and the laptop computer peeking out of it. "But boy, that would be really stupid of me. I'd never get my book done in time if I got caught."

Megan laughed. "I guess there's that."

"I guess Sadhbh would be in it for revenge, huh?" Stephanie got up and finally went to order a coffee, asking Liam if he knew whether their downstairs office was occupied. He shook his head and when she came back, it was to gather up her belongings. "I'm going to go downstairs to write. You can come hang out, if you want?"

"I might, yeah." If the others were coming over, Megan might get a chance to talk to them before Detective Reese caught up to yell at her for interfering. If they weren't, at least she'd be hidden from Detective Reese catching up to yell at her for interfering. "I'll get another coffee and be down in a minute."

Stephanie waved and Megan went up to the counter, watching Liam pulling levers and tapping used grinds into the rubbish and wiping down the thing that they always cleared with a burst of steam before wiping it. It was probably a steamer, Megan thought, amused, but she'd never worked as a barista and regarded the entire process of creating a commercially produced coffee as vaguely magical. "Another mocha?" he said. "You'll be climbing the walls."

"I know, but I like them better than anything else and it's too early for a peanut butter slice." She glanced longingly at the peanut butter and caramel cake in the glass-fronted display case, then, firmly, reminding herself, added, "And I just finished a scone. I don't need cake."

"Does anyone ever really *need* cake?" Liam asked philosophically. "Go on, order a slice now and have it later when you've solved this whole bloody mess."

"You have such faith in me. No, I'll wait until later." Her phone rang as she paid for the mocha, an American number coming up on it. Liam indicated he'd bring the drink to her, and she went back to the seat she'd had near the door, as reception in the basement was terrible. "This is Megan."

"Megan, hi, this is Derek Jacobson again."

"Oh! Hi, is everything okay? They can't have a coroner's report yet, can they?"

"No, they only just left with—" Jacobson's voice

cracked. "With her body. But they were asking me questions about how fast she'd gotten sick and one of them said—I don't think I was supposed to hear it—that he'd put money on her having been drinking antifreeze."

"*Antifreeze?*" Megan's gut recoiled at the idea. "No way. She couldn't have just been drinking straight antifreeze, could she?"

"Apparently it's sweet," Derek said. "I heard them saying you could mix it with anything sweet and you wouldn't necessarily know you were drinking it. It takes . . . they said a hundred milliliters, but I don't know how much that is."

"About half a cup." Megan's coffee arrived and she gave Liam a weak smile as she said, "She had at least six shots last night and you said they were doubles?" to Derek. "That's eighteen ounces, that's more than two cups. If they were even a quarter antifreeze, that would be a lethal dose, but I don't know if you'd taste it? My God. She could have drunk a huge amount, or just enough to kill her, probably. Who would do that?"

"I'd say that girl with the impossible name, but I think she'd have been happier to use a knife."

"Sadhbh," Megan said. "Juliet said she looked like she was in a race with Claire to see who could get alcohol poisoning first, yeah. Challenging somebody to a drinking contest could be a really good way to get them to—"

"Drink antifreeze until they died," Derek said flatly. "It sounded like a bad way to die, Ms. Malone."

"I'm so sorry." Megan's stomach roiled again. "You said they were doing an autopsy?"

Derek made a bitter sound. "Yeah, so we'll know for sure after that. But the cop sounded pretty confident and the other one wouldn't take his bet."

"Right. Well, thanks for letting me know. Look, if you want to just get out of there while you deal with whatever calls you need to, I'm at the café. Accents, on Stephen Street Lower."

"I could use a pub, not a café," he said, clearly not really kidding. "But thanks. Maybe."

"Take care," Megan said, meaning it more than usual as she hung up. She didn't even know if Claire Woodward had family who needed to be contacted, much less what other responsibilities her editor might be expected to take on in the wake of her death, but she didn't envy him any of it. The door beside her swung open and she glanced up to see Sadhbh storm in. The young woman swept past without even noticing her, heading directly downstairs without stopping to order a drink.

Anie, on her way up the stairs, pressed into the wall to let the customer pass, then came up with her eyebrows lifted. "Someone's in a mood."

"Is she often?" Megan asked.

"Nah, I'd say she's nice enough. Usually tips whatever's left from her fiver if she pays with cash. She was close with Bláthnaid, though." Anie shook her head. "You know that."

"I do, and I guess it's reason enough to come in like a thundercloud. She said she'd be celebrating Claire's death, though."

"That's mean." Anie went back to work with a sniff that made Megan smile, although she didn't much blame Sadhbh. She was gathering her own stuff up to go downstairs when a graying man in his fifties came into the café, shaking his head as Anie stepped up to the counter and offered him a smile. He looked around the café, frowned, and went downstairs with much the same energy Sadhbh had displayed, although perhaps a little less grumpy. A minute or two later he came back up, his expression lightening as his gaze landed on Megan.

He approached vigorously and she looked around, wondering who he wanted. He looked vaguely familiar, but not enough to talk to her, not until he said, "Excuse me, Megan Malone? I'm Aidan Collins with the *Irish Daily Star.*"

Megan recognized him with a sinking sensation, then. He'd been one of the tabloid reporters at Claire's disastrous book signing, just a couple of days ago. "We're doing an exclusive on the Dublin murder driver, and I'd like to know if you have any comment on the death of your latest client."

CHAPTER 18

"How do you even *know* about that?" Megan asked in disbelief, then, more importantly, said, "How did you know where to *find* me? No, I don't have any comment!"

"Ah, c'mere now," Collins said in a disarmingly pleasant way. He had the look of an Irish da, a little paunchy with pinches of pink in his cheeks and a sparkle to his eyes. "It's not too hard to find somebody when a murder driver video of you putting a girl in a closet is trending on Twitter."

"Oh my God, it is?" Megan opened her phone, then put it down firmly, clenched her hands around her mocha, and crushed her eyes shut. "No. No, go away, I'm not looking, I have nothing to say." She was going to kill whomever it was who had gone ahead and filmed her earlier, though.

No, she wasn't going to kill them. She *was* going to have to somehow cut that phrase out of her vocabulary, if people were going to keep dying around her. Which they weren't, because she'd promised Jelena, but given the past couple of years, Megan was all too aware that wasn't a promise she could keep. It wasn't like *she* was the one murdering people, which she would theoretically have had some control over.

"What's it like being embroiled in so many murders?" Collins asked, still with that charming note that somehow made Megan want to answer him. "It must be hard, a nice young woman like yourself—"

Megan's eyes popped open despite herself, so she could peer at him skeptically. He was in maybe his late fifties, *maybe* as much as fifteen years older than herself. Calling her a young woman seemed like laying it on a little thick, but he went on without missing a beat. "—caught up in so much nastiness. Would you say it's just case after case of wrong place, wrong time, or is it something about your own self that draws these types to you?"

"W—" Megan managed to cut herself off after the single consonant, then shook her head again. "I'm not interested in talking to you, Mr. Collins. Please leave me alone."

"If you don't talk to me, you'll end up talking to someone else," Collins said cheerfully. "Might as well give me the scoop, love. I'm here first and all. And if you do talk to me, I'll tell the rest of them that are on their way that you've moved on and aren't here anymore."

"Oh, that's dirty pool, Mr. Collins." Megan took a sip of coffee instead of saying anything else, but Collins grinned like he knew he'd gotten through her defenses and it was all downhill for her from there. She wasn't sure he was wrong, unfortunately.

"C'mere now," he repeated. "Tell me all about it. What do you think of this Woodward woman? A piece of work, from what I've heard."

Megan eyed him over her coffee cup. It was such an obvious ploy. She would ask, he'd say something, then they'd be in a conversation and she'd let something slip. Trying to outplay him at his own game was a *terrible* idea.

She said, "What have you heard?" anyway, and Collins's smile flashed as he leaned in conspiratorially.

"Popular but not well-liked, if you know what I mean. Able to throw her publishing power around and make people dance to her tune, so's you couldn't tell the difference between friends and sycophants, but she only had use for anybody as long as they were propping her up. After that show you put on at the book signing the other night, it's a wonder she had a word to say to you, from how I hear she was."

Megan, with great effort, said, "Huh," and nothing else.

Collins's eyes lit with amusement. "Ah, you're determined to be a challenge, are ye. All right, love, have it your own way, you will anyway. I'm only saying it'd be easy enough to imply you'd had a hand in her death. You were with her last night, weren't you, and herself dead this morning?"

"How do you *know* that?" Megan asked again, then winced, suddenly too aware she'd been caught on his fishing line.

His grin sparked again, though his tone was serious enough. "So do you think she killed that poor girl on the Monday?"

Megan, trying to keep her voice soft and steady, said, "I don't know who killed Bláthnaid O'Leary, but I hope they're found and brought to justice. I really don't have anything else to say to you, Mr. Collins."

"All right, all right." He put his phone away and sat back, examining her. "Tough nut, aren't you?"

"If I have to be." Megan took another sip of coffee, trying desperately not to say more. Collins was comfortably personal, obviously good at drawing people into conversation. "You remind me of Bertie Ahern."

Collins's eyebrows shot toward his receding hairline. "The old Taoiseach? Do I, now? How's that?"

"I saw him once across a parking lot and did a double take when I recognized him," Megan said. Ahern had been what news outlets outside of Ireland tended to refer to as the prime minister—although *taoiseach* actually translated to something like *leader*—of Ireland for a decade. He'd gone down in something of a corruption scandal, but had the charm to carry him through with a nickname of Teflon Taoiseach. "He saw me notice him and gave me the wink and the nod, like our seeing each other was a secret of our own. It was ridiculous, and I knew it, but it still felt like I'd had a moment with the man. You're a little like that."

Collins laughed. "I'm flattered, so I am. Would you be giving up your story to auld Bertie, though?"

"No," Megan said, smiling now. "Charm and trust-worthiness aren't the same thing. I'm sorry, Mr. Collins, but I really don't have anything to say to you."

"All right, love. If you say so." Collins got up, pat-ting his pockets to make sure he had everything he needed. "Let me ask you this, though, Ms. Malone. Do you like being the murder driver? You're fierce notorious now, you know."

"Goodbye, Mr. Collins," Megan said firmly. He chuckled and exited, leaving Megan to slump in her seat and hope to God that he was wrong about anybody else trying to find her for an interview. Her phone buzzed and she took it out, finding a text from Paul that said **They're talking about you on 98 FM.**

So much for hoping nobody would want to in-terview her. Megan texted a horrified emoji back at him and put her phone away. Maybe she and Je-lena could retire to a small, otherwise uninhab-ited island in the Azores, or something. Not that Megan was entirely sure where the Azores were, but presumably if she couldn't locate them, they wouldn't have heard about her being a murder driver. She took her phone out again, checked their location, and mumbled, "Huh, Portugal, huh, who knew," and read a little more. Enough to learn that the uninhabited islands were *of vol-canic origin*, which she assumed meant "not nice to live on."

Well, that would keep people from coming to bother them, anyway. Megan started to send a text to Jelena to ask if she wanted to move to the

Azores, but got a newsboard notification highlighting Claire's death before she finished, and paused, studying it.

If Claire hadn't been well-liked professionally, that opened up the number of people who might want to murder her. It still limited them to people who were in Ireland, obviously, but it could bring Kiki Rogers into play. Megan, more or less under her breath, said, "She seems like the type," then remembered Derek had said Kiki wasn't too broken up about Claire's death. It made publicity easier, he'd said. "Seems like the type and has motive," Megan said aloud. She opened a notes file on her phone, writing that down instead of just texting it to Paul. Then, since she had the file open anyway, she wrote down everybody else that she could think of, too.

Stephanie—career envy, Sadhbh—revenge, Juliet—protecting son (nobody thinks this), Paul—defending Niamh?!, Adrian???, Derek—idk, she's a pain? and then finally, looking over the notes, she added, *me—don't want to be a book series* and then, *Jelena—doesn't want me to be a book series!*

Alarmingly, looking at the list, it occurred to Megan that while antifreeze wasn't difficult to come by, as a professional driver, she had really easy access to it. There were certainly bottles at the garage, not that Ireland often got cold enough to justify using it. Still, it was part of basic vehicle maintenance, so she arguably had both motive and means, although she hadn't been anywhere near Claire's drinks until the author was already on the last one.

Sadhbh had come in at the same time as the drinks, at the Duke. She could have spiked them, maybe, although Megan couldn't imagine a server letting anybody obviously put anything into a drink. The others had mostly been giving Claire a wide berth, although Derek had been the stalwart at her side. She put a dubious *opportunity* beside his name in her notes. Troublesome or not, Claire Woodward's books made money, and killing the golden goose seemed impractical.

Of course, she'd think Kiki Rogers would feel that way, too. And Kiki hadn't been at the pub crawl. Megan looked up *antifreeze poisoning* and groaned. Given how much Claire had drunk, she could have been poisoned during the pub crawl, but it was almost as likely she'd ingested the antifreeze earlier.

Assuming the garda's supposition was even right, and that it had been antifreeze that killed Claire. Autopsies themselves didn't take long, but getting into the queue for one and getting the results back could take weeks. Derek had mentioned skipping to the front of the line, but Megan didn't know how long that would take, even with the best of intentions.

Under her breath again, and mostly to the phone, she said, "Maybe *how* doesn't matter as much as *why*," and looked at her lists again. Sadhbh seemed most likely on the surface, but that left the question of who had killed Bláthnaid O'Leary, because Megan felt fairly confident Sadhbh hadn't. Not that *feelings* were to be trusted in an investigation, but barring everything else, killing Bláthnaid would leave Sadhbh short one housemate, and with Dublin rent being what it was, Megan bet she didn't want to do that.

The door opened with a rustle of bells and Sadhbh herself came back in, glancing around without noticing Megan before she went to the counter and ordered. Anie said she'd bring it down, and Sadhbh marched downstairs without ever seeing Megan. Megan, grinning a bit, settled deeper into her chair to see if the rest of them would come in without noticing her, and a couple of minutes later, Adrian did. He looked much more wrung-out than Sadhbh, as if this was all taking its toll on him.

Or, Megan thought as he ordered a large Americano, maybe he was just hungover. He kept glancing toward the stairs like he was late for a very important date, and hurried off as soon as his order went through. Megan abruptly remembered reading Trixie Belden mystery books when she was a kid, and how she'd spent ages trying to be observant the way Trixie, who wanted to be a detective, had trained herself to be. Clearly neither Adrian nor Sadhbh had ever had any such childhood ambitions. Either that or they were exceptionally bad at detecting. Megan grinned over her notes, then startled and laughed a minute later when Juliet said, "Megan," immediately upon entering.

"Juliet. I don't suppose you read Trixie Belden as a kid?"

Juliet's eyebrows rose and she shook her head in polite confusion. Megan laughed again and shook her head, too. "No, they were American books, probably. Nothing, never mind. What's the story?"

Juliet glanced toward the downstairs, then took the still-empty seat across from Megan, obviously not intending to stay long. "Well, I can't say I'm shedding any tears over her death, but I'd like to know what's going on, all the same. Have you solved it yet, murder driver?"

Megan smiled briefly. "No, but I've just about eliminated you as a suspect, for what it's worth."

"Have you now." Juliet's eyebrows rose very high. "Why's that?"

"Everyone thinks you're too thorough to leave any loose ends. A body, for example."

Juliet opened her mouth and closed it again, a smirk slowly arising. "So I might have done it and thrown everyone off the scent by being sloppy."

"I suggested that," Megan said with another quick smile. "It was rejected as a theory, based on leaving things messy would send you spare."

Juliet narrowly avoided flapping her jaw again, pursing her lips instead. "Part of me wants to object, and the rest of me thinks they know me too well. I suppose a crime of passion . . ."

"Well, that's what I said, but the others felt pretty confident that you'd tidy up after a crime of passion, too."

"And what do you think?"

"I think there are better candidates, especially given that everybody is so confident you'd make sure nobody ever found the body."

"Is it wrong to be a wee small bit pleased about that?"

"I don't know, I sort of feel like people thinking you would actually get away with murder is a kind of bizarre feather in your cap. Did you?"

Juliet looked startled, then laughed sharply. "No. Neither got away with it nor murdered anyone. I wouldn't have any reason to kill Claire, anyway."

"Bláthnaid, though?"

"Well now." Juliet gave Megan an appraising examination. "You wouldn't be asking if they hadn't told you about Aaron and her."

Megan shrugged her eyebrows. "Do the gardaí know about that?"

"I'd be lying if I said I'd told them, but if they've told you, someone's told the guards, no doubt. Look, there was no love lost between me and herself, but if I'd been going to murder her, I wouldn't have waited four or five months." As soon as she spoke she clearly reconsidered, lips pursed again. "I suppose it would throw the scent off. I didn't kill her, though. Either of them. In the end, the damage is done to Aaron's career, and revenge wouldn't get him anywhere. And I didn't like Claire, but I wouldn't have a reason to kill her."

"She had film industry friends," Megan said. "She could have spread rumors about Aaron being hard to work with."

"She could, but she'd have had to know he existed, and Claire Woodward only knew she her own self and those that could help her existed. She was nice to you, wasn't she. She hadn't the time of day for me, and I'm not losing any sleep over that. Are the rest of them downstairs?"

Megan nodded. "Sadhbh and Adrian came in a few minutes before you did."

"Grand." Juliet stood with the air of someone who had finished her business. "I hope you or the

guards figure it out, but it's no problem of mine."
She went to order coffee, leaving Megan to open
up her notes again, sigh, and then rise to leave.
Unless one of the writers had killed at least one of
the victims, there wasn't much left to be done at
the café, and apparently she could be found if she
stayed there.

Her phone rang as she left, Jelena's picture
coming up. Megan, smiling as she answered, said,
"Hey, babe, what's the story?"

"They're talking about you on the news, Megan."
Jelena sounded strained. "'Murder driver curse
strikes again' kinds of things. They know my name."

"Jesus, what—" Megan opened the news app on
her phone again, set it to local news, and saw *murder driver* in the local trends. "Oh my God, Yella.
I'm sorry. I'll be right home to—I don't know.
Talk about it."

"What good is talking going to do? I'm calling
Paul. At least we can rage about dating famous
people!"

"I didn't want to be famous!"

"I don't want you to be! At least Paul knew what
he was getting into!"

"I'm not sure—" Megan broke off the protestation, recognizing it wasn't particularly useful, especially right then, to debate whether it was really
possible to know what you were getting into if you
started dating a film star. "I'm not sure I can fix
this," she said instead, "but I'll try, Yella. You didn't
ask for it, and it's not fair. I'm sorry."

"Just solve the damn case, or stop trying, either
way, so we can go back to our lives, Megan." Jelena's accent was stronger than usual, and Megan's

heart twisted painfully at the frustration in her voice.

"I'm trying. I'm sorry, Yella." But Jelena had hung up by the end of that, and Megan couldn't blame her.

Her phone rang again almost immediately. Megan let out an inarticulate yell, shouted, "Who uses phones for *calling* so much anymore?" and answered with a snarled, "*What?*"

Derek Jacobson's apologetic tone came across the line. "Megan, it's Derek again. I'm sorry I keep calling. I just don't know who else to talk to. Kiki, I guess, but she's eyeball deep in spinning this for the press and I don't even know how to tell her what they just found."

Megan's stomach dropped and she looked for somewhere to sit, even knowing the sidewalk was all she'd find. "What's happened now?"

"They got into her computer," Derek said helplessly. "Megan, they found Claire's suicide note."

CHAPTER 19

Megan heard her own laugh like it was someone else's distant voice; a shrill, uncontrolled sound. "*What?*"

"They had me read it to see if it sounded like her," Derek said hoarsely. "There was a lot of dramatic flair, but . . ."

"But writer." Megan's shrill laugh had disappeared into a tightly closed throat that she could barely force words through. "What did it say?"

"I took a screenshot." Derek sounded ashamed. "They'd probably arrest me or something if they knew, but I'll send it to you. It was a confession, Megan. She said she'd copied Bláthnaid's work and then killed her, and that she couldn't live with the guilt so she was going to kill herself next. It was written last night."

"Oh my." Megan swallowed a curse and backed up to a wall for some support. "Oh my God," she said a moment later, when she felt a little more in control of her language. "Yeah, send it to me, please?" As she asked, she had the surreal realization she had absolutely no right to see it, but he'd offered, and she wouldn't learn anything if she didn't accept the offer. It wasn't that she didn't think the guards could do their job, but it wasn't their lives being turned upside down by sudden unexpected notoriety, either. "Are you okay?"

She could almost hear him shake his head. "I never thought she was the type. But that's a stupid thing to say. No one ever seems like the type, do they? We're always shocked when something like this happens. I'd just—" His voice went choked. "I'd known her for so long. I've been her editor since the beginning. She never—oh, God, what am I going to tell Kiki?"

"I have no idea," Megan said, a wave of sympathy washing through her own shock. "I'm sorry, Derek." Her phone blipped with an incoming text. She glanced at it, saw it was the screenshot he'd mentioned, and realized too late that a murder-suicide meant the case was actually solved. She almost physically reeled, taken aback by the idea. "I guess . . . at least now we have answers?"

Derek's silence sounded confused for a moment before he choked off a laugh-like sob. "I guess. I guess so. I hate these answers, Megan."

"I know." Megan's heart hurt for him, even if he was all but a stranger. "I know, but I don't know . . . I don't know what else to say."

"Nothing to be said," he replied miserably. "I've got to call Kiki. I think I have to get out of here.

Back to my own hotel, or—I don't know. Is it too early to start drinking?"

"Probably, after everybody tying one on last night," Megan said ruefully, then winced at how cavalier that sounded in context of the tragedy he was trying to cope with.

He gave another of the choked-off laughs. "You're probably right. I'm at the Clarence if you need me. Or I will be."

"All right. Call if you need a friendly ear." Megan hung up and stared down the little street the café sat on, like some kind of satisfactory resolution would appear if she scowled hard enough.

None did, and after a minute she stalked up to George's Street to catch a bus home.

She'd read Claire's suicide note twice before she got home, and stopped looking at it only because it wasn't really going to tell her anything new. The dogs rushed her when she came, but Jelena, on the phone, gave her a capital-L *look* and went into the bedroom to finish her conversation. Megan sat on the floor with the dogs for a while, making an effort not to listen, not that she could hear more than Jelena's occasionally muffled voice. Eventually she got up to wash her hands and find some lunch, while the dogs clung to her ankles in hopes of a treat. Megan said, "Nope," softly, and held her resolve only because she was eating leftover takeaway and it wasn't suitable for delicate doggy tummies.

Jelena eventually emerged and Megan gestured

to the food she hadn't put away yet. "Want me to heat you up something?"

"No, but thank you." Jelena sat across the table from her, worry marks wrinkling her forehead. "Have you looked at the news, Megan? At the stories about you?"

Megan shook her head. "No, but it should die down pretty fast now. Claire's editor called me a while ago." She took a deep breath. "They found a suicide note, one that confessed to Bláthnaid's murder, so I guess . . . I guess it's all settled."

Jelena's eyes popped. "Claire Woodward killed herself?"

"That's what the note says. Derek—I'm sure he shouldn't have, but he sent me a screenshot of it." Megan unlocked her phone and gave it to Jelena as she put out an expectant hand.

"Holy shit," Jelena breathed after a minute. "What the—is this real?"

"It came from her computer and the file is time-stamped last night, so I guess so."

Jelena handed the phone back, frowning. "She seemed too self-centered to kill herself."

"That's kind of what Derek thought, but I guess you really never know."

"So that's . . . it." Jelena sat back, forehead creased again, this time with surprise and confusion.

Megan nodded. "That's it. It's over. I'm sorry I got—I'm sorry I *let* myself get dragged into it, Jelena."

"I know." Jelena's frown stayed in place, though, as she studied Megan's phone like it held some secret. "Doesn't it seem very convenient?"

"Yes!" The word burst out of Megan so suddenly

it surprised even her. She clapped her hands over her mouth, then parted her fingers enough to mumble, "I was trying not to let myself think that, but *yes*. It's so tidy. Maybe it's just tidy. Maybe it just works that way this time."

"Let me see the note again." Jelena opened the picture again when Megan gave her the phone, then rubbed two fingers between her eyebrows. "Megan, I know there are only so many things people can say in a suicide note, but I think I've read part of this before." She circled a section with her finger before pushing the phone back to Megan, who read the whole note again with a sick, sad feeling in her gut.

> *I've been lying for so long now I don't know how to stop unless I stop everything. Everything is crumbling around me, from my career plans to my friendships, because it turns out none of them were my friends anyway. They were only people I used to try to make myself feel better, and when that stopped working, I realized I had nothing left.*
>
> *All I've ever wanted was to be loved, to be trusted, to be adored. Now I've ruined even my legacy. People will wonder if I wrote my own stories, like they wonder whether Shakespeare did. Well, in this case, I admit it. I didn't.*
>
> *Bláthnaid O'Leary was an amazing writer with a terrific book idea, and I stole it. I had power and connections and my last book didn't do as well as my publisher hoped, so when I saw the work Bláthnaid was producing, I took it and said it was my own. It was easy. It even felt good, at first, but I had no idea she'd sent it to an editor.*

*Honestly, I only needed another few weeks, until
the book was actually published, and then she
would have looked like a fool for trying to claim
I'd taken her work.*

*I got so angry, though. Now I see how stupid
that was, but then I felt like it was her fault that
my life was coming apart. She had an early class,
so I asked her to meet me before the café opened so
we could talk about it, and I strangled her and
put her in the closet. I don't know what I was
thinking. I should have dumped her in the river.
But it's too late now.*

*It's too late for anything, now. The world I
knew has come to an end. All that I have in front
of me is a final battle, one that will reshape the future, if not for me, then for others. I believe that
future is a better one, so I go to it boldly, confident
that I will, in the end, be remembered for this act
more than any other.*

*I hope so. I pray so. My life is without meaning,
otherwise, and that, my beloveds, is too bitter a pill
to swallow.*

*I doubt Bláthnaid's family or friends can for-
give me, and I don't blame them for that. The best
I can do is offer them a vengeance they otherwise
wouldn't have, by giving them my death alongside
hers.*

Jelena had circled the penultimate and ante-
penultimate paragraphs, and underlined the final
sentence. "I'm not crazy, Megan, I think I've read
that before."

"Where?"

"I'm trying to remember." Jelena picked up her own phone, flipping through open apps dismissively, until she took a sudden sharp breath. "Oh, I know. I was reading that fan fiction. The one I was telling you about?"

"The one where somebody got frustrated with Stephanie not finishing her series fast enough and wrote the last book themselves?" Megan shook her head, momentarily distracted by the very idea again. "I still can't believe people do that."

"When people love something they want to be a part of it in some way," Jelena said absently, skimming through a file on her phone.

"No, I get that, it's more the impatience, I guess. Not that I have any idea how long it takes to write a book, but I guess I'd want to wait to see what the author did first." Megan grinned. "And then maybe go 'oh my god, no, that's wrong,' and fix it later."

Jelena smiled briefly. "That's called fix-it fic. Here! Here it is." She came to Megan's side of the table so they could both peer at her screen together. "The story is that they're at war and the heroine's side has lost in all but name, and she thinks her girlfriend is dead. They're about to face the last fight and of course she saves them all, but right now she believes she's lost her power and the only thing left that she can do is hold the line for a little longer, so other people might escape. See, it starts here." She pointed, directing Megan's gaze to the lines she wanted her to read, and Megan put her chin in her hands, skimming them, then rereading them more carefully.

But it's too late now. It's too late for Turia, whose face still haunts my dreams. It's too late for anything, now. The world I knew has come to an end. It came to an end with her. All that I have in front of me is a final battle, one that will reshape the future, if not for me, then for others. I believe that future is a better one, so I go to it boldly, confident that I will, in the end, be remembered for this act more than any other.

I hope so. I pray so. My life is without meaning, otherwise. The best I can do is try to offer them a hope they otherwise wouldn't have, by giving them my death alongside Turia's. I can, I will, stand between them and the oncoming onslaught, and when I fall, at least I can rest easy, knowing my beloved awaits me in a better world.

"Oh yeah," Megan said in dismay. "Oh, yeah, that's really the same, isn't it? Like you couldn't really pretend that was a coincidence."

"Why would Claire Woodward plagiarize a fic of Stephanie's work for her own suicide note?" Jelena demanded as she sat again. Dip leaned against her leg, whining, and she leaned down to rub him, still talking to Megan. "Why would she plagiarize it at all? It's the last time you get to say anything to the world, right? Would you really use somebody else's words?"

"I guess if I thought somebody else could say it better I might, but if I was a writer, probably not? But . . ." Megan slumped in her seat and exhaled, looking at her own now-black phone screen. "But if she didn't kill herself, then who killed her?

Somebody with access to her computer? In theory, that would just be the owner of the B and B or something, right? Except if she really did die from drinking antifreeze—"

"What?" Jelena sounded rightfully horrified, and Megan broke off to explain what Claire's editor had overheard about her death. "I don't think I'd kill myself that way!"

"It sounds like a really brutal way to die," Megan admitted. "But I guess if you had access to it, it would at least work?"

"Well, is there a garage at the B and B? Would they have bottles of antifreeze lying around?"

"I don't know, but you can buy it at Tesco, if it comes to it."

Jelena squinted at her. "Why do you even know that?"

"Because I drive cars for a living, probably. Um. Crap. Jelena, we'd better call Paul—"

"Who isn't on the case," Jelena reminded her, but Megan spread her hands.

"I don't have Detective Reese's number, and I'm pretty sure Paul will pass on the message. You might have solved this, you know."

Jelena shook her head. "I unsolved it. The guards can solve it."

A worried knot clenched Megan's stomach. "I'm sure they will."

"You don't sound sure."

"I'll talk to Paul," Megan said, instead of trying to convince either of them that she was, in fact, sure the gardaí would solve what was, without Jelena's input, a nice, tidy case. She got up as she dialed the phone, stepping over Thong, who then ran between her legs, apparently trying to kill her as she went to the couch.

Paul picked up with a wary, "Don't tell me someone else is dead," and Megan shook her head, forgetting he couldn't see her.

"No. There was a suicide note confessing to the murder, b—"

"Oh, tank God." Paul went deeply Irish there, dropping his H entirely, and Megan smiled, despite knowing she had to break some bad news.

"But there's a catch," Megan went on. "Part of Claire's suicide note is plagiarized, Paul."

The silence before his eventual, "What?" was broad enough to drive a truck through.

"It's plagiarized," Megan repeated. "From a piece of fan fiction Jelena read recently."

Paul took a breath and audibly held it before saying, "Fan fiction?" in deceptively mild tones.

"Stories written in other creators' already developed worlds. Like a TV show. People write stories using characters from their favorite TV shows. *Star Trek* or whatever."

"I thought those were . . ." He fell silent. "Called something else. When you buy books of *Star Trek* at the shop."

"No, those *are* something else," Megan agreed. "They're like authorized tie-ins, or something. Fan fiction isn't sanctioned. It's just people writing stories because they love the characters and want to, and then they post them online so other people can read them."

"That sounds illegal."

"It kind of is, but I guess most creators let it go

unless you try to make money off it. Anyway, the point is—"

"Yes," Paul said a little grimly. "Do tell me the point."

"—that Claire's note definitely copied some fic based off Stephanie Burgis's series."

Bourke, after another long silence, said, "*Shite.* You're sure, Megan?"

"Yella, can you screenshot that page of the story and send it to Paul, and I'll forward the suicide note to him?"

Jelena said, "Tak, yes," as Paul, despairing, said, "Why do you even have a copy of the note, Megan?" with a wild fluctuation of emphasis, as if he couldn't decide which word most needed stressing.

"Her editor took it and sent it to me. Hang on, we're sending them, okay . . . there."

"All right, I've—grand, they're here, I—" Paul said, "Shite," again more softly as he obviously read the texts. "I'll ring Reese. Megan, you're supposed to be keeping yourself *out* of this!"

"I'm evidently very bad at that!"

"Well . . ." Resigned frustration filled his voice. "Thank you. And don't do it again."

"That's clearly not a promise I can keep."

Paul mumbled something and hung up, leaving Megan to lower the phone and glance nervously toward Jelena, who sat at the table with her face in her hands. "Yella . . ."

"There's nothing you can say, Megan. This time it's my fault. I'm the one who recognized the sentences."

"I wouldn't say that's your *fault*," Megan said helplessly. "And you might have just stopped some-

body from getting away with murder, which is kind
of a big deal."

"Not one that I wanted anything to do with,
though." Jelena lifted her head far enough to expose her eyes, though she looked across the table
at nothingness instead of at Megan. "Now we wait,
right? We wait to see if Detective Reese solves the
case. But what if she dismisses it?"

"She won't," Megan said with more confidence
than she felt. "Paul won't let her, anyway. God, how
awful for Stephanie. She mentioned knowing
there was fic about her work, but can you imagine
finding out somebody had used it to fake somebody's suici—"

"Megan?"

"She knows there's fic," Megan said slowly. "And
she said she's finally figured out the story so she
can finish her series by the deadline *next week.* Jelena, is that fic any good?"

"Pretty good," she said. "Good enough to keep
reading, anyway. Why?"

Megan stood up, chills running through her.
"What if she's using it? What if *she's* plagiarizing,
and Claire found out? Maybe it wasn't an accident
there was a section from it in the suicide note.
Maybe it was meant to be a last dig at a dead
woman. Jelena, what if Stephanie Burgis killed
Claire?"

CHAPTER 20

"Megan, no." Jelena stood, too, dismay turning her cheeks pink.

"Megan, yes! I'm just going to go—I won't confront Stephanie, Jelena. I promise. I'm just going to go talk to the B and B landlord and see if anybody there saw Stephanie, and maybe talk to the other writers to ask if Stephanie had any chance to get to Claire's drinks alone. She's got a car, she probably has antifreeze in the trunk, I mean, the boot, or something. I'll just poke around a little, I promise!"

"That's what Detective Reese is supposed to do!"

"I know, but who knows how long that'll take, assuming she even thinks this is a lead worth following?" Megan tried for her best winning smile. "You told me to solve this so we could get back to our lives, right? I'm trying!"

"That was before we found a lead for the detectives to follow!" Jelena sat down in despair, face in her hands again, and Megan came over to crouch beside her.

"I promise I won't confront Stephanie, okay? I just—"

"You just want to figure it out," Jelena said into her hands. "More than you want to do what I ask you to do. To stay away from it. More than you believe the guards will do their jobs. Do you know, Megan, that the world doesn't stop turning if you don't supervise it?" She dropped her hands, looking down at Megan unhappily. "They'll do their jobs. The killer will be caught. You've done everything you're supposed to do. More. Can't you just let it go?"

Megan leaned forward until her forehead was against Jelena's thigh and mumbled, "I hate not knowing."

"You'll know enough," Jelena protested. "You'll know if the killer is caught, and why they did it. Isn't that enough? Do you have to be there in the moment?"

"But what if they don't listen to us," Megan said quietly, then shook her head and pulled a smile together for her girlfriend. "No. No, you're right, and I'm sorry. I should chill. I—"

Her phone rang and Jelena said, "If that's Paul calling to say Detective Reese isn't following up on the lead, I will pull his toenails out."

Megan slunk to the phone, head lowered like one of the dogs when they got in trouble, and saw the American number coming through. "It's probably Derek Jacobson. Should I answer?"

Jelena threw her hands up and Megan, wishing that meant something more positive than "I can't stop you," answered the phone.

"I'm sorry I keep calling," Derek said miserably. "I get one thing done and then I'm overwhelmed. She doesn't even have any next of kin, so either I do it or no one does."

"What about Kiki?" Megan asked cautiously, and felt she deserved the derisive snort she got in response, although Derek followed it up with a hasty, "To be fair, she's got a lot on her plate now, too, with all of this happening, and Claire's not—wasn't—the only PR project going on."

"I'm sure you have other things on your plate, too," Megan said. "And I know this was supposed to be a kind of working holiday for you. Some holiday, huh? Look, let me check with my girlfriend and if it's okay with her, I'll come over to help you keep things moving. I know having somebody die overseas is complicated, and it can't be any easier if you're not actually related to them." She looked up to see Jelena shrugging with resigned acceptance. "Just for a while," Megan said both to Jelena and Derek.

Jelena shrugged again, then sighed and nodded, and Derek, in Megan's ear, made a sound of relief. "Thank you. Just having somebody here who's not panicking will probably help."

"I'll be there in a while." Megan hung up and said, "Are you sure?"

"If you're helping him sort out Claire's details, you're not investigating," Jelena said. "And it is hard, dealing with a death overseas. You remember, from the last time."

Megan nodded. The last client who'd died under mysterious circumstances had been American, and her family had been under a tight deadline to return to the States. It hadn't been something Megan would want to deal with. "Still, it's not my problem," she offered, and Jelena flattened her mouth.

"No, but you'll feel bad if you don't go help him and I'll feel bad if I make you not go help him, so go help him."

"You're a star, Yella."

Jelena made a face. "You'll make it up to me. Go on, before I change my mind."

Megan kissed her and grabbed a coat on the way out the door, promising, "I'll keep you updated and won't do anything exciting."

To her relief, Jelena's laugh was the last thing she heard as the door closed.

It didn't take long to get to the establishment known locally as Bono's hotel, although technically, Megan thought the entire U2 band owned the Clarence, which sat right on the edge of Temple Bar and faced the River Liffey. The band had bought it decades earlier to what Megan had the impression was the general derision of the Irish public, and refurbished it into a luxury boutique hotel. Megan thought they still owned it, but even if they didn't, social memory meant it would be Bono's hotel until the end of time. She lingered in the lobby, looking around appreciatively before taking the lift up to Derek's room.

His muffled acknowledgement preceded him appearing at the door by about a minute, when she knocked. Megan spent the wait time studying the bold patterns of the hall floor and wondering if it would turn out his room covered half the hotel's floor. It turned out to be an only ordinarily sized hotel room, with startlingly red wallpaper and decor to match. The Liffey, framed by two bridges and bright with morning sunshine, glittered outside his windows, between which a couple of comfortable chairs and a cozy table sat. The table had scribbled-on papers and a large vase shoved to one side as if to make room for the papers, and one of the chairs looked recently sat-in. Either the quays outside were quiet, or the room was well-soundproofed, as Megan heard hardly a sound of traffic as she entered the room. "This is great. I've never been inside the Clarence before."

"I'm sure staying at U2's hotel is an American-tourist-trappy thing to do, but it's nice, it's central, and it's the only thing that's gone right in this whole damn trip." Derek ushered her all the way in and sat with the air of a man overwhelmed by despair.

"Maybe it is tourist-trappy, but it's a nice room and if you might only have the chance to get here once, why not go all out? I always do the hop-on-hop-off bus tours if I'm going to a city for the first time. It's incredibly touristy, but it gives you a good overview and helps you decide what you want to do, especially if you're not there for long."

"Exactly," Derek said, as if justified. "I did one of those down in Cork after I got back Monday morning and wanted to do one here, but everything exploded."

"I did one in London once," Megan said, remembering with a sudden grin. "A friend of mine and I, we did the tour and we went by this little alley that was filled with police and people in suits and we were all like 'oh ho-ho, someone very important must live there, ha-ha-ha,' and thought we were really funny. Except later we went by the same place again on foot and realized it was Downing Street."

Derek's laugh cracked through the room. "Well, you weren't wrong, then!"

"We weren't," Megan agreed, amused. "I had no idea it was an alley, though. Who puts the prime minister in an alley?"

"The British, apparently. Look, why don't you sit down. Have you had breakfast? I can order room service. I'm stuck," he said in frustration. "The US embassy can't register a death abroad until it's open, and the holiday weekend means that's not until Tuesday, and of course I can't have her shipped back to the States until this whole investigation is closed. I'm having her cremated," he added grimly. "Nobody else is around to care, and I just can't cope with the idea of bcing responsible for a whole body getting back to the States and then buried."

"Good," Megan said, sitting in a pleasantly comfortable leather chair. "That's one thing. Have you contacted a funeral director here, to deal with all of that?"

"I've called—" He looked for a card, then held

it up between two fingers. "Massey Brothers? They seemed nice. They're arranging for the body to be released to them whenever that can happen. I hope I won't have to wait in Ireland for all of this to get done. Is that terrible?"

Megan shook her head sympathetically. "No. You have a life and a job of your own, and it's all right to be frustrated at it being interrupted."

"It's not like it's her fault! I don't mean to—" Tears rose in Derek's eyes and he wiped his hand over his face with an exhausted action. "Sorry."

"It's all right," Megan said again. "You knew her a long time, didn't you? It's okay to be upset about her death and also frustrated that dealing with the details has landed on you."

"You're very good at this," Derek said in a low voice. "Being calm and reassuring."

"It's a strangely large part of the job," Megan admitted. "Not usually because someone's died, although we're hired for funerals, too, so sometimes it's exactly that. But unobtrusive calm is what most people want from their drivers."

"Except the ones who ask for the murder driver specifically?"

Megan chuckled. "Yeah. And I'm afraid there's a lot of those right now. Claire really raised my profile."

Derek winced. "Some people would like that. You're obviously not one of them, so sorry about that."

"I'll cope." She would have to. "Tell you what: Make one phone call, then tell me one thing you did in Cork. I haven't spent much time there. We'll get through your list that way."

"I got in Saturday and went to Blarney Castle," Derek said as he got his phone. "Ever been there?"

Megan laughed. "Once, when I was young. I did the whole kiss-the-Blarney-stone thing and everything. I had no idea it was a four-story drop with a couple rusty bars of iron between you and certain death. I don't know what they do now, but at the time there was a tiny, frail Irishman who looked about ninety-eight years of age who would hold your ankles while you bent backward over the death drop and I thought, 'This is one of the stupidest things I've ever done in my life.' I'd never do it again, but it was fun."

"There's now a large, sturdy Irishman who holds your middle," Derek reported. "And I'd still never do it again. But it *was* fun. Beautiful grounds. I spent most of the day hiking around them so I wouldn't fall asleep, then went back to my hotel room. All right. I'll call and then tell you about the Butter Museum."

"The what?" Megan laughed again, and let him make his calls. It took a while, one leading to another while he wrote notes and obviously contacted some people in America, which led to a few wrenching conversations. He finally put the phone down, rubbed his face, and eventually said, "It's just around the corner from the Shandon Bells. I went up to ring them, because if I was going to do the tourist thing I wanted to do all of it, right? When I came down I found the Butter Museum and thought something like, 'Well, that's ridiculous, I should go in.' And it is ridiculous, but it's also weirdly great. It's the history of butter. Irish butter, especially, but butter. Did you know Kerrygold is Ireland's biggest food export?"

Megan's eyebrows rose. "I did not know that."

"Me either. Anyway, you should go if you're down in Cork again. It's great."

"I will! Did you go out to Fota?"

"I did. A pelican stared me down. Sometimes it's easy to remember that birds are dinosaurs." Derek smiled briefly. "Although I guess it's just as well they're the only kinds of dinosaurs at the wildlife park, or it'd get very *Jurassic World* really fast."

Megan grinned and opened her phone file again, looking over the notes she'd taken earlier as Derek went back to his phone calls. There still weren't any revelations in them, although she studied what she had written about Stephanie more carefully. There was no reason to suspect she'd killed Claire over being discovered as a plagiarizer, except it made a certain amount of sense. There were no other clues in the suicide note Derek had forwarded on to her, either. When he finished his next call, Megan cautiously said, "There's something Jelena noticed about the note Claire left."

"What's that?"

"Part of it was taken from a fan fiction written about some of Stephanie's characters."

Derek put his phone down, blood draining from his face. "What?"

"Jelena just finished reading it a few days ago," Megan explained. "And when she read the note she thought it sounded familiar, and found the section in the fic that it was taken from. I know Stephanie knows there *is* fan fiction about her stuff, and she says she doesn't read it, but I can't help wondering."

"Wondering if it wasn't a murder-suicide after all? You think Stephanie killed Claire?" Derek asked hoarsely.

Megan nodded. "I keep imagining. But I can't figure out how she would have written a suicide note on Claire's computer. I was going to go over to the B and B and ask if anybody saw Stephanie last night, but you called and I came here instead."

"I know she's—" Derek sounded strained. "I know her editor. We've talked about the frustration of Stephanie not getting that last book done in a timely manner. I know she's been under a lot of stress about it, but . . . you think she read the fic and decided to use it, and Claire found out, don't you."

"It seems plausible. The only piece that doesn't fit is how to get the note onto Claire's computer. She'd either have to go there or have access to her cloud files, I guess, but they didn't like each other that much, so I don't see why she would have. I could see *Bláthnaid* maybe having some degree of cloud access, since Claire was mentoring her, but not Stephanie." Megan opened the suicide note screenshot again, shaking her head. "And the time stamp is practically during the pub crawl still. I guess if Sadhbh had access to Bláthnaid's computer or phone she might have done it, but then Sadhbh and Stephanie would have to be in it together and it just starts getting too complicated. There's got to be a better Occam's razor solution."

"The Occam's razor solution is that Claire killed Bláthnaid, then herself," Derek pointed out, and Megan gave a low, unhappy chuckle.

"Yeah, I guess you're right. It just seems too pat, especially with the note being plagiarized." Megan let her phone screen go dark again and made a face. "Anyway, I'm sorry. I shouldn't be piling this on you, and it's all supposition anyway. You have more than enough to deal with already."

"You *are* the murder driver," Derek said. "You wouldn't have gotten the nickname if you didn't keep poking at these things, I guess. I have one more call," he added. "You just being here has helped me get through them. Let me take you out to lunch after I've made this one?"

Megan's stomach rumbled at the idea. She pressed a hand over it, grinning. "I guess I think that sounds like a good plan." She turned her attention back to her phone, glancing over the suicide note screenshot one more time before opening a game, mostly so she wasn't listening too hard to Derek's call. She could feel her mind worrying at the note again, like something else was wrong, but within a few minutes, the puzzle game took over her concentration. She'd almost reached a high score when it crashed, the whole screen shrinking like it had been pinched down, then wobbling before shutting off entirely. Megan muttered, reopening it before her hands went cold on the surface of her screen.

The suicide note was a *screenshot*.

It wasn't a picture of a computer screen, not something that had been taken by using the phone as a camera to photograph a separate object. Megan would probably call that a screenshot, too, for shorthand, but the image Derek had sent was an actual phone screenshot, cropped down so it didn't have the battery or network information at the top, but still tall and narrow like a phone screen, without the weird rainbow interference that taking pictures of computer screens usually produced. It looked, in essence, like the screenshot Jelena had taken of the fan fiction so she could send it on to Paul.

Derek Jacobson, Claire's editor, was a lot more likely to have access to Claire's cloud files than Stephanie Burgis was.

And he'd gotten *back* to Cork on Monday morning, before his hop-on-hop-off tour.

He hung up, muttered, and said, "Sorry, I need to do one more call after all," and Megan, trying to sound casual, waved her hand.

"That's fine, but you owe me another adventure-in-Cork story, then. Where'd you go Monday?"

"Uh. Cashel." Derek emphasized the first syllable properly, which would have impressed Megan if her stomach wasn't churning.

"Oh, cool, you did the whole tour of the castle? Did you go to Hore Abbey, too?"

"Just the castle."

Megan nodded, then waved again, feeling like she looked and sounded like her stress levels had shot through the roof. "Okay, my wanderlust is vicariously sated. Back to work." She text Paul with **you need to call me RIGHT NOW** and tried to work her way through suddenly raging thoughts.

Cashel, in County Tipperary, was over an hour's drive from Cork, and while she didn't know what time the castle on the hill opened for business, she was certain it wasn't before nine in the morning, because virtually *no* Irish-based tourism attractions opened before nine. She'd done the tour herself, and even at a quick, fast-guided pace it was an easy hour's worth of exploration around the centuries-old ruins. Even assuming Derek had arrived at the stroke of nine and left immediately after looking around, getting back to Cork in the morning was unlikely. Maybe, if he'd been Irish, she could have accepted it, as "morning" in Ireland tended to mean "before lunch," which could be as late as 2:00, but Derek, an American, was more likely to mean before noon.

Maybe he *had* gone to Cashel, and done a Cork bus tour at half eleven.

But maybe he'd answered a Sunday evening call from his agitated writer, come up to Dublin to help with a murder, and gone back to Cork with no one the wiser. Claire would have had a much easier time getting Bláthnaid's body into that closet with assistance, and if Derek knew, or suspected, that Claire had plagiarized Bláthnaid's book, making sure the girl was dead would probably have made his life easier.

Megan's heart spasmed in her chest as her phone rang, Paul's number coming up. Relief swept her and she croaked, "Sorry, I'll go into the hall to take this so I don't interfere with your call," toward Derek.

"Mmmhmm."

She answered the phone on the way to the door, saying, "Paul, hi, I—" and something hit her incredibly hard on the back of the head.

CHAPTER 21

There was pain and dimness, not quite darkness, as the world faded out without entirely letting go. Megan fell forward, hitting her forehead on the door and sending a wave of dizzy nausea through her. She couldn't hear properly, ears ringing, and although her throat hurt, she couldn't quite remember having cried out. She crashed to the floor, unable to get an arm up to cradle her head as she fell, but somehow she landed on her biceps anyway, cushioning her skull from a third hit. She knew Derek was right there, but she felt so terrible she couldn't really bring herself to care. He stepped closer, a foot lifting to catch her in the ribs. Her back hit something. The hotel door, the wall beside it, she couldn't tell, but she threw up.

Derek yowled with dismay and skittered backward, like saving his shoes from spattered vomit was more important than killing her. Megan, through dazed queasiness, was grateful enough to almost think that was funny. She was also fairly certain laughing would make her throw up again. She tried to sit up and did vomit again, earning another squeal of horror from Claire's editor. She couldn't see her phone. She couldn't see much, really. Her vision kept swimming in and out. Mostly out. The room seemed a lot darker than it had a minute ago. "I was right, huh?"

"I don't know how you figured it out," Derek snarled.

Megan cackled, which made her head hurt even more and her stomach roil with protest again. If she could keep barfing in Derek's direction, she might stay alive long enough for—she didn't know what. Even if her phone hadn't shut off or broken, Paul didn't know where she was, and a confession from Derek wouldn't give her much satisfaction if it was posthumous. At least not if it was her posthumousness. She didn't care much, just then, if it was Derek's posthumousness. Although she guessed he couldn't confess if he was dead.

Thoughts were clearly not her friend right now. She tried to scrape them out of the circle they were running in, and croaked, "The screenshot. You—" Another cackle escaped her. It made her head throb horribly, and she threw up again. There wasn't really anything left to throw up, at this point, but she managed to spatter it anyway. "Wanted to brag. Didn't you. Couldn't stand. People not knowing. How clever you were. What'd you . . . hit me with." She tried to focus on him again, and thought maybe the blue-greenish blur on the floor beside him was the glass vase that had been on the table between the windows. "Oh wow. Lucky I'm not . . . dead."

"Well, I'm gonna have to fix that, aren't I," Derek snarled. He stepped forward, still obviously trying to avoid the puke on the floor, and hauled Megan to her feet.

She vomited again, this time all over him, and he shrieked like a child, dropping her in disgust. In so far as she could think, Megan wondered what he'd expected, given she'd thrown up every time she moved several times in a row now.

If she breathed very, very slowly, she could just about put a whole thought together. "I—complicated it too much, didn't I? Claire didn't—hide in the closet at Accents. She just—turned off the security cameras. Called you. Probably—stole a front door key to the café. Or maybe copied one. Or skelenton. Skelenton." Megan bared her teeth, trying to say the word correctly. She sounded like Claire had, in the throes of drunkenness.

"Oooh!" Her voice rose high and piercing enough to make it feel like the entire inside of her head was probably bleeding. "Oooh! Did you *really* hear the guards saying it was antifreeze or were you just so clever with yourself that you pleased—oooh, that's not right." She couldn't get the words to come out correctly. Just recognizing they were wrong took almost more effort than she could sustain.

Derek crouched a few feet away, just far enough to not get thrown up on again. "I might have hit you hard enough to kill you, after all. Why don't you take a little nap, Megan? I'm sure you'll feel much better when you wake up."

"Mmmm*no*, that's bad, that's bad." Megan forced

herself to sit up, wishing her head didn't hurt so much it made the rest of her body ache in sympathy. "Did they? Antifreeze?"

"Not yet, but they *will*," he hissed. "God, that whining bitch! She was so afraid they'd catch us, she was going to confess! You can't get away with something if you confess! I started spiking her coffee and her sodas with antifreeze yesterday morning. Twelve to twenty-four hours for acute symptoms, death to follow, if untreated. It's not my *fault*. I just had to make sure she wasn't going to *tell* on us. I encouraged her to get shit-faced on the pub crawl. It was really easy to top off her drinks with antifreeze."

"Your flasket. Tisket, tasket, green and bellow yasket. Yellow basket!" Megan corrected herself. Every time her head throbbed, her vision narrowed down to a pinprick. "Flask. It was in your flask. At the pub. Thought I saw you drink from it, though."

"A sip won't hurt even a skinny little guy like me," Derek said with a sneer.

"Ooh. Smart." Megan even meant that, and through the spikes of pain in her head she saw his mouth tighten smugly.

"I burned the traces out of the flask, too. Nothing left in there but whiskey. Nobody'll pin it on me."

Megan took a slow, deep breath through her nose, partly trying to stay awake and mostly trying to see if she thought she had the strength, or coordination, to surge forward and tackle him. "Clever," she said again. "You . . . drove from Cork?"

"And have the rental car under my own name on the roads?" Derek sneered. "No. I used ride-shares back and forth. Paid cash for the gas both ways."

"Security cramas," Megan said, and barely kept herself from shaking her head, which would hurt. "Cameras," she repeated more carefully. "On the tolls?"

"Weren't going to matter if nobody knew to look," Derek said bitterly. "Claire and her damn skeleton keys. She was obsessed, but since she could open the café, hiding the body in there seemed like a good enough idea. Stupid girl," he added. "It was so easy to lure her. Claire told her I was flying in to talk to her, that she was obviously a great writer, so I wanted to get ahead of any other offers, and she believed it. Claire told her the café was open early for them because she was famous, and the idiot just came over to die."

"Who plagiarized who?" Megan was proud of herself for getting the big word out on the first try. Her head didn't hurt any less, but she thought she might be able to do one swift, sudden burst of movement. She shifted position very, very carefully first, though, trying to see if she could move without throwing up.

Derek snarled a warning and she lifted the fingertips of one hand, trying to assure him she was only getting more comfortable. She didn't quite throw up, which was an improvement, although she had to clench her teeth against bile. Derek's snarl turned into a nasty smile. "Yeah, you just need a little nap, don't you. It'll be very sad, how you fell and hit your head and died." He finally rose, as if convinced he didn't need to kill her himself, and Megan watched in dismay as he walked away and began to distastefully strip his vomit-coated shirt off.

"Claire's been plagiarizing her entire career," he said airily, over his shoulder. "She's not a genius at changing her voice from one book to another. She's a hack who can't tell a story of her own. But she *could* find amazing stories to rip off, and had a knack for polishing them into something the public would gobble down. She's the one who *told* Stephanie about the fan-written stories based on her books. I thought it would point the finger nicely at Stephanie, if anyone noticed that, but truthfully, I didn't expect anybody would."

"Did Stephanie have anything to do with Claire's death?" Megan finally found her phone, facedown in puke and, when she turned it over, no longer connected to the call from Paul Bourke. The screen was badly cracked and she supposed she'd lost the connection when she fell and dropped it.

"I'm afraid not. I suspect she's using the fic Claire pointed her toward to finish her book, and that's a whole exciting kettle of fish, but she's not a killer." Derek studied his shirt grimly. "I suppose all of this will have to go into a public trash can. Ugh, what a waste. If you'll excuse me, Megan, I think I'll leave you to pass out in a pool of your own vomit while I shower."

Megan let her eyes close, although she was afraid that might prove to be a terrible mistake. It felt so much better with them closed. All she needed to do was rest for a *minute*, and then she could get up and deal with Derek and the police and . . . and get a new phone, because hers was disgusting. Derek actually did go into the bathroom. Megan ground her teeth together, which hurt her entire head incredibly badly, and rearranged herself into a crawling position. Her head weighed a thousand throbbing tons, and the only thing that got her moving was a profound desire to *not* collapse in a pool of her own vomit.

The room, which had seemed perfectly reasonable in size when she arrived, had somehow become roughly the width of the Atlantic, but somehow she crawled, fairly steadily, all the way across it to the telephone. The shower was still running when she pulled the phone from its cradle, hit the front desk button, and whispered, "Help. He attacked me and I think I'm dying," to the woman who answered.

In retrospect, the pounding on the door had probably not happened instantaneously, although it certainly seemed like it from Megan's point of view. She assumed she'd fallen asleep, only to be wakened two or three minutes later by the frantic knocking. Derek burst out of the bathroom naked and Megan yelled, "Help!" before she threw up again, hoping they'd open the door before he picked up the vase and bashed her skull with it again.

They did, a woman opening the door so a burly young man could dash in. Derek screamed loudly enough that the young man checked himself, visibly confused, but Megan croaked, "Help," again. The kid found her with his gaze, went both pale and angry, and grabbed Derek by the throat to shove him up against a wall. Derek flailed and yelled, but the young man had easy reach on him and kept him pinned effortlessly.

The woman who'd opened the door propped it open and pushed past both of them to crouch next to Megan, her face a wrinkle of fear and worry. "You're all right now, love. I've called the ambulance."

"Police?" Megan's head hurt so much, and Derek kept yelling. She wanted to stuff a sock in his mouth.

"Them, too. Can I look at your eyes? You've a concussion, love, you know that? Can you talk?"

"Detective Bourke."

Shock darted across the woman's face. "*You're* a guard?"

Megan couldn't help a giggle, although she regretted it to the very bottom of her soul. "No. Please ask for Detective Paul Bourke. Pearce . . . Street Garda station. Tell him Megan's okay." She considered that last bit and added, "ish," in the name of accuracy. Okay*ish* was better than she thought she'd be ten minutes ago, though, so she'd take it.

"Oh! Is he your boyfriend, chicken? I'll ring straightaway."

"Should I let him put some clothes on, Molly?" The kid holding Derek was now trying to look anywhere but at his captive.

Molly, standing to take her phone from a pocket, sniffed. "I'd say not. Let him wave it in all its glory . . ." She paused, eyeing Derek critically. ". . . or not . . . for the guards when they get here." A moment later she was on the phone, asking for Detective Inspector Paul Bourke, whose alarmed voice Megan could hear over the phone as he answered. "Your wan's here, Detective," Molly told him with the unflappable calm of a woman who's seen it all. "A bit worse for the wear and you'll want to coddle her some, but I'd say she'll be right as rain after the doctors have seen to her." She paused, then said, "The Clarence Hotel, love, that's where 'here' is. Some American lunatic attacked her in his bedroom."

"Derek," Megan whispered. "Derek Jacobson. Claire's editor."

Molly repeated that to Paul, who obviously demanded Megan be put on the phone. "I don't know, love, her pupils are three different sizes—yes, love, see, that was a joke—now shut yer gob, Detective, there's no good using language like that with me—" She sighed and crouched again, putting her phone on speaker and holding it toward Megan. "He's got a mouth on him, yer man does. Here she is, Detective."

"Megan?" Bourke's voice rose and broke on the two syllables.

"'m fine, Paul. Derek Jacobson killed them both." Megan's head throbbed magnificently and she wanted very, very badly to sleep. "Then he hit me in the head with a vase. It hurts."

"She's concussed," Molly announced loudly.

Bourke made a noise that sounded like he was imagining throttling her. "Did you go *confront* him, Megan?" His voice was very, very loud, even over the phone. Megan winced and tried to lie down, only to discover she was already lying down. Somehow that was such a disappointment tears filled her eyes.

"Here now, you're making her cry, you gobshite."

"Din't confront him," Megan mumbled. "I was helping him with . . . stuff . . . an' figured it out. I'm gonna sleep now."

"No!" Bourke's voice broke again, this time with alarm. "Don't let her sleep, Ms. Regan."

"Do you think I don't know that," Molly Regan said in offense. There were sirens in the background now, almost drowning out Derek's ongoing shrieks of protest, and Megan didn't remember very much again in between noticing them and waking up to a too-harsh overhead light and a nearby background of blue curtains. Unfamiliar, but easily recognizable noises filled the background: beeping, intercoms in a hallway, voices rising and falling in the room with her. Jelena sat at her side in a padded chair that nonetheless looked uncomfortable. Megan held still a few long seconds, trying to be sure moving wouldn't hurt, and also counting the number of Jelenas at her side.

After a minute, fairly certain she was only seeing one Jelena, Megan said, "Yella?" hoarsely, and Jelena looked up from her book with a relieved gasp.

"Megan! Oh, you're awake, thank goodness." She moved like she would come in for a kiss, then reconsidered and took Megan's hand to kiss the back of it instead. Megan, despite being back to single vision, was relieved. The idea of somebody's face coming at her fast right then seemed nauseating, at best. Jelena, squeezing her hand, said, "How do you feel?"

"Less bad than the last time I remember feeling anything," Megan replied, her voice still rough. Jelena got her a cup of water that she sipped at gratefully before sinking back into the bed. "I'm at the hospital?"

"The Mater," Jelena confirmed. "God, Megan, you scared us."

"I think I scared me, too. What'd I miss?"

"Derek Jacobson's been arrested and confessed." Jelena pulled her forehead down to the back of Megan's hand, saying, "And I thought sending you over to help him was the *safe* choice."

"It's not your fault." Megan curled her fingers around Jelena's, helplessly trying to offer comfort. "It just finally hit me that the screenshot wasn't a photograph of a computer screen. I feel like an idiot for not realizing it right away. He had access to Claire's cloud files?"

"Full access," Jelena mumbled, then looked up without unfolding herself, so she could keep Megan's hand tucked beneath her chin. "He even admitted he wasn't supposed to. There's a *For Derek* folder in there that's his. But the rest of her files weren't password-protected from that folder, so he just wrote the note and put it into her most recents. They would have figured it out, Paul says. But you beat them to it."

"I'm very sorry," Megan said sincerely. "I was really not trying to and as soon as I was sure I tried to leave."

"And got your head bashed." Tears filled Jelena's eyes. "I'm so glad you're okay, Megan."

"Me, too." Megan paused. "*Am* I okay?"

"Nasty concussion," Jelena said with a fragile smile through the tears. "They kept you awake several hours yesterday—"

"Oh, is it tomorrow?" Megan frowned, trying to make sense of that, then let it go, assuming Jelena would understand.

And she obviously did, her smile turning into an almost-equally-fragile laugh. "Yes, it's tomorrow. Sunday. They finally let you go to sleep late last night. I've been here since yesterday afternoon."

Megan squinted, regretted it, and closed her eyes to try to remember the events Jelena described. She had the very vaguest sense of people looking in her eyes with bright light and insisting on talking to her when all she really wanted to do was sleep, and a slightly clearer sense of a lot of beeping and intercom-sounding background noise, which, to be fair, was still going on. "I don't really remember, but okay."

"You got hit really hard. You're off work for at least two weeks. Orla," Jelena said ruefully, "is *spitting* mad."

"What about you?"

Jelena sighed and ducked her head over Megan's hand again. "I'm just glad you're all right. I know you weren't trying to solve this one by going to Derek's hotel. Oh, and the film production of Claire's book *Last Dance at Sunset* got canceled over plagiarism accusations, so it's just as well Niamh didn't get the part anyway."

"Uh-huh. She's gonna star in the murder driver TV series anyway." Megan thought she was funny, but Jelena's eyes widened as she looked up at Megan through her lashes.

"You're the main story on the tabloid websites, Megan. *Driven To It: Another Murder Solved!* and things like that. There are pictures. There are pictures of *us.*"

"Oh my God," Megan said in real horror. "I get knocked unconscious once and wake up to being the star of *The Truman Show*?"

"Well, no, he was famous his whole life and didn't find out until late," Jelena said thoughtfully. "I can't think of a movie where someone just wakes up famous and has to deal with it. *Notting Hill,* kind of."

"Yes, except you're Hugh Grant in that and I'm Julia Roberts, except yesterday I was Hugh Grant."

"No, you were more famous than Hugh Grant, yesterday." Jelena squinted, then laughed. "No, you weren't, but you know what I'm trying to say."

"Right. Yesterday I was more famous because of the murder driver thing than Hugh Grant was in the movie world before Julia Roberts walked into his bookstore. Now that we've got that settled, am I allowed to go home?"

"Let me check." Jelena kissed her knuckles again and got up to go to the nurses' station, while Megan looked for her phone, then remembered it had last been seen broken in a puddle of vomit. Maybe she didn't want it anyway.

Jelena came back to say, "They'll try to discharge you this afternoon, after a doctor has looked at you again. In the meantime, you're supposed to rest."

"Okay." Megan closed her eyes obediently, but

they popped open again. "Wait, do you know if Stephanie is plagiarizing that fan fic for her final book?"

"Why on earth would I know that? I certainly wouldn't do any plagiarizing, though, if I'd just been on the edges of all this."

"Maybe if I get out of here early enough we could go over to the café and see if they're there."

"Megan." Jelena sat, folded her arms across her chest, and stared at her. "Are you mad?"

"I just hate loose ends!"

"There are no loose ends! The murders are solved! The guards have arrested the killer! And we are just going to go home, forget about the murder driver, and try to live happily ever after!"

"Oh." Megan sat up carefully, pleased to discover it mostly didn't hurt, and reached for Jelena's hand to pull her close. "Well. Okay. I have to admit that sounds pretty nice."

"Yes. It does." Jelena leaned in to give her a gentle kiss, then crawled onto the bed to wrap Megan in a hug. "So don't mess it up, Megan Malone."

Megan smiled and relaxed into Jelena's arms. "I'll try not to."

DEATH OF AN IRISH MUMMY
By Catie Murphy

Squiring a self-proclaimed heiress around Dublin has got limo driver Megan Malone's Irish up—until she finds the woman dead . . .

American-born Cherise Williams believes herself to be heir to an old Irish earldom, and she's come to Dublin to claim her heritage. Under the circumstances, Megan's boss Olga at Leprechaun Limos has no qualms about overcharging the brash Texas transplant for their services. Megan chauffeurs Cherise to the ancient St. Michan's Church, where the woman intends to get a wee little DNA sample from the mummified earls—much to the horror of the priest.

But before she can desecrate the dead, Cherise Williams is murdered—just as her three daughters arrive to also claim their birthright. With rumors of famine-era treasure on the lands owned by the old Williams family and the promise of riches for the heirs, greed seems a likely motive. But when Orla surprisingly becomes the Garda's prime suspect, Megan attempts to steer the investigation away from her boss and solve the murder with the help of the dashing Detective Bourke. With a killer who's not wrapped too tight, she'll need to proceed with caution—or she could go from driving a limo to riding in a hearse . . .

Look for *Death of an Irish Mummy*, on sale now!

CHAPTER 1

The body lay in a coffin eighteen inches too small, its legs broken and folded under so it would fit.

Megan stood on her tiptoes, peering down at it in fascinated horror. Dust-gray and naturally mummified, the body in the box, nicknamed "the Crusader," must have been a giant—especially for his era—while he lived, some eight hundred years ago. How he'd come to rest in the crypt at St. Michan's Church in Dublin was beyond Megan's ken.

Next to him, in a better-fitted coffin, lay someone missing both feet and his right hand. Megan didn't quite dare ask if he'd gone into the grave that way or if his parts had been . . . *misplaced* . . . over the centuries. Given that there was a tiny woman called "the Nun" lying beside them both, Megan assumed nobody in ancient, Catholic Ireland would have had the nerve to liberate the fellow of his limbs under her supervision. The fact that he was buried here, in the church, suggested he'd been a decent sort of fellow in life, although he was known, according to both the tour guide and the plaques in the crypt, as "the Thief." The final body, a woman, was referred to only as "the Unknown," which, Megan felt, just figured.

"Are any of these the earl?" A brash American voice bounced off the crypt's limestone walls and echoed unpleasantly in the small bones of Megan's ears. She, being Texas-born and not quite three years in Ireland, knew from brash Americans. Cherise Williams fell squarely into that bracket. Megan had been driving Mrs. Williams around Dublin for two days, and recognized the brief, teeth-baring grimace the young tour guide exhibited after only knowing the woman for ten minutes.

Like Megan had done dozens of times herself, the guide turned his grimace into a smile as he shook his head. "No, ma'am, the earls are interred, but not among the mummies on display. As you can imagine, the church can hardly condone breaking open coffins to admire the mummies, so those we see here are . . ."

He hesitated just briefly, and Megan, unable to help herself, suggested, "Free-range?"

The poor kid, who was probably twenty years Megan's junior, gave her a startled glance backed by horror. As he struggled to control his expression, Megan realized the horror was at the fear he might burst out laughing, although he managed to keep his voice mostly under control as he said, "Em . . . well, yes. Free-range would . . . yes, you could say that. *I* wouldn't," he said, like he was trying to convince himself, "but you could. Their coffins have slipped, decayed, or been damaged over the centuries, and in those cases we've chosen not to . . ." He shot Megan another moderately appalled look, but went along with her analogy. "Not to re-cage them, as it were."

"But I need the *earl's* DNA," Mrs. Williams said in stentorian tones.

"Yes, ma'am, but you understand I can't just open a coffin at the behest of every visitor to the vault—"

"Well, what about one of these?" Mrs. Williams made an impatient gesture at the wall, where nooks and vaults held crumbling coffins of various sizes, and the floor, where a variety of wooden coffins had succumbed enough to age that mummified legs and arms poked out here or there.

"Yes, ma'am, some of these *are* the earls of Leitrim, but—"

"Well, let me have one, then! I only need a sample. It's not as if I'm going to carry an entire skeleton out of here in my handbag, young man; don't be absurd."

The kid cast Megan a despairing glance. She responded with a sigh, taking one step closer to Cherise Williams. "We'd better be leaving soon to get to your two p.m. appointment, Mrs. Williams. The one you're meant to be speaking with officials about this, instead of a tour guide. You know how difficult it is for young men to say no to the ladies. We wouldn't want to get him in trouble." She *wanted* to say it was difficult for young men to say no to women who reminded them of their mothers, but Cherise Adelaide Williams wore her sixty-three years like a well-bandaged wound and seemed like the sort who could imagine no one thought her old enough to be a twenty-year-old's mom.

Just like that, the guide's gaze softened into a sparkle and he bestowed an absolutely winsome smile on Mrs. Williams. His voice dropped into a confiding murmur as he offered her his arm, which she took without hesitation. "Sure and she's right, though, ma'am. It's breaking me own heart to see the distress in yer lovely blue eyes, but if I lose this job it's me whole future gone, yis know how it is. It's true university's not as dear in Ireland as I hear it is back in the States, but when you're a lad all alone, making his own way in the world, it's dear enough so. I'd be desperate altogether without the good faith of the brothers at St. Michan's and I know a darling woman like yourself would never want to see a lad lost at sea like." He escorted her toward and up the stairway, both of them ducking under the stone arch that led to the graveyard. He laid the Irish on so thick as they mounted the rough stone stairs that Megan lifted her feet unnecessarily high as she followed them, like she might otherwise get some of the flattery stuck on her feet.

By the time she'd exited the steel cellar doors that led underground, the guide had jollied Mrs. Williams into smiles and fluttering eyelashes. "We have a minute, don't we?" she cooed at Megan. "Peter here wants to show me the church's interior. Maybe I can convince the pastor"—The tour guide bit his tongue to stop himself correcting Mrs. Williams on the topic of priests versus pastors,

an act of restraint Megan commended him for—
"to let me have a finger bone or something, instead of going through all this bothersome legal
nonsense."

"Of course, Mrs. Williams." Megan could imagine no scenario in which that would happen, but
she followed the flutterer and the flatterer into the
church.

Parts of St. Michan's Church looked magnificently old from the exterior. Its foundation dated
from Dublin's Viking era, and a tower and partial
nave had survived since the seventeenth century.
They looked like it, too, all irregular grey stones
and thick mortar. The rest of the nave had been
repaired with concrete blocks that, to Megan's eye,
could have been as recent as the 1970s, although
apparently they were actually from the early 1800s.
She expected the interior to be equally old-fashioned,
but its clean, cream walls and dark pews looked as
modern as any church she'd ever seen. Arched
stained glass windows let light spill in, and a pipe
organ—one that Handel, composer of the *Messiah*,
had evidently played on—dominated one end of
the nave. Megan shook her head, astonished at the
contrast with the narrow halls and sunken nooks
of the crypts below.

But Dublin was like that, as she'd slowly discovered over the years she'd lived there. Modern con-
structions sat on top of ancient sites, and builders
were forever digging up the remains of Viking set-
tlements when they started new projects. Even this
church, well over three hundred years old, was
predated by the original chapel, built a thousand

years ago. According to the literature, the ground had been consecrated five hundred years before *that*.

Any temples or building sites that old in the States had been razed to the ground, and all the people who'd used them, murdered, around about the same time St. Michan's had been built.

"Cheerful," Megan told herself, under her breath. Peter the tour guide had introduced Mrs. Williams to the priest, who currently had the look of a man weathering a storm. He actually leaned toward Mrs. Williams a little, as if bracing himself against the onslaught of her determination, and if he'd had more hair, Megan would have imagined she could see it waving in Mrs. Williams's breeze. He had to be in his seventies, with a slim build that had long ago gone wiry, and a short beard on a strong jaw that looked like it had held a line in many arguments more important than this one.

"—grandfather, the Earl of Leitrim—" Cherise Williams persisted in saying *Lye-trum*, though the Irish county was pronounced *Leetrim*. Megan—a fellow Texan—couldn't tell if Williams didn't know how it was said, or if her accent simply did things to the word that weren't meant to be done. Everyone who had encountered the *Lye-trum* pronunciation had repeated *Leetrim* back with increasing firmness and volume, while also somehow being slightly too polite to directly correct the error. So far the attempted corrections hadn't taken, leaving Megan to suspect the other Texan didn't hear a difference in what she said and what everyone else did.

The priest had interrupted with a genuinely startled, "Your *great-grandfather*?" and Mrs. Williams simpered, putting her hand out like she expected it to be kissed.

"That's right. I'm the heir to the Earldom of Lyetrum."

The tour guide and the priest both shot Megan glances of desperate incredulity while Mrs. Williams batted her eyelashes. Megan widened her eyes and shrugged in response. A week earlier she hadn't known Leitrim (or anywhere else in Ireland, for that matter) had ever had any earls. Then Mrs. Williams, styling herself *Countess* Williams, had called to book a car with Leprechaun Limos, the driving service Megan worked for. Megan's boss, who was perhaps the least gullible person Megan had ever met, had taken the self-styled countess at her word and charged her three times the usual going rate for a driver. Megan had looked up the earls of Leitrim, and been subjected to Mrs. Williams's explanation more than once since she'd collected her up at the airport. In fact, Mrs. Williams had launched into it again, spinning a fairy tale that drew the priest and Peter's attention back to her.

"—never knew my great-grandfather, of course, and my granddaddy died in the war, but his wife, my granny Elsie, she used to tell a few stories about Great-Granddaddy, because she knew him before he died. She said he always did sound Irish as the day was long, and how he used to tell tall tales about being a nobleman's son. We'd play at being princesses and knights, when we were little, because we believed we had the blood of kings." Mrs. Williams dipped a hand into a purse large enough to contain the Alamo and extracted a small book, its yellowed pages thick with age and a faded blue-floral print fabric cover held shut with a tarnished gold lock. The key dangled from a thin, pale red ribbon tucked between the pages, and Mrs. Williams deftly slid it around to open the book with. She opened it to well-worn pages and displayed it to a priest and a tour guide who clearly had no idea of, and less genuine interest in, what they were looking at.

"Granny Elsie never seemed to take it at all seriously, but after she died we found this in her belongings. It's all the stories Great-Granddaddy Patrick used to tell her, right down to the place he was the earl of, Lyetrum. She said he never wanted to go back because of all the troubles there, but that was then and this is now, isn't it! So all I need is a bit of one of the old earls' bones, so I can prove I'm the heir, you see?"

As if against his will, the priest said, "What about your father?"

Creases fell into Cherise Williams's face, deep lines that cut through her makeup and drew the corners of her mouth down. "Daddy died a long time ago, and the Edgeworth name went with him. If I'd only known it meant something, of course, I'd have kept it, but when I got married I changed my name. Everyone did in those days. But my girls and I, we're the last of the Edgeworth blood. My middle daughter, Raquel, is coming in this afternoon to be with me for all of this. We meant to fly together, but there was an emergency at work." She turned a tragic, blue-eyed gaze on Megan, who was surprised to be remembered. "Ms. Malone is going to get her at the airport while I speak with the people at vital statistics about getting a DNA sample from the mummies here, aren't you, Ms. Malone?"

"I am, ma'am." Megan was reasonably certain the Irish version of vital statistics was called something else, but neither she nor the two Irish-born men in the church seemed inclined to correct Cherise on the matter. "And I don't mean to pressure you, Mrs. Williams, but we really should be going. I'd hate to be late collecting Ms. Williams."

Cherise Williams gave the priest one last fluttering glance of shy hope, but he, sensing rescue, remained resolute. "I do dearly hope you find what you need at the Central Statistics Office, Mrs. Williams."

"I'm sure I shall." Mrs. Williams sniffed and tossed her artistically graying hair. "I'm told the Irish love to be accommodating, and no one can resist the Williams charm." She swept out of the church, leaving Megan to exchange a weak, wry glance with two Irish people who had proven neither accommodating nor susceptible to the Williams charm. Then she hastened out in Mrs. Williams's wake, scurrying to reach the car quickly enough to open the door for her client. "I can't imagine why they couldn't just—" Mrs. Williams waved a hand as she settled into the vehicle. "Surely a little finger bone wouldn't be missed."

"Well," Megan said as gently as she could, as she got into the Lincoln's front seat, "I suppose we'd have to think about how *we* would feel if someone wanted to just take a finger bone from *our* grandfather's hand."

"That's just it!" Mrs. Williams proclaimed. "He *is* my grandfather! Or one of them is. The last earl was my great-granduncle, so it's his father who was my direct ancestor."

"But your immediate grandpa. The one who was married to Grandma Elsie." Megan pulled out into traffic, albeit not much of it. The River Liffey lay off to their right, beyond the light-rail Luas tracks, and she forbore to mention that Mrs. Williams would probably get to Rathmines, where her appointment with the vital statistics office was, faster on the tram than in Megan's car.

"No one would want Granddaddy's finger!" Mrs. Williams replied, shocked. "What a horrible idea, Ms. Malone. What on earth could you be thinking, suggesting somebody go and steal Granddaddy's finger!"

"My apologies, Mrs. Williams," Megan said, straight-faced. "I can't imagine what got into me." She drove them across the tracks and pulled onto the quays (a word she still had trouble saying *keys*), offering bits of information about the scenery when Cherise Williams had to pause for breath while scolding her for the imaginary sin of violating the sanctity of her poor sainted grandfather's body. "Here's Ha'penny Bridge. It was the first bridge across the Liffey, and cost a ha'penny to cross—up there is Trinity College, I suppose it's possible the earls of Leitrim were educated there— entering the old Georgian center of Dublin, made popular when the Duke of Leinster moved to the unfashionable southern side of the city—"

"To be a duchess," Mrs. Williams sighed. "Now wouldn't that be something?"

"Countess is more than most of us can hope to aspire to." Megan smiled at the woman in the rearview mirror, and Mrs. Williams, evidently assuaged, listened to the rest of Megan's tour-guide spiel in comparative silence. Half a block from the clunky-looking statistics office building, Megan broke off to say, "Now, I just want to verify, Mrs. Williams, that I'll be bringing Ms. Williams back to your hotel, and you'll be meeting us there? You're certain you don't need me to collect you here at the office?"

"I'm sure, honey. You go get Raquel and I'll see you tomorrow morning when we drive up to *Lye*trum."

Megan, wincing, said, "Leitrim," under her breath and pulled in under the ugly statistics building to let Mrs. Williams out. "You have the company's number if you decide you need a lift. Don't be afraid to use it."

"Thanks, honey. Oh! And you take my extra room key, so Ray-ray can go right in." Mrs. Williams handed the key over, despite Megan's protestations, and disappeared inside the building. Megan, letting out a breath of relief, drove out to the airport in blissful silence, not even turning the radio on. Raquel Williams's flight was almost an hour late, so Megan got a passingly decent coffee and a truly terrible croissant from one of the airport cafés, and sat beside arrivals to wait for her client.

She would have known Raquel as Cherise's daughter even if Raquel hadn't waved when she saw Megan's placard. She was taller than her mother, with rich auburn hair that didn't match her eyebrows, but with the same strong facial shape that Cherise had. Her hair was worn in a much looser, more modern style than Cherise's hairsprayed football helmet, but otherwise she was her mother's younger doppelgänger, down to the pronunciation of Leitrim. She swept up to Megan, said, "Hi, I'm Raquel Williams, the heir apparent to Lyetrum, and I just can't wait to see this whole darn gorgeous Emerald Isle."

"Megan Malone. It's nice to meet you, Ms. Williams. I've dropped your mother off at—"

"Oh my gosh, you're American too! Are you from Texas?" Raquel leaned across the barrier to hug Megan, who stiffened in surprise and found an awkward smile for the other woman.

"I am, yes. From Austin. And here's your room key, from your mother."

"Oh, wasn't that nice of her? And woo-hoo! Keep Austin weird, honey! I live there now myself, but Mama's from El Paso. Who'd have ever thought an earl would settle in Texas, huh?" Raquel Williams tucked the key in a pocket and came around the barrier rolling a suitcase large enough to pack three-quarters of a household into and wrangling a huge purse along with a carry-on. "Not that he did right away, of course. It was New York first, but when his son died in the war, he took sick and Gigi Elsie—that's his daughter-in-law, our great-great-grandma Elsie—took him down to El Paso, where she'd always wanted to live, and heck fire, here we are. How's Mama?"

Megan smiled. "She's just fine. Visiting the statistics office now in hopes of getting permission to get a DNA test done on one of the mummies. I'll take this, if you like, ma'am." She nodded toward the enormous suitcase.

"Oh heck fire, sure thing, but you'd better call me Raquel or you'll have me feeling old as sin." Raquel swung the suitcase Megan's way and smiled. "I've never been out of Texas before, this is all a big old adventure for me. How did you end up here?"

"I had citizenship through my grandfather, so they couldn't keep me out." Megan smiled again and gestured for Raquel to walk along with her as they headed for the hired cars parking lot. "Not quite as fancy as a connection to the earls of Leitrim, but it's worked for me."

"*Leetrim?* Oh my gosh, is that how they say it here? We've had it all wrong all this time! Won't Mama have a laugh!" Raquel chattered merrily, her Texan accent washing over Megan in a more familiar, friendly way than her mother's did, as they reached the car and drove back to Dublin. Raquel peppered her with questions about the scenery, Leitrim's history—Megan wasn't much help there—and whether the Irish were really as superstitious as she'd heard.

"It's not that they're superstitious," Megan said with a smile. "It's that you wouldn't *really* want to build a road through a fairy ring, would you?"

Laughter pealed from the back seat. "Gotcha, right. Look, I don't mean to be rude, but are we almost there? I forgot to use the ladies' before I left the airport."

"Just a few more minutes, and you can run right in to use the toilets in the lobby while I get your luggage," Megan promised.

Raquel breathed, "Thank goodness," and, a few minutes later when they arrived, did just that. She met Megan at the hotel's front doors, an apologetic smile in place, afterward. "Thank goodness for public restrooms. Would you mind helping me bring the luggage up? I hate to bother—" She nodded at the bustling lobby, full of people already doing jobs.

"I don't mind at all. It's room four-oh-three." They took the lifts up, Raquel in the lead as they entered a narrow hall with dark blue carpeting.

"Oh, isn't this terrific, it's so *atmospheric*, isn't it?"

"A lot of Dublin is. Old buildings, lots of history. It's one of the reasons I love it."

"I can see why." Raquel slipped the key in the door, and, pushing it open, smashed the corner into her dead mother's hip.

ACKNOWLEDGMENTS

I have so many complex feelings about writing this author's note.

Accents, the beloved cafe at which this book is set, is real. Or was, pre-pandemic; they closed permanently in mid-2020, and I've missed them constantly since. I'd always intended to set the fourth Dublin Driver book there, though, and I decided I was going to ANYWAY, despite the vagaries of the real world, so this book is as much a memorial as an homage to a place I spent so very, very many hours working. The staff there very kindly lent me their names, so everyone who works at the fictional Accents worked at the real one.

The writer's group is loosely based on my own group, whose goal is always "get together and make sure we're getting some writing done," although to the best of my knowledge, none of us have killed anybody (in Accents or anywhere else). My eternal thanks are due to Stephanie Burgis, Juliet McKenna, and Adrian Tchaikovsky, who also all lent me their names, and who are all actual novelists whose books you should check out. (They are not, however, the people in my writing group! Or, I suspect, murderers.)

I owe a great debt of gratitude to Twitter users _mawhrin, muczachan, and blotosmetek who helped me with Jelena's bits of interspersed Polish, and indeed to my infinitely patient writer's group,

Sarah, Susan, and Ruth, who still put up with a lot of me going "Okay but is this a proper Irish way to say that" about many, many things.

Beyond that, my thanks and adoration are always due to my family, who make sure I get time to write and are generally altogether lovely people. <3

-Catie